Dylan's Song

DYLAN'S SONG
By p.m.terrell

Published by
Drake Valley Press
USA

Published by Drake Valley Press

Cover design from photographs by Pamela June Kimmell, www.pamelajunekimmell.com

ISBN 978-1-935970-07-1 (Trade Paperback)
ISBN 978-1-935970-08-8 (eBook)

Author's website: www.pmterrell.com
Angelfish website: www.vickisangelfish.blogspot.com

Other Books by p.m.terrell

Black Swamp Mysteries:

Exit 22 (2008)

Vicki's Key (2012)

Secrets of a Dangerous Woman (2012)

Dylan's Song (2013)

The Pendulum Files (2014)

Other Books:

Kickback (2002)

The China Conspiracy (2003)

Ricochet (2006)

Take the Mystery out of Promoting Your Book (2006)

Songbirds are Free (2007)

River Passage (2009)

The Banker's Greed (2011)

What Critics Are Saying

Suspense Magazine says p.m.terrell's books are "powerfully written and masterfully suspenseful; you have to hang on for the ride of your life."

Jersey Girl Book Reviews says of *Vicki's Key*, "A riveting suspense thriller with enough thrills, chills and action-packed adventure to give you an adrenaline rush... The author has created a cast of characters that are realistic and complex. Their interactions make the story that much more compelling and powerful."

Midwest Book Review says, "Terrell is a master at skillfully combining drama, action, suspense and romance to engage the reader in an adrenaline rush of page turning adventure... It is a refreshing experience to read good writing. You can always count on p. m. terrell to come through with a good story."

Between the Lines Reviews says, "The multitudes of mystery writers increase on a daily basis, but it's always a bit like coming home when you can reach for that familiar name and know that there's quality page-turning excitement just beyond the cover of a p.m. terrell novel."

Syndicated reviewer Simon Barrett says, "As a reader you are swept along on a magic carpet ride of writing wizardry."

The Book Blues says, "Just when you think p.m.terrell is the best she can be, she gets better!"

Author Kathy Gandy says, "Terrell displays a unique knack for getting into the minds of her characters, making them come alive on the pages of her books… a must-read for everyone who loves mysteries. I can't wait for the next installment of the Black Swamp Mysteries Series."

Bengal Book Reviews says p.m.terrell's books are "riveting… spellbinding… sexy, intense, stay-up-all-night until you are done thrillers!"

Special Thanks

To Pamela June Kimmell for use of her Ireland photographs for the cover of *Dylan's Song*, and for her valuable input during the writing and editorial stages;

And to all the fans who eagerly await each new novel. Without you, I'd have to get a real job.

Book 4 in the Black Swamp Mysteries Series

1

The ancient stone walls were cold to the touch but as Vicki Boyd descended into the bowels of the hulking bastion, she felt a heat so intense that beads of perspiration formed across her brow. The staircase coiled like a snake, preventing her from viewing more than a few feet in front of her. Earlier she'd passed by tiny windows cut into the stone, offering glimpses of the Irish landscape against a dusky sky; but they had ceased, leaving her with the sense that she was now below ground level.

Sconces appeared around every other turn, the flames from blackened torches weaving as though a breeze licked at them, though the air was perfectly still. Shadows danced against the stone and she instinctively recoiled as if she was encountering another being. Even though she quickly realized that it was just another flicker, it was not enough to calm her pounding heart.

The air was thick with smoke from crude tallow and as she continued downward, she found it increasingly more difficult to breathe. There was a presence in this air; darker than the soot, lower than the subterranean depths to which she descended. It was an aura of evil, heavy and distinct, taunting her as it encircled her.

It crawled against her skin, making her scratch at her arms in protest. It nipped at the base of her neck, causing her to peer behind her, expecting to see an apparition at her heels. It played tricks with her eyes until she thought she saw things that were not there. And it whispered words against her ear, expressions she could not decipher but which were unmistakably human.

"Tell me what you see."

She heard the voice, soft and melodious as only an Irish accent can be, as if she was wearing an earpiece. In another place and time, she might have rushed into Dylan's waiting arms. Instead, she steadied her breathing before describing the winding staircase and stone walls and the oppressive atmosphere. Her words were measured like a soldier reporting back to a commander. As she spoke, the calmness of her own voice gave her the strength to continue until the walls fanned out and she found herself in an antechamber.

She stood for a moment as her eyes struggled to adjust to the weak light. She soon realized she was standing on a circular platform made of ancient stone. Like spokes of a wheel, four paths appeared around her: three hallways that threaded through the dungeons and the staircase from which she had just descended.

She described the area and waited for instructions but knew there could be none. Sam and Dylan knew less about her position than she, and it would be up to her alone to decide which path to take.

After a moment, she continued into the hallway directly in front of her. It was serpentine and confusing, muddling her natural compass until she no longer knew how she had arrived at her present location.

Just when she had decided she had taken the wrong route, she realized the walls were opening up on either side of her. She stopped to examine her surroundings and found herself staring at metal bars. The realization struck her that this was a dungeon in which prisoners were once held, and she struggled to guard herself against the invisible demons that still seemed to inhabit this dank, dark place.

She forced herself to peer inside each cell until she was relatively certain it was empty. But as she strained to see into the recesses of the gloomy rooms, she couldn't be sure there wasn't someone lying in the corners, balled up and motionless. Instinct told her to move on after a cursory examination and she continued to follow the meandering hall.

Deep in the bowels of this building that seemed to have no beginning and no end, she found the man for whom she searched.

He sat near the center of a cell, his knees drawn up against his chest and his head tucked inside his arms, creating a cocoon.

She stepped through the bars as she described the scene to Dylan and Sam. As she approached, the man raised his head and looked past her into the looming shadows. His face and hands were streaked with grime. His hair was light brown, the straight locks barely reaching past his dingy shirt collar, the strands caked with dirt; the only comb they'd seen had obviously been his own fingers, which left indentations along their route.

She bent to her knees in front of him and described his intense, intelligent gray eyes, a slightly crooked nose, and a firm jaw covered in an unkempt beard. She stopped herself from describing the expression of reluctant resignation, the veil that crept over his eyes and darkened them, the set of the mouth that told her he'd been captive for far too long.

"Look for a scar above the left brow," Sam said quietly. She leaned forward and searched his face for the telltale scar. It was then that she realized how dark the cell was and how difficult his circumstances. Finally, she confirmed the small scar above the brow.

"Latitude and longitude." Sam's voice sounded emotionless but she knew how anxious he was; how eager they all had been to find the fellow CIA operative that had been missing for months. Stephen Anders had been tracking a known terrorist across Europe, following him from London to Ireland. And there, on the outskirts of Dublin, they both had vanished.

She looked to her palm and stared at a GPS held there. As she read off the exact latitude and longitude, she knew within minutes a satellite would be trained on this enormous structure. She wanted to convey to the man that his captivity was coming to an end, but he continued to stare past her into the darkness.

His eyes widened at the same moment as she heard the voices and she reluctantly turned away from him and followed his gaze.

"Four men," she reported, "possibly more." She cocked her head as if the gesture allowed her to hear more clearly. "They're not Irish," she added.

"Middle Eastern." It was said as a statement but Vicki sensed that Sam was expecting confirmation.

After a moment, she said, "No. They're German."

"German?" Sam did not attempt to conceal his surprise.

"Yes," she said, her voice firm. "German." Instinctively, she moved further into the shadows, while she waited for them to emerge even though she knew they could not see her.

Their voices grew louder as they moved closer. Then a glow appeared at an angle from their cell; a light that danced and swayed like the torches had in the stairway. As the men emerged, she realized two of them carried torches; one to lead the way and the other taking up the rear. They illuminated the area around them quite well and she began to describe the men to Sam.

They wore field gray uniforms with wide black belts and tall boots. As she recognized the way the pants billowed before disappearing into the boots, her mouth went dry. Her eyes swept upward, knowing as she stared at them that her own expression must be incredulous. Even before she saw the collar insignia and shoulder boards, there could be no mistake of their identity. The red armband with the distinctive swastika left no doubt.

She could feel Sam's confusion as she described the uniforms. Yet she knew these were not reenactors of some sort. Their fit, chiseled appearance and the strong, almost harsh inflections in their voices were as easily recognizable as the Nazi symbols they wore.

They did not stop at Stephen Anders' cell but continued past it as if they were unaware of his presence.

As Vicki watched them, she could feel her jaw dropping and the blood draining from her face. She felt a wave of fear and panic as palpable as though she was a political prisoner in a den of German soldiers. But as she watched them wide-eyed, they abruptly disappeared.

She gasped, her hand instinctively moving to her mouth. She continued to stare at the hall, now dark and empty. As she moved closer to the cell bars, she stared in the direction they'd been moving. They had not rounded a corner or ducked into an adjoining cell. They had simply vanished.

She watched the hall for some time, waiting for them to reemerge but the only sounds were those of rats scurrying in the dark recesses.

Finally, she turned back to Stephen.

He was no longer sitting in the center of the cell. He was huddled into a far corner, his body curled tightly as if he was making a determined effort to fade into the background. He didn't move but remained as still as a statue; not even his breathing caused his chest to rise or fall. His face was buried in the crook of his arm and had she not seen him earlier, she realized she would have passed right by this cell without detecting him there in the farthest shadows.

After several tense moments, he finally stirred. His head rose slowly until only his eyes emerged above the bent arm. They were wide and unblinking, the white completely surrounding the iris. He moaned; a quiet but tortured lament that echoed against his confined space until it seemed as if a chorus was rising. He quickly raised both hands to his mouth, clamping his lips together as if he had no control over his voice but to physically stifle it.

Vicki remained perfectly still as she watched his body convulse. "He's terrified," she reported back to Sam and Dylan. "He looks like he's just seen a ghost."

"You?" Dylan asked.

She hesitated. "No. He hasn't seen me." She raised one arm and slowly waved it. He continued staring past her into the hallway. "He can't see me. But he saw—*them*." Incredulous, she looked to the hallway herself, narrowing her eyes as though she could will the men to reappear if only she focused hard enough. But the hall remained empty.

She turned again to Stephen. He was whimpering now. As she watched his large, muscled shoulders begin to shake and the tears roll down his cheeks, she could feel his internal struggle. He wanted to release the tension, the fear, the anxiety, the terror; but he forced himself again to remain perfectly quiet, stifling his sobs with beefy hands that squeezed against his mouth until she could no longer hear his cries.

"Get him out of here, Sam," she said. Her own voice was firm. "Get him out of here. *Now.*"

2

Vicki put the finishing touches on her sketch and held it at arm's length to view the final product. As Sam had directed, she'd completed diagrams of the stairwell, the meandering halls, a close-up portrait of Stephen Anders and one of him in his cell. Now she was finishing the final illustration of the men she'd seen wearing German uniforms.

"Vicki!" Her name was called with optimistic exuberance.

She laid the drawing in her lap as she looked across the porch. In contrast to the dank, dreary confines of her remote mission, North Carolina was awash with color. The flowers had long since ceased blossoming as Halloween beckoned, the blooms replaced with the brilliant red of maple trees, the orange leaves of the oak and the yellow ones of the birch. On their front door was a massive wreath with all of fall's brilliant colors, the gold mesh ribbons streaming down to catch the gentle breeze.

Summer's humidity had been replaced with cooler temperatures and blue skies dotted with cotton candy clouds. It had been the perfect weather for walks through historic downtown Lumberton with only a thin sweater needed to protect against cool breezes.

"Darlin'," Dylan said as he joined her on the porch. "You *must* come and see this." He brushed away a lock of black hair that strayed across his brow, leaving her to stare at his crescent-shaped hazel eyes. They seemed to change color with the seasons and his mood; today they were flecked with gold as if they, too, were celebrating autumn. They twinkled as he reached for her hand.

"What is it?" Though reluctant to leave her comfortable seat on the porch swing, she knew she'd never be able to resist Dylan's enthusiasm. She set aside her work, anchoring it with her lap desk, as he reached for her hand.

"It's a once-in-a-lifetime experience," he said, his Irish accent sounding more lyrical as his excitement grew. He took her hand and urged her down the steps and into the yard.

"What is it?" Vicki repeated, laughing.

They stopped at the edge of the driveway and Dylan pointed. His pickup truck was parked a few feet from a garage that appeared to be one gust away from toppling. Originally built nearly one hundred years earlier, it had once housed a carriage. It had barely been capable of containing Vicki's small car but recently she'd begun fearing it would collapse on top of it. Now her car remained parked in the driveway beside Dylan's truck.

He walked her to the edge of his vehicle, where cables were stretched from a winch to the four corners of the garage roof.

Vicki's smile was fading as she asked, "What are you planning to do?"

"It's goin' to be grand," Dylan said enthusiastically. "I can't repair it, you know. It wasn't built with the same solid structure as the house. It was an afterthought; I'm convinced o' it."

A dark blue sedan pulled alongside the curb as Dylan eagerly checked the tightness of the cables. Vicki kept one skeptical eye on Dylan as she watched Sam approach the house. Taking in the activity about to unfold, his brows creased.

"You see," Dylan said to them both, his voice growing almost breathless, "in just a few seconds, the entire structure will come down. Just like in the movies. I've cleared out everythin' that was in it. You should see the boxes o' memorabilia I found! It's quite extraordinary."

"But," Vicki said hesitantly, "what are you going to do with all the—wood and roofing and—"

"Oh, don't you worry about that. I've arranged for it all to be picked up and hauled away. All I must do is get the whole thin' on the ground."

Sam crossed his arms. "This I've got to see."

"You can't be serious. How do you know—?"

"I've thought the whole thin' out," Dylan said, waving away her objection. "Look. You and Sam go stand on the porch, out o' the way, and watch."

"Isn't a winch supposed to have just one cable?" Sam asked.

"Aye," Dylan answered, "but I've designed this ingenious method of usin' four. It's goin' to be grand."

"I don't think—" Vicki began, but her words were brushed away as both Sam and Dylan escorted her back to the porch. Once they were deposited at the railing, Dylan returned to the truck and climbed inside.

"I don't like this at all," Vicki said.

Sam chuckled. "This I've got to see," he repeated.

Dylan started the engine and looked through the windshield once more at the crumbling garage. The cables were strung to the four edges of the roof along what appeared to be the structure's most solid pieces of wood. He glanced back at Sam and Vicki. Apparently satisfied that they were at a safe distance, he put the truck in reverse and began to back up.

The truck wheels spun in place and for a moment, Vicki thought his effort would end there as it appeared that the vehicle would be no match for even a decrepit, rotting building. But then a sound began that could only be likened to gale force winds strafing tree bark. It grew in intensity as the truck began slowly backing up.

Vicki recoiled from the porch railing just as the nearest corner of the roof began to tilt. Afraid to stand where debris might fly into her but unable to tear her eyes away from impending disaster, she instinctively covered her mouth with both hands as the roof seemed to dance in one direction and then another.

The engine revved up higher and as the truck continued backing down the driveway, the entire roof began to wobble. It appeared for a moment as if it would lift off the building and fly toward the truck. Then it stopped even as Dylan continued in reverse. Vicki held her breath as it suddenly dropped.

The impact collapsed the entire right side of the garage in a plume of dust that rose above the treetops. The sound was deafening as wood struck the concrete foundation. A small scream escaped from Vicki's lips as she rushed backward to evade the dust cloud. But it appeared to follow her, wrapping around the corner of the house as Sam joined her at the opposite end of the porch. Soon she was unable to see anything more than a few inches away and as the grime landed on her skin, she raised her shirt tail to cover her face from the assault. She turned her back to the driveway, closed her eyes and waited for things to settle.

After a moment, she peeked around the material to find Sam back at the railing, his dark hair, still short from his recent surgery, covered in so much dust that he appeared to have aged twenty years. The engine was still revving and despite her better judgment, she returned to the railing and glanced toward the garage.

One side was on the ground, the walls folded underneath the roof like an accordion. The other side was proving more difficult and as Dylan inched the truck closer to the street, cars stopped to watch. The strain of the engine was undeniable and Vicki marveled that Dylan hadn't given up. But just as she thought the demonstration had done all the damage it could do, the other side swayed and toppled forward with an explosive shower of debris. It happened so suddenly that neither Vicki nor Sam had been able to move and now they found themselves covered in thick dust.

She tried to guard her face with her arm as a high-pitched ping erupted. Sam slammed her against the wall, shielding her with his body. She heard the sound of glass breaking, followed by another ping and then the excruciating sound of metal against metal.

The truck engine stopped revving and she peeked around Sam's protective arm to see a cable lying across the windshield and a hook embedded in the truck's grille. She could barely see Dylan moving inside, his figure not much more than a silhouette against the debris-covered window. He turned off the truck and opened the door but before he could step out, a third and then a fourth ping sounded.

He ducked back inside, covering his head with his arms as the last two cables flew through the air. One cracked the windshield with such ferocity that Vicki was afraid the glass had covered Dylan inside; but as the dust settled and she could see once more, she realized he was unscathed. The fourth cable had somehow wrapped itself around the open door.

It was deathly silent now.

Sam moved cautiously away from her and inched toward the railing, where he glanced at Dylan before turning to stare in the direction of the garage. Seeing him visibly relax, Vicki guardedly joined him.

The garage had collapsed into a heap of cinderblocks, cedar siding and drywall, all covered in a thick powder that had managed to blot out the sun and sky. The roof remained nearly intact but it now sat only a foot or two off the ground.

A movement caught her eye and she turned to watch Dylan climb out of the truck. He walked slowly to the front, where he examined coolant leaking onto the driveway. Then realizing the two of them were looking, he walked toward them.

"Are you alright?" he called.

"Yes," Vicki said shakily.

Sam remained silent as he stood like a gray ghost of his former self.

"I'm fine, too," Dylan said cheerily. "The truck stopped the cables." He gestured toward the end of the driveway. "I told you it would be grand!"

Sam finished washing his face. As he turned to accept the towel Vicki offered him, he glanced at Dylan. "Congratulations." He wiped his face and tried to brush off the debris from his clothes onto the laundry room floor. "You're now officially a redneck."

"Well," Dylan said as he stepped up to the laundry sink, "I'm not quite certain what a redneck is. But thank you."

Vicki glared at Sam. "Really?" she said sarcastically. Then, "What brings you here today anyway, Sam?"

As Dylan wiped his face clean, Sam glanced from one to the other. "I came to talk to both of you."

"That doesn't sound good," Dylan said.

Benita appeared in the doorway. Seeing the floor, she shook her head and clucked her tongue.

"Not to worry, Bennie. I'll clean it up," Dylan said.

"Go," she said, gesturing to the doorway. As they filed past her, she looked at their dusty hair and clothes. "That's what showers are for," she said in her heavy Mexican accent.

"She's getting a bit bossy, isn't she?" Sam said as they wandered into the kitchen. Pulling out a chair, he plopped a briefcase onto the table. In the midst of all the activity, Vicki hadn't even noticed it. Now he pulled out an iPad and accessed the Internet.

Dylan pulled a pitcher of iced tea from the refrigerator while Vicki gathered some glasses and filled them with ice. As they joined him, Sam was opening an aerial photograph of Ireland.

"You get those sketches for me?" he asked as he peered over reading glasses perched at the end of his nose.

"Yes. I've done them all."

Sam pointed at an area on the eastern edge of the island. "This is where our operative disappeared," he said.

"Dublin." Dylan said it flatly and Vicki glanced in his direction. He continued looking at the map and didn't meet her eyes. His face seemed darker than usual and his smile had faded.

"That's right. And this," he continued, pointing near the center of the island, "is the longitude and latitude you gave us."

Vicki looked at the map and then at Sam. He seemed to be waiting for her response, but she wasn't sure what kind of answer he was looking for.

"Let me see that," Dylan said, turning the iPad toward him. He frowned and then looked at Vicki. "This is where you pointed them to?"

"I guess. I don't see aerial maps in my missions." She turned to Sam. "What's wrong? He wasn't there?"

Sam turned to Dylan. "You were there, watching and listening. What type of structure did Vicki describe?"

"Well, it's quite obvious, don't ya think?" Sam didn't respond and Dylan continued, "It was a castle. Ireland has a number o' 'em."

"How many?" Sam interjected.

Dylan shrugged. "Hundreds. They date back to the days o' the Norman invasion. Possibly before. The lords owned 'em. Sometimes they governed a small territory and sometimes it was quite large."

"And there are hundreds of them?" Sam seemed to grow paler.

"I'm sure. Many o' 'em are in ruins but you can't go far without comin' upon one." He jabbed his finger at the map. "But I'll be tellin' you one thin'. There are no castles right there." He pointed to the same area Sam had identified.

"How can you be sure?"

"There are no castles there?" Vicki interrupted. "This is the longitude and latitude I gave you, and there are *no* castles there?"

Dylan shook his head slowly. As he opened his mouth to speak, Vicki interrupted again. "What about a manor house? A big house? A big building?"

He continued shaking his head.

"How can you be sure?" Sam pressed.

"That area," he said, moving his finger around the center of the island, "That precise area consists o' bogs."

"Bogs?"

"Bogs. Móin is what we call 'em there. You're talkin' about an area nearly a thousand square kilometers."

"But couldn't there have been a castle there, someone who once owned and lorded over the bogs?" Vicki asked.

Dylan chuckled. "You can't build a castle in a bog, lass. It would be akin to buildin' a house in a quagmire."

"You mean it's a swamp?" Sam asked.

"Not exactly. That particular area is farmed for its peat, which is used for fuel. But at the time of the Norman invasion and for centuries afterward, it would 'ave been nearly impenetrable."

"You're sure about that?"

Dylan nodded.

"But how can you be so sure?" Vicki asked.

"Because he was raised there," Sam answered for Dylan.

Dylan looked at Sam but didn't respond.

"Isn't that right, Dylan?"

He appeared to be choosing his words carefully. "I wasn't raised in a bog," he said. "I'd not be knowin' anyone who was. But I grew up right on the edge o' it."

"You farmed it, didn't you?"

He cocked his head. "Aye. I farmed it. It's a big industry in Ireland. As you know. And I'm not knowin' why you're askin' me these questions since it's clear you already know the answers."

"Our men can't get into this area," Sam said. "Between the landscape itself and the difficulty navigating through there... We're at a loss here. We trained the satellites on the longitude and latitude Vicki gave us, right down to the degree. And all that's there is—"

"Peat," Dylan finished.

"Wait a minute," Vicki said, pulling the map toward her. She zoomed in on the area. "Couldn't there have been a castle ruin there? Any type of structure?"

"I'm tellin' ya, Darlin'," Dylan said, "There are no castles there. And there never were."

3

Vicki pressed her back against Dylan's muscled chest. This was one of her favorite times of the day, she thought as Dylan sleepily draped his arm around her. Instinctively, she wrapped her arm around his and allowed her fingers to trace the outline of his powerfully built bicep.

The days were getting shorter now; where once the sunlight would already have lightened the room, it was still hazy, the furniture hard to see in the semi-gloom.

"Do you know when you'll leave for Ireland?" she asked.

He groaned and for a moment, she thought he might not answer. Then he rolled onto his back and rubbed his eyes. "I told Sam I wasn't goin'. I'll tell you the same."

She turned around to face him. "But you can't refuse a mission."

"I can't, can't I? Well, I did. So that's that."

"But don't you want to go home again? Visit—"

"Visit who? A mother who hasn't once attempted to contact me since I left? Me father, who I've not seen since he abandoned us in America? Ooh, that's right, he wouldn't be in Ireland, now would he?"

Vicki rolled onto her stomach and propped her head on his chest. "You don't have to get so testy."

"It's a 'ail o' a way for a man to wake up, bein' nagged about doin' somethin' he already said he wouldn't do."

"Are you accusing me of nagging you?"

He gently extricated himself from her as he sat up and dropped his long legs over the side of the bed. "Pay me no mind," he said as he rose. "I've overslept. And I've got some men comin' straight-away to get all the debris hauled away."

He made his way into the bathroom and a moment later she heard the shower running. She sat up, propping the pillows against the headboard. It wasn't like Dylan to be so irritable; he was usually so good humored. But he'd been in a dark mood ever since Sam gave him the mission: travel to Ireland, find the missing CIA operative, extract him and get him safely back to the States. The details, he said, would follow soon. But Dylan was adamant: he wasn't going.

His cell phone rang and Vicki leaned across the bed to answer it. She was aware of only two people who had his number— Sam and herself. But as she grabbed the phone from the nightstand, the caller identification seemed strange; there were too many numbers.

"Sam?" she answered.

"I'll be beggin' your pardon," came a lilting male voice, "it appears I've dialed a wrong number."

"Wait," Vicki said hastily, "Were you looking for Dylan Maguire?"

There was a hesitation on the other end of the line. "Dylan— I suppose that's what he's goin' by now, 'eh? I know him as Mick. Mick Maguire."

It was odd to hear the Irish voice on the phone; stranger still was the reference to the man she loved as Mick.

"He's in the shower," she said. "I'm Vicki. I'm his girlfriend. Can I take a message?"

"His girlfriend." The voice was softer. It was obvious she'd surprised him and now she could almost feel the wheels turning. "M' name's Father Rowan."

"*Father* Rowan."

"I'll not be knowin' if Mick ever mentioned me to you?"

Vicki glanced toward the bathroom as the shower was turned off. "I'm afraid not."

"I'm a friend o' the family. He gave me this number in the event o' an emergency."

Vicki sat up straighter and began to rummage for something to write with. "Yes?"

"Would you get a message to him, please?"

"Of course." She found a pad of paper and hunted for a pen.

"Would you be informin' him—his grandmother, his m'am, she's—well, her days are numbered."

"Excuse me?" She stopped searching for the pen and stared toward the bathroom door. It was slightly ajar and she glimpsed Dylan as he moved.

"She's soon to leave this world," he said. His voice was deep and a bit raspy. "She wants to see him one last time. I've called to beckon him home."

"His grandmother—"

"His mum's mum. She raised him since he was a tyke. And it's her dyin' wish to see him once more. I know he's not likely to be wantin' to return—but please, ask him to telephone me. He'll be regrettin' it if he doesn't come home."

"Of course I'll tell him," she said. Her own voice had grown softer.

"You 'ave m' gratitude, Miss Vicki." With that, the phone clicked off.

She glanced up to see Dylan standing in the doorway.

"Is that Sam callin' me already?" he asked, poorly concealing his irritation. Before she could respond, he walked past her into the walk-in closet.

She set the phone on the nightstand and followed him, stopping in the doorway to watch him pull on his jeans. "No. It wasn't Sam."

He sat on the bench as he pulled on his socks.

"It was Father Rowan."

"What?" Dylan stopped with his hand in mid-air, the sock dangling.

"Do you know a Father Rowan?"

He stared at her. His eyes betrayed a myriad of emotions; emotions, Vicki thought, which he preferred to keep hidden. But they were there and undeniable. After a moment, he licked his lips as though they'd gone dry. "Of course I know Father Rowan." He looked to the sock and then to his naked foot before turning his attention back to Vicki. "But why would he be phonin' me?"

She kneeled on the floor in front of him and rested a hand on his knee as she looked up at him.

"It's me mum, isn't it?"

"No. It's your grandmother—your 'm'am'?"

"Mam. Short for Maimeó." He waved his hand. "It's what I called me grandmother."

"She's sick, Dylan."

"She didn't pass?"

"No. But Father Rowan said her days were numbered. And she wants to see you."

He abruptly began pulling on his socks. Vicki leaned away from him as he put on his boots. His mood seemed to have changed from one of shock to one of aggravation. And she didn't understand it.

He stood and crossed to the far side of the closet, where he grabbed a shirt off a hanger. "Sam put you up to this, did he?" he demanded.

"What?"

"Pretendin' someone called so you could convince me to go to Ireland?"

"*What?*" She felt the heat rising in her cheeks. "That was not Sam on the phone. Check the caller i.d. if you don't believe me. It was Father Rowan. He said your Mam wanted to see you right away. She's dying, Dylan. I wouldn't make up a thing like that."

He brushed past her into the bedroom. As she followed, he moved quickly to the hallway as if eager to dismiss her.

"You've got to go," she pleaded. "Don't you see? It's a sign."

He was already out the door when he turned around and popped his head back in. "A sign? A sign, you say? A sign o' what? That me past won't stay in the past?" Without waiting for a response, he turned abruptly and hurried down the stairs. She started to follow him but realizing she wasn't dressed, she quickly donned a robe as she rushed after him.

"It's not about you," she said, catching up with him at the bottom of the stairs. "It's about an old woman who's dying. And her dying wish is to see you again. How can you be so cruel?"

"How can I—" He began to sputter. "You don't know what you're talkin' about, Woman."

She felt dizzy and she grabbed the newel post to steady herself. A wave of nausea swept over her and she closed her eyes and willed herself to remain in control. When she reopened them, Dylan was watching her curiously. She swallowed hard. "You can see her once more before she dies. You may never get another chance."

The front door opened and Sam walked in. Seeing them standing at the bottom of the stairs, Vicki in disarray, he stopped in his tracks. "Am I interrupting something?"

Dylan threw his hands up in disgust and started toward the kitchen.

"Dylan got a call this morning," Vicki explained as she started after him. "His grandmother is dying and she wants to see him."

"That's perfect!" Sam said.

Vicki halted to glare at him before continuing to follow Dylan.

"It's not perfect that she's dying," Sam muttered. "But it's perfect that she's in Ireland." He hurried after them. "He can see his grandmother and complete this mission."

"I said I wasn't goin' to Ireland!" Dylan bellowed.

They converged in the kitchen. His face was flushed in a way Vicki hadn't seen since he pummeled an attacker nearly to death in the back yard.

"I don't recall *asking* you," Sam said, his own voice rising. "You work for me now. It's an *order*."

"Well, I don't take orders from the likes o' you!" He stepped toward Sam menacingly. Then something washed over his face, softening it. He mumbled something under his breath as he turned away. "I said I'm not goin'. And that means I'm not goin'. If you want to arrest me, keep me cooped up in that—cell— again, go right ahead. Have at it."

"Why are you so adamant about not going back?" Vicki said. "I don't understand."

He strode to the back door. With his hand almost on the knob, he stopped abruptly and turned around to face them. "The flight is a hundred hours long."

"It's six hours," Sam said.

"I'll have jet lag for weeks!"

"Two days, tops." Sam's voice was becoming quizzical.

"Are you afraid of flying?" Vicki asked.

"*No!*" he bellowed. He opened the kitchen door. "The weather there is atrocious!"

"I can't believe you're acting like this is such an inconvenience for you when your own flesh and blood is dying!" Vicki shouted.

"In me whole life," he said as if he hadn't heard her, "it's rained once." He held up his finger. "One time!"

"Really?" Vicki said. "Once?"

"*And it's lasted for thirty years!*" With that, he marched outside and slammed the door behind him.

Vicki and Sam stared at the door for a long moment without speaking. Then she turned to him. "I'm at a loss here."

He continued staring at the kitchen door as if he hadn't heard her.

"Do you know why he doesn't want to see Ireland again?" Vicki asked.

"He can't refuse a mission," Sam said quietly. "You can't pick and choose your missions in this line of work."

Vicki turned to stand directly in front of him.

"Do you know," she said in a stronger voice, "why he doesn't want to see Ireland again?"

He looked at her as if seeing her for the first time.

"You know, don't you?"

He looked away from her. His eyes roamed the kitchen as though he was searching for something. Vicki stood her ground until he said, "No. I have my suspicions; that's all."

"Is he wanted?" When Sam didn't answer, she pressed, "If he goes to Ireland, will he be arrested?"

"No." Sam pulled out a chair and gestured for Vicki to take it. She hesitated until he pulled out another one and sat down heavily. "Before we hired him, we went over his background with a fine toothed comb. If he'd ever had a parking ticket, we would have known about it. He isn't wanted for anything in Ireland. Or anywhere else, for that matter."

Vicki visibly relaxed.

"That's not to say he's never done anything wrong. Just that he's never been caught. No subpoenas. No arrest records."

They remained silent for a moment, each with their own thoughts.

Vicki looked at Sam. "But you know why he doesn't want to go back."

"He'll have to tell you himself," Sam said, rising. "All I have is a suspicion. And suspicions could be wrong. I'm not going to lead you down the wrong path."

"But—"

"Get dressed. You and I have someplace to go."

4

"What's going on, Sam?" Vicki asked as she settled into a rocking chair.

Sam opened the wrapper on the egg sandwich he'd just purchased at the Fayetteville Airport café. "Want some?" he offered.

Vicki shook her head. "I'm feeling a bit queasy."

As he joined her in the corner of the airport, sitting heavily into a rocking chair opposite her, she turned her attention to the wide open view displayed through large plate glass windows. Beyond them, passengers hurried from the parking lot to the building while others walked more slowly back to their vehicles, often chatting with lovers, families and friends that they appeared not to have seen in some time. It might have been the perfect spot to while away the morning. But as Vicki waited for Sam to answer her question, she knew this destination had been prearranged.

Sam glanced at his watch. "We have about half an hour," he said, "if the plane's on time."

"What plane?"

He waved his hand as if to dismiss her questions. "I'll fill you in on all the details later. But first things first. I think you should go."

"Go where?"

"To Ireland."

"What?"

"You heard me." He leveled his eyes at her. She remembered when they used to be deep brown but now they were ringed with blue. He looked tired but then, he always looked tired and bored. She had no idea how old Sam was, but she suspected he was nearing the end of his career. "We both know Dylan is going to Ireland, like it or not. I need him for an important mission. And his grandmother needs him. He might think he doesn't want to see her; but if he doesn't, he'll regret it for the rest of his life."

"That's exactly what the priest said." She turned away. There had been a time when she'd tried to leave the agency. She knew now that no one left without their express permission. And no one turned down an assignment.

"And this could be your only opportunity to see where he grew up. More importantly, to meet the woman who raised him."

"You really believe he won't go back again?"

He shrugged. "He's got a past there, Vicki. My guess is he came to America because he was running from something. I can get him there for this mission but I can't make him see his grandmother. And I doubt if he'll go back there on his own."

A group of passengers swarmed through the gate on their way to baggage claim. Vicki looked quizzically at Sam.

"Not our flight," he said.

"How can you be so sure?"

He held up his cell phone. "I'll get a text when they've landed."

"So—why do you want me to go? I'm not a ground operative."

"I wouldn't have you working the same mission as Dylan. Your mission can be done anywhere: find the missing agent."

"Then why—?"

"You're going to be his front. Look, he's going back to the village—or a close proximity—where he grew up. If he shows up alone, even if he claims to be there to see his grandmother, it might raise questions if he suddenly looks like a tourist. But with you along—you're his love interest. He's bringing you back to meet his family—what little family he's got—and of course he'll want to show you around Ireland."

"You think he'll go along with it?"

Sam shrugged. "I'm not asking him. Look, I can assign a female agent to go with him. But you're already familiar with the case. And you wouldn't be in any danger. When the time comes for him to extract the agent, you're to remain behind. I'll give instructions to Dylan to get him and the agent to a safe house. Once the agent is back in our custody and headed back to the States, Dylan is free to get back to you. Finish your little 'vacation' and head back to the States a day or two later."

"But he doesn't want to go."

"I'm telling you, he's going."

"Is there someone there he doesn't want me to know about?"

Sam cracked his knuckles before answering. "If you're asking if he left a girlfriend behind, I'm pretty sure the answer is 'no.' Did he leave a string of broken hearts? Maybe." He stared into Vicki's eyes as if to make his point. "But there is no one there waiting for him; no girlfriend or wife in the wings. And I have no doubt he loves only you."

Vicki leaned back in the rocker. Logistically, there were a dozen reasons why she shouldn't go, not the least of which was the angelfish business. But her stomach was beginning to flip-flop inside her with excitement. Ireland had, truthfully, never been on her list of places to visit but it was due to the fact that she'd never known anything about it. Now that Sam was providing her with this opportunity, it seemed the perfect time for a romantic getaway—even if a CIA mission and a dying relative were part of the complicated equation.

"Ah," Sam said, reaching for his cell phone as it began to vibrate. "They're here."

"Are you planning to tell me why I'm here? Or am I supposed to be surprised?"

"Oh, you'll be surprised, alright." He texted a response and then rested the cell on his knee. "I need for you to listen closely."

"I'm listening."

"A young lady is about to step off that plane. She's going to be escorted by a U.S. Marshal. She'll be wearing an ankle bracelet and she's under house arrest—"

"Brenda?" She leaned forward, her eyes wide.

"She's not on a 'get out of jail free' card, Vicki. You got that? She's facing some serious charges."

"Then how—"

"We're working with the FBI. Crooked politicians fall into their jurisdiction, not ours."

"But—"

"We have the list of politicians. It's Brenda's job to fill in the blanks. Don't get yourself caught up in it, Vicki. It's none of your business."

She nodded. Her mouth felt dry and she found her gaze drifting from Sam's eyes to the security gate.

"I've arranged for her to be under the custody of two CIA agents. You got that, Vicki? Not her sister and her sister's boyfriend. *Two CIA agents.*" He waited for that to sink in before continuing. "If she escapes one more time—even if she's immediately caught—it's over for her. She will spend the rest of her life in prison."

"Does she understand that?"

"She had to understand it before she was released to the U.S. Marshals."

"And she agreed not to attempt an escape?"

"She did." He rose from the rocking chair. "And you and I both know her word is worth nothing."

"Then why—?"

"I was your only family before she showed up. And let's face it, I'm a lousy family."

"I wouldn't say—"

"I would. So here's your chance to have your sister with you. She can go anywhere as long as she is in your custody and Dylan's. Leave Lumberton and I need to know about it."

"But Ireland—"

"She's going with you."

Vicki's jaw dropped. "You've got to kidding."

"You don't want her? I can put her right back on that plane."

"This is a lot to process, Sam. Dylan's going to Ireland only he says he's not. You've just told me I'm going and I'll be his front. Now you're handing me my felon sister and saying babysit her, too, while I'm at it?"

"She's not a felon—yet. She hasn't stood trial. And she's not going to cause any problems," Sam said. "And I think she'd be good to have around."

"Because I will be in danger?"

"Because you're gonna need someone."

"I'll have Dylan."

"Besides Dylan."

A flash of billowing copper hair caught her attention and she turned to watch Brenda escorted through the security gate. She strolled side by side with a handsome, chiseled man who appeared to be in his thirties. And from the looks of it, Brenda had been slapping on the charm pretty heavily. She exuded sensuality, even from this distance.

As they drew closer, she realized Brenda's right hand and the agent's left were concealed under his jacket, as if he'd casually tossed it over his arm. But Vicki knew even before they had reached the rocking chairs that underneath that jacket, Brenda was handcuffed to him.

"You're Jacob Brunn, I presume?" Sam said, rising to meet them.

As the Marshal nodded, a slow smile crept across Brenda's face. "Well, well," she said, lifting one brow, "I just love these little field trips. You just never know who you might run into."

Vicki rose, stepping toward her sister.

"I'd give you a great big hug," Brenda said, "but Jacob here doesn't want to let me go." She held up her right hand under his jacket. Though Vicki couldn't see the handcuffs, the meaning was clear.

Sam reached for a pen inside his jacket. "You've got paperwork for me?"

As he signed the necessary papers, Marshal Brunn unlocked himself from the handcuff. "Which one of you—?"

"It won't be necessary," Sam said without looking up. "You can uncuff her."

"But—"

"She's not going anywhere."

He unlocked the cuff, though it was clear to Vicki that he did so reluctantly.

Brenda rubbed her wrist. "So sorry we have to end things here," she said. "It was such a lovely flight."

As the Marshal's cheeks began to redden, Sam said, "Take her to the car, Vicki. I'll be right behind you." He turned back to the paperwork.

"It's good to have you back," Vicki said when they were out of earshot.

"Thanks for saving my life," Brenda replied. She'd become more somber as they rounded the corner and moved out of the men's line of sight, the mask of bravado slipping away.

"What are sisters for?" Vicki quipped.

"I never got the chance to thank you," she said as if she hadn't heard her. "When I regained consciousness, they told me what had happened—what you'd done. But they wouldn't let me talk to you."

"I didn't know where you were," Vicki said. "Sam kept telling me you were okay—but he wouldn't even give me an address where I could write you."

"I was in federal prison," she said. "A medical ward but a prison is a prison."

"Oh," Vicki said, stopping short of the car. "Your bags."

Brenda laughed. "You're joking, right? All I own is what I'm wearing."

"Well," she said, "we'll take care of that."

She appeared to be ready for a witty retort but fell silent as Sam approached. He seemed deep in thought and started to speak before he'd even reached the car.

"You are not free and clear," he said. His voice had taken on an edge like a father lecturing a teenager. "You still face charges that could put you away for a long time."

"Tell me something I don't know," Brenda said.

He leveled his eyes at her. "If you try to run—if you try to disappear—we will hunt you down. And you will spend the rest of your life in a ten foot cell." He waited for this to sink in.

When she didn't respond, he continued, "Vicki and Dylan are responsible for you. You get away from them and not only are their careers over, but I will make sure they stand trial for aiding and abetting a criminal."

Vicki felt the blood draining from her face. Sam did not look at her but kept his eyes locked on Brenda's. Surely he's going overboard with this, she thought. Or was he serious?

Brenda remained perfectly silent.

After a moment, Sam said, "You got that?"

She nodded.

"Do you have a problem with it?"

She opened her mouth, her brow arched as it always did right before she responded with bluster. But she clamped her mouth shut, apparently thinking better of the idea. "No," she said quietly. "I don't have a problem with it."

He stared at her for a long moment before hitting the button on the remote. As the doors unlocked, Vicki breathed a sigh of relief. But before she could open the back door, Sam tossed the keys to her. "You're driving," he barked. "She's sitting up front with you." With that, he opened the back door and climbed in.

The driveway felt foreign as Vicki pulled Sam's sedan beside the house. Gone was the garage with its dangerous slant; gone also was the pile of debris. In its place was a wide open area that allowed her to see through to the neighbor's yard. Sandy was working near her grill in shorts that didn't quite cover her derriere. The heat rose in Vicki's cheeks as the blond called out to Dylan, sashaying her hips as she did so.

Dylan stood at the end of the driveway on the concrete foundation where the garage had stood. He had a broom in his hand and had obviously been cleaning the last of the debris and dust from the pad. He turned as the car moved into the driveway. His mouth was set and his eyes narrowed. Sandy was still talking as he made a deliberate approach, setting the broom against the side porch as he neared the car.

Vicki had barely come to her feet when he asked, "Where 'ave you been?"

The back door opened and Sam climbed out. "I took her to Fayetteville."

Dylan pulled Vicki to him. "Don't ever leave without tellin' me where you're goin'." He said it with his mouth close to her ear, his lips brushing her hair. "I was worried about you."

A third door opened and as Vicki drew far enough from Dylan to look him in the eye, their attention was drawn to the hood of the car, where Brenda was leaning toward them. "What sweet little lovebirds," she said.

"Tell me she's not really there," Dylan said without taking his eyes off her.

"She's been placed into our custody," Vicki said quietly.

"Did you know this?" Dylan's voice was taking on an edge.

"She didn't know anything," Sam said, closing the car door. "She didn't know we were picking up her sister until she stepped off the plane."

"You placed this—this woman," Dylan sputtered, "in our custody again, knowin' she's a flight risk?"

"It's great to see you, too, Irish," Brenda quipped.

Sam waved his hand as if dismissing his concern. "She's not going anywhere. She knows if she tries, it's curtains—for all of you."

"For *all* of us," Dylan repeated. "*All* of us. Don't be paintin' me with the same brush as—as *her*."

Brenda took a step backward. Her mouth was set as if she was ready to open the door and climb back into the car.

"Let's everybody stay calm," Vicki said. Her voice was firm. "Brenda is wearing an ankle bracelet. She's being monitored. She'll stay in my old room and she won't be any trouble." She glanced toward Brenda. "Will you?"

"She's right," Brenda said.

"Stay away from me," Dylan said, pointing his finger at her. Without taking his eyes off her, he said in a louder voice, "I'll have nothin' to do w'her."

"Okay," Vicki said. "We're clear on that. You won't even know Brenda is in the house. Will he, Brenda?"

Before she could answer, Sam opened the driver's door and started to climb in.

"Where do ya think you're goin'?" Dylan asked.

"You all have too many issues for me," Sam said, getting in and starting the engine. "Besides, I have a cat now. I have to go home and feed her."

Before anyone could object, he backed the car down the driveway, leaving Brenda and Dylan staring at each other like boxers at opposite ends of the ring—and Vicki as a hapless referee in the middle.

5

Vicki opened the bathroom door to the master bedroom to find Brenda sitting on the edge of her bed.

"Where's Dylan?" Vicki asked.

"Outside," Brenda said, her eyes widening. She studied Vicki's face, leaning forward to try and catch her eye, but she seemed intent on avoiding her gaze. "What's that in your hand?"

Vicki didn't answer but walked slowly to the bed and sat down beside her. She held a blue and white stick in her hands. She continued to stare at it as if dumbfounded.

"What is that?" Brenda pressed. "Don't tell me you're—"

"I'm pregnant," Vicki blurted. Her lower lip trembled and she bit into it to keep it still.

"You're wrong."

She held the instrument so Brenda could see it. "It's the third one I've taken. Three different brands. This one says 'Pregnant' or 'Not Pregnant.'" Her hands trembled. "I *am* pregnant."

Brenda pushed her hair off her forehead. "Does Dylan know?"

"No." Her voice became firm. "And don't you tell him."

"I wouldn't dream of it. Not after the reception he gave me."

"I have to be the one to tell him," Vicki continued as though she hadn't heard her. "And I have to choose just the right time."

"What does that mean, 'just the right time'?"

Vicki gazed into her sister's eyes. They were wide; a golden amber color that she knew mirrored her own. The vision blurred as her eyes filled with tears. "He doesn't want children."

"I don't believe you," Brenda said, reaching for a tissue.

Vicki allowed her sister to wipe the tears off her cheeks. "He said he'd rather be put in front of a firing squad."

Brenda stopped to stare into her eyes. "He said what?"

"You heard me. He said he hates children."

"You were arguing."

"No. We were just talking."

"And he feels that strongly?"

Vicki nodded.

"Then why—?"

"We weren't trying."

"Then weren't you using—?"

"Of course we were." She waved the instrument in the air. "Obviously, it's not one hundred percent effective."

"My God." Brenda placed her hands in her lap. She looked stunned. "Dylan hates children," she repeated as if she was trying to let it soak in, "and you weren't trying to get pregnant. It just happened."

Vicki groaned and leaned back until she was lying prone on the bed.

Brenda turned to look down on her. "What are you going to do?"

"I'm going to tell Dylan—when the time is right."

"But—what are you going to do?"

The full implication of Brenda's words hit her and she rose to her elbows. "I'm going to have it." Her sister didn't respond and Vicki added, "With or without Dylan. Hopefully, with him."

Before she could answer, the sound of the door slamming downstairs jarred both of them. Heavy footsteps sounded on the stairs and as it became clear that Dylan was heading toward the bedroom, Brenda grabbed the pregnancy tester and slid it into her pocket.

"I told you," he was bellowing, "I'm not goin' to Ireland. I meant it then. And I mean it now."

Sam's voice was lower but just as insistent. "I'm not asking you. It's a direct order."

"And I don't take orders. From you or anybody else!"

They reached the bedroom door at the same time. As Dylan saw Brenda sitting on the edge of the bed, he appeared to be half a step away from turning around and heading back downstairs. Instead, he pointed at her. "What about 'er?" he yelled. "Aren't we supposed to be babysittin' *her*?"

"She's going with you."

"*She is?*"

"I am?"

"Oh, that's just grand, I want you to know! It wasn't enough for her to torment me in me own house and home. Now I've got to traipse around the world w' 'er in me pocket?"

Sam, Vicki and Brenda were silent as they stared at him.

"Besides," Dylan continued, "I can't leave. What about all the babies in the fish house? I've got hundreds o' 'em! Thousands, even! They'll all die without me here to care for 'em!"

"I'll take care of them," Sam said quietly.

"*You'll* take care o' 'em?"

"That's right."

"Do you even know how? Have you ever owned a fish in your life?"

"I have a cat."

"You have a cat." He jabbed his finger in Sam's direction. "He has a cat. Well, you can't put down a dish o' milk for a tank full o' baby fish. Do you know how to test the water? Do you know how to change it without suckin' up all the babies in the hose? Do you know what and when to feed 'em? Do you—?"

"You'll tell me. And I'll do it. And I won't lose any of your fish."

"That's right. You won't be losin' any o' the fish on account o' you won't be carin' for 'em. They're my responsibility and I'm not leavin' 'em."

"It's only for a few days. Four days, maybe five. Tops."

Dylan strode across the bedroom toward the bathroom door

as Brenda glanced furtively in Vicki's direction. Her mouth barely moved but Vicki knew exactly what she wanted to know. She shook her head. The box was in the wastebasket under the sink.

Dylan whipped around. "I told you," he yelled at Sam, "I'm not goin' to Ireland. And that's the final word on the matter! When I said I'm not goin' to Ireland, I meant *I'm not goin' to Ireland!*"

6

Vicki leaned her head against the soft cushion and gazed out the tiny window onto the airstrip. It was barely eight o'clock but already the sun had set, leaving behind a faint trail of red-orange along the distant horizon. The moon was full and bright, the variations in its surface glowing in alternating white and blue tones; stars were already beginning to twinkle in the clear night sky.

She was dead tired. It had been an exhausting day filled with last minute preparations for the quick trip to Ireland. Sam had driven them to Fort Bragg, where they'd boarded an Army helicopter which, in turn, delivered them to Andrews Air Force Base. Now they were on a private jet getting ready to depart for the last leg over the Atlantic.

In the end, it wasn't Sam or Vicki who had persuaded Dylan to return home; it was Father Rowan. He'd telephoned again and when Dylan had answered the call, he'd become very quiet. He'd wandered outside where he had paced the driveway as Vicki watched unnoticed at the window. He'd remained on the phone for nearly an hour and appeared to be speaking very little but listening intently. When he returned to the house after the call, he'd announced in a hushed voice that he would go—and then promptly began preparations.

Brenda sighed in the window seat next to her and reclined her seat. "Gotta admit," she said, "this sure beats commercial flights."

Vicki smiled. It certainly did. Their seats reclined into narrow beds and of the twelve seats she counted it appeared they would be the only passengers. A pilot and co-pilot had greeted them as they'd climbed aboard; she'd wondered if they were CIA agents themselves or perhaps military pilots but knew better than to ask. They'd simply confirmed their destination—a private airstrip on the west coast operated by a military contractor. Once there, they would be provided with a rental car. And then they'd be on their own.

"What a shame Chris couldn't go with us."

"Where is he?" Vicki asked.

"You didn't watch the news earlier?" She shrugged. "He's testifying before a Congressional subcommittee. Something to do with his old boss… Can't imagine what that is." She batted her eyes in faux innocence. "And wouldn't I just love having him along."

Dylan sighed and opened his laptop in the aisle seat on the other side of Vicki. Sam had presented it to him during his training but she'd never seen him use it. Now he seemed eager to log onto the Internet.

"What are you doing?" Vicki turned to him sleepily.

"Surveillance," he said solemnly. His voice was low and subdued as he brought up a live video of the fish room. He'd insisted on installing the cameras before they left.

"Surveillance, huh?" When he didn't respond, she said, "You can trust Sam, you know."

"I gave 'im the book I'd given you when you were just startin' to learn the fish business. And I'll be monitorin' the situation from Ireland. I'll not be comin' home to find thousands o' cadavers litterin' the tanks."

Vicki leaned her cheek against Dylan's shoulder as she placed her hand on his bicep. The fish room was awash in a cool blue light; tank after tank of angels breeding, wigglers struggling to make the transition from egg to fry; and babies of all sizes determined to survive. The mortality rate was high among angelfish unless water conditions were kept just right and her stomach tightened as she thought of leaving them.

She turned her attention from the screen to Dylan as she gently ran her hand along his five o'clock shadow. He closed his eyes and leaned into her palm. He was gorgeous, she thought; even in semi-repose, his dimples were deep, his jaw squared and his skin at once tough and supple. His black brows were thick and his lashes long and slightly curled. He opened his eyes and kissed her hand with tender lips and when he looked at her, his hazel eyes shone.

He closed the laptop and leaned in toward her. "It would be lookin' as though we have company," he whispered, nodding toward the window.

Vicki followed his gaze. The sky had darkened further so only the taillights were visible as a vehicle pulled slowly past them and stopped near the cockpit. "You remember what Sam told us."

"We're returnin' to Ireland to see to me Mam," Dylan responded instantly. "And I'll be showin' you a bit o' the isle whilst we're there."

"Dylan," Vicki said softly.

"Aye, Darlin'?"

She smiled at the melodious lilt to his voice. He wasn't happy about returning to his homeland but he had resigned himself to going, however reluctantly. For herself, she felt an excitement she hadn't experienced in years—if ever. This was going to be the vacation of a lifetime—even if it would be dominated by a CIA mission and his grandmother's illness.

And she was happy. Happier than she'd been at any time in her life.

"Was there somethin' you were wantin' to say?" Dylan asked. He held her hand, squeezing it lovingly, and she turned her attention to her petite hand in his much larger, stronger one.

"Yes. There's something I need to tell you."

Vicki felt Brenda shift on the other side of her and could sense her listening intently. She gazed into Dylan's eyes. They were tired but he smiled, causing them to turn into half-moons—

a shape she associated with his warm, ready laughter and good humor. He was going to be such a good father.

The sound of voices reached their ears as the pilot and co-pilot greeted the other passengers. In another moment, their privacy would be gone. "Yes," she said. "I wanted to tell you—"

"Good God Almighty." Dylan turned away from her, his face turning dark as three small boys ran through the plane. They seemed oblivious to their presence as they sat in each empty seat in turn, remaining only a few seconds before popping up and moving to the next one. Their voices filled the small cabin and even Vicki was aghast at the total lack of parental supervision.

"Of all the planes in all the world," Dylan said with no attempt to hide his irritation, "They felt the need to badger me w' buggers for an entire night o' hell. I'd rather 'ave been put afore a firin' squad."

A man and woman boarded next; the man appeared to be in his fifties and was stout and solemn. He nodded in their direction but immediately focused on finding a spot for his carryon luggage. His wife appeared much younger; she was slender with shoulder-length platinum hair. She selected two seats for herself and her husband and settled in without so much as a glance in their direction—or their children's.

The door was closed and the sound of the engine changed. The co-pilot stood in the doorway. "Welcome aboard," he said. "I'll have to ask each of you to remain seated with your seat belts on until we're in the air—"

"Thank God someone has a bit o' sense," Dylan muttered.

"Once we're in the air, you're free to move about the cabin," he continued.

Dylan groaned. "He could'a left off the latter. Now we'll have these blasted nippers runnin' around us all the cursed night."

Vicki settled into her seat, accepting a blanket Brenda silently offered her, and tried to ignore the sinking feeling in the pit of her stomach.

The co-pilot continued his spiel and then retreated to the cockpit. With the three boys now in seats but continuing to point and shout about every imagined landmark they thought they could spot through the windows, they taxied down the runway.

Within a few seconds, they were lifting off and then navigating eastward toward the Atlantic.

Dylan grabbed a pillow and slid it behind his head. Reclining, he turned to Vicki. "What was it you were wantin' to say to me afore we were so rudely interrupted?"

Vicki hesitated. "I just wanted to say 'thank you.' I'm glad you agreed to go."

The boys jumped up as the plane leveled off and Dylan pulled a blanket up to his ears. "Christ Almighty!" he said before closing his eyes.

Vicki sank her head into the pillow. Out of the corner of her eye, she glimpsed Brenda's face turned toward her. She twisted in her seat until she was face to face with her. Her sister had undoubtedly heard the conversation. Her eyes were wide and knowing, unblinking as she looked Vicki in the eye. Her lips were slightly parted as if she wanted to say something but didn't quite know how or what to say.

Vicki closed her eyes and sighed. If God was merciful, she would soon be fast asleep—and wouldn't awaken until they were landing on the Emerald Isle. She felt Dylan groping for her hand; finding it, he intertwined his fingers in hers as they both drifted off to sleep.

7

The drone of the engine morphed into the sound of breathing, the ragged exhales causing the hair on the back of her neck to prickle. She opened her eyes to find the cabin replaced with the castle's winding stone stairs. The odor of reconstituted air was now moldy and damp; the bluish haze of nighttime cabin lighting replaced with an undulating yellow vapor from wall sconces. She could sense the smoke irritating her sinuses; could feel the dank air weighing down her hair and causing an uneasy sweat to break out across her brow.

She steeled herself and whipped around, expecting to see someone directly behind her. The uncomfortable sense of breathing on her neck instantly stopped, as if she'd turned away from the source. But he was still there; she could feel him with every ounce of her body. And he was evil.

She wanted to race up the stairs toward the surface, to emerge into the light of day and into Dylan's arms. But something sinister hung a few steps above her; she couldn't see it but she knew it was there. To go back would be to pass through it and the mere thought of it caused her knees to buckle.

She caught herself by shakily placing her hands on opposite stone walls. They were mildewed and she instantly recoiled from the slimy texture of stone sweating and fungus creeping. It was as if the walls themselves had come alive.

Forcing herself to continue downward, the narrowing serpentine stairs created claustrophobia that threatened to send her screaming in hysteria. Stephen Anders' trepidation still permeated the air as he'd been led down these stairs, surrounded by his captors, not knowing whether they would torture him, kill him, or leave him to die alone in the depths of the subterranean dungeons.

She knew even before reaching his cell that he was huddled in its corner as mice and vermin scuttled around him. He had a dry, hacking cough that invaded his lungs from the damp, unhealthy air and now his chest felt compressed. He'd lost weight and would lose more and though he forced himself to pace, each day found him growing weaker until the mere thought of standing had become too much.

When Vicki first heard the voices, they sounded like mere wisps of air; for even the atmosphere in the dark, condemned dungeons had a thick and oppressive life of its own. It whispered like apparitions forever doomed to eternity in this prison, brushing like lips against her ears, breathing hot on the back of her neck while sending cold chills up her spine. The air had grown increasingly frigid and she hugged herself against the cold. Continuing ever deeper, she wanted to return to the surface but seemed unable to do so as if her free will had been ripped from her.

But as she moved ever deeper, she realized the sounds *were* voices. She halted mid-step. They were approaching her from below on narrow, uneven stone steps that were barely wide enough for a single person. And there was nowhere to hide.

The logical part of her mind tried to convince her that they could not see her; she was there in spirit only. But the emotional structure of her psyche panicked and wavered with the fear that they would torture her as they had tortured him.

She couldn't blink and she couldn't move. She could only stand transfixed as they approached.

She squeezed her eyes and forced herself to remember her CIA training. It had never been enough to simply travel in her mind. To journey without remembering was just as bad as not having traveled at all. Her training rushed into her core; it had become second nature to memorize her surroundings down to the smallest detail. She knew once she awakened from this nightmarish existence she would be required to draw every ounce of detail she could recall.

She listened to their accents, expecting to hear the coarseness of the German language on their tongues. But she heard instead a familiar one.

One sounded as though it was from America's Deep South. It had the cadence, almost like poetry in motion. The other was more difficult to discern; perhaps Midwestern. She wanted the rhythm, the intonation, the accents emblazoned on her mind; she would be called to identify it, she was certain of that, even though she could not decipher their exact words.

When they appeared around the corner, she gasped in surprise but their pace never wavered. When the first one walked through her, she felt the sensation of her breath being sucked out of her. In its place was an inky blackness, something cheerless and sinister. She felt pain inflicted; a satisfaction from exacting it; a yearning to be more menacing, an evil that wanted to consume.

He was of medium height and slender. Yet when he passed through, she could feel his muscular arms and legs and knew he had the fortitude to withstand physical hardship. His skin was swarthy, his face long and lean. A unibrow dominated his facial features, sitting like a thick shelf above dark, deeply inset eyes.

She hadn't recovered from the onslaught of evil emotion before the second man crossed through her and the wickedness engulfed her tenfold. He didn't want to murder quickly; he wanted to torture slowly, to dismember and to laugh in the face of another's pain. He wanted answers and he would get them. There was no national pride there, no sense of protecting political ideology; no impression of defending family, home or country. There was only a mercenary, one bred to kill and maim.

His emotions made it more difficult for her to memorize his physical characteristics. She struggled to stare into eyes the color of gunmetal, to register the dark hair cut so short that she barely realized the hair on both temples were receding, and to compare his short, squat frame to his associate. He had a slight potbelly but he, like the other, was fit and ready for whatever physical punishment Life might throw at him. He was nearly past when she realized half a brow was missing from a strange, jagged scar.

They stopped on the stairs as if listening and she found herself caught just below them, struggling to breathe, unable to escape, incapable of defending herself. She wanted to rush down the stairs and along the meandering halls until she'd reached Stephen Anders and freed him. And she wanted to run screaming up the stairs to the sunlight that must be there somewhere, never to return to this hell again.

Stephen was calling out to her with his mind, pleading with her to rescue him, beseeching her to find him, praying this would end. He was losing a sense of who he was and what he stood for; his wife's face had long since blurred until he no longer remembered her; he couldn't recollect where he'd been before this place and couldn't envision ever leaving. He tried to recall the alphabet in the five languages he knew until only one remained; he attempted to recite verses of scripture but they seemed to escape him now.

She was losing him. And he was losing himself.

She felt his essence grow thinner until she could no longer feel him. He was dying. They would come across the Atlantic to free him but they would be too late.

The men began their ascent once more and she whirled around, ready to rush down the stairs to Stephen when she ran abruptly into a third man.

Unlike the others, he did not move through her but glared at her as if she was there in flesh and blood. He had stopped a step or two beneath her but still he towered over her; his shoulders were broad, stretching nearly from one side of the stairwell to the other. His hair was long, reaching to his shoulders in red waves. His brows were thick and unruly, the long strands of an older but not yet elderly man. His eyes were a vivid blue, the lids folding on them, as he glowered at her. He was dressed in strange stockings that ended just below the knee, where a skirt of some kind joined it. A deep blue cape was carefully arranged over his shoulders, the thick material intensifying his hulking image.

His eyes did not waver from hers as he shouted in a thick, authoritative voice, "Garda! Garda!"

She awakened in a pool of perspiration, her heart thumping wildly in her chest, her eyes sandy and lidded as if she'd kept them open all night.

"Are you alright, Darlin'?"

She stared at Dylan, her mouth dry. He had been leaning forward as if peering down the aisle, his blanket and pillow gone and his seat erect.

"Did you 'ave a bad dream, Vicki?" he asked. He pointed toward the windows on the opposite side of the aisle. "No matter, Darlin'. That's Ireland there. Looks like we'll be landin' close to the coast near one of the mountainous regions. Though I suppose they're just hills when compared to what you 'ave in the States…"

Vicki slowly raised her seat. Her back throbbed in protest at her unnatural sleeping position and she squinted as her eyes adjusted to the light. It was morning; the start of a new day.

And, she realized as she struggled to control her juddering heartbeat, every day mattered to Stephen Anders.

8

Vicki stared westward as she waited for the men to unload their luggage. They'd landed at the extreme edge of the island; perched high above a vast ocean that swelled tumultuously as if just underneath the surface a war was raging. The waves crashed against the cliffs with such vengeance that even at this height the sound was undeniable. The ocean wanted in like an insistent stranger pounding on the door in the middle of an otherwise still night.

Her stomach churned as the light penetrated her lids and she turned away from the chaotic roil of the sea.

In this direction, jagged cliffs rose from valleys made both vivid and surreal from the multitude of green shades that assaulted her eyes before the lush landscape gave way to gray rock that appeared both majestic and foreboding. A narrow road perilously close to the edge snaked its way around the cliffs, which in turn rested against a sky so pale that it was nearly white.

But as she searched for clouds, she saw none. "It's not raining," she said to Dylan as he joined her on the makeshift tarmac.

He made a strange sound akin to a chortle as he set down a large suitcase speckled with country stickers announcing their status as world travelers. Sam had delivered it the day before,

opening it to reveal a compartment with a combination scanner-
printer-copier-fax, a spot for Dylan's laptop, a hidden section
for his CIA weapon and a variety of tools that Vicki did not
want to think about. "Don't be countin' on it stayin' this way,"
he said as he eyed the skies. "The gods are toyin' w'ya, is all. It'll
rain straight-away."

She turned toward Brenda, who was watching a limousine
pull away. Three little boys' faces were pressed against the window
glass and all three mouths were moving. "I'd hate to be in that
car right now," Vicki giggled.

"That poor chauffeur," Brenda agreed. Then she turned
toward Dylan with a half-grin. "So, where's our limo?"

Before he could answer, the co-pilot called out. "Mr.
Maguire."

"Aye?"

"Here are your stamped passports. We've set your bags as
you directed." He pointed toward the tail end of the plane.

"And the automobile?" Dylan asked.

The man held out a key. "On the other side of the plane.
Fueled up and ready to go."

Dylan reached for the key with one hand as he pulled out
his wallet, but the man waved as he backed away. "No tips. Enjoy
your vacation, Mr. Maguire. Ladies."

"Ladies," Dylan repeated, gesturing toward the bags.

They fell in beside him. As reality sank in, Vicki felt unsettled.
She had just traveled to another country for the first time in her
life and already they were on their own.

There were only three bags waiting for them; they'd packed
light, as Sam had instructed. They each grabbed a bag and
continued around the plane. Dylan headed straight for the tiniest
car Vicki had ever seen.

"What is this?" Brenda said, stopping alongside it.

Dylan glanced at her but didn't answer. Instead, he opened
the passenger side door on the left, adjusted the seat so it leaned
forward and crammed his electronics case into the back.

As he walked around to the driver's door, Brenda said,
"Where am I supposed to sit? On the roof?"

"There's a back seat," he said, adjusting the front seat so she could climb in. "And there's space beside you for our bags. If not, you can hold one in your lap."

"This is a joke, isn't it?" Brenda continued. "They get a limo and we get—a bicycle on tires?"

"I requested the smallest car possible," Dylan said, taking Vicki's bag from her and tossing it into the back seat. "We're goin' into a rural area, one where the roads are not that good— and not that passable."

Vicki glanced in the direction of the narrow road winding along the cliffs as Dylan continued, "You wouldn't want to be in a sizable vehicle and find y'self starin' into the grille o' a farmer's truck in the same lane as you."

"Well, what do we do when we're staring at a truck in this thing?"

Dylan took Brenda's bag and added it to Vicki's before tossing his in. "We move out o' the way. Now get in."

Vicki and Brenda exchanged glances. Then Brenda climbed in, pulling one bag into her lap and scooting another bag onto the floorboard. The seat seemed more suited to a small child and as Vicki slipped into the front seat, she felt a pang of guilt for Brenda's discomfort.

"Make y'selves comfortable," Dylan said as he started the engine and adjusted his seat. "We've a long drive ahead o' us."

It wasn't long before she realized just how right Dylan had been. She felt herself hanging onto the grab-handles as he drove along the narrow road, at times leaning inward as if her weight could move the vehicle closer to the relative safety of the shoulder on the other side.

"You're lookin' a bit green," Dylan said, glancing at her.

"I don't like this height," Vicki said. She pointed at the road as Dylan looked at her more closely. "Do *not* take your eyes off the road."

"Ooh," Dylan breathed.

"Why did you do that?" she asked nervously.

"Do what?"

"Breathe like that."

"Here we go again."

"What does that mean?"

"It means you're micromanagin' me breathin'. And we're finally a bonafide couple."

"What do you mean?"

"It means you're tellin' me how to drive and you keep askin' me what I mean. Do you want to drive?"

"No. I'm afraid of this road. It's not even hardly a road. It's *dirt*."

"Then allow me to drive. I've not gone off a cliff yet."

Vicki leaned into the seatback. She glanced toward Brenda, who was grinning mischievously. She appeared to be enjoying the ride, pressing her face close to the glass so she could see the sheer drop below and the turbulent gray ocean waves pounding just beneath them.

Vicki realized from her vantage point that she could see the roads ahead; they were moving southeast toward flatter ground and into the country's interior. As the minutes turned to an hour and then two, the cliffs were replaced with rolling countryside. Though the roads never became wider, she no longer felt as if her life was endangered. At times they were paved but more often, they found themselves on dirt or gravel roads and sometimes nothing more than twin tire paths.

They stopped for a late breakfast in a quaint and tiny village. A bus filled with tourists was just letting out, the tour guide directing everyone to look at a sunken road that appeared to have been made from wood.

"It *is* a wood road," Dylan whispered to her conspiratorially. When he smiled, his eyes twinkled. "It's made o' oak. They say it was laid around 148 B.C."

"Why would they make a road out of oak?" Brenda asked quizzically.

"It's a bog road. The only way they could travel through the bogs was to make a road out o' somethin' other than the earth."

"So we're close to the bogs?" Vicki asked.

"Aye. We're nearin' the River Shannon and the area you pointed out to Sam is between the Rivers Shannon and Liffey."

"Are we going to be driving on that oak road?"

Dylan laughed. "Hardly, Darlin'. It's preserved. Historical treasure, you know."

She thought between the long flight and the drive, she would be famished but when they settled into a café, the aroma of food cooking made her queasy. Under Brenda's inquiring glance and Dylan's slightly furrowed brow, she settled on Irish oatmeal and soda bread. When the food arrived, she tried not to look at Brenda's and Dylan's heaping plates of rashers, bangers, black and white pudding and eggs—and she excused herself when Dylan began educating Brenda on the use of blood in the black pudding.

"Are you feelin' alright, Darlin'?" Dylan asked when she returned.

"Jet lag," Vicki said, sliding into the booth.

"Ah." He watched her for a moment. "It usually settles in a few hours after arrival. But don't worry; it'll pass quickly. Within two or three days."

"Wonderful," Brenda said. She leveled a questioning gaze at Vicki but when Dylan glanced up again, she averted her eyes.

When they left the café a short time later, they stretched their legs as they walked along the village's main street. The place was alive with tourists; she must have detected languages from every continent. They were taking photographs of beautiful cathedrals that seemed to appear on every corner, sandwiched in between the pubs and specialty shops.

The air was brisk; when Vicki shivered, Dylan insisted they head back to the car so Vicki and Brenda could don their jackets. He didn't seem affected by the cold; if anything, it invigorated him.

As Vicki pulled a heavy sweater from her suitcase and slipped it on, she glanced at Dylan. He'd been irritable from the moment Sam had mentioned returning here. But now he appeared to move between moods; at varying times, he seemed animated, telling of places and events and people. At other times, he seemed alone with his thoughts, even pensive.

He was, after all, going to see his grandmother and she steeled herself for what could be an emotional reunion. She didn't know how close to death his Mam would be, though Father Rowan had made it sound urgent that they come quickly. They might even be attending a funeral within the next day or two. She hoped Stephen Anders' funeral wouldn't be a second one.

9

It was mid-afternoon when they came across a diminutive one-lane bridge over a gently winding brook. Dylan stopped halfway across and looked down at the water below. His face was dark, his forehead lined.

"What is it?" Vicki asked.

"Just lookin'," he responded.

Both Vicki and Brenda followed his gaze but all Vicki could see was the water flowing idyllically across large stones as it wound its way toward lower ground. It was crystal clear and appeared shallow enough to skip across the stones from one side to the other without getting more than the bottoms of their shoes wet. In the distance was a single cottage set amid tall grasses that bent and swayed with the breeze.

After a moment, Dylan continued across the bridge, only to stop on the other side of it. He pulled onto the grass at the side of the road and stared at the cottage.

"Is this where we're staying?" Brenda asked, leaning forward to look at the tiny structure.

"No!" Dylan nearly barked his response. His voice was so forceful that Vicki spun around to look at him. He didn't move but continued to stare out the window as if he was memorizing every detail. She turned slightly to lock eyes with Brenda, who returned her gaze with an equal amount of curiosity and astonishment.

A long, awkward moment of silence ensued before Dylan opened his door. "Stay here," he directed.

"What did I say that stuck up his craw?" Brenda breathed as he walked away from the car.

"It wasn't you," Vicki answered. "I'm sure of it." She felt a strange sensation beginning in the pit of her stomach and reaching through her gut. The grass began to sway more violently as if the wind had picked up and as she looked toward the tops of the trees, they bent toward the car, their branches seeming to reach out to her.

She rolled down the window, expecting to feel the wind against her face but there was none. "That's strange," she murmured. She poked her arm out the window. The air was perfectly still.

But as she looked again to the tops of the trees, they twisted toward her. She could hear the wind now; it began as a whistle but as she listened, she realized it was more of a hum. And then she recognized a cadence as though a woman's soft voice was wafting through the trees toward her.

She turned to say something to Brenda when she saw a woman's face peering in through Dylan's window at them. She was young, perhaps in her early twenties. Her eyes were larger than most, very round and very blue. Her features were petite and her frame was slight. As Vicki stared at her, her long blond hair began to catch on the breeze and swirl around her.

And then she vanished.

"Did you see that?" Vicki managed to croak.

"See what?"

Vicki stared out the window and Brenda followed her gaze away from Dylan and the cottage to the other side of the road.

"That dog?" Brenda asked.

She had been so intent on the woman's image that she hadn't noticed a large black and white dog watching them from a knoll. It moved from paw to paw as though restless; its head was dipped low and the eyes averted upward as it observed them. Even from this distance, she could tell its eyes were light-colored; instead of the brown eyes she expected to see, they appeared blue. He locked his gaze on Vicki and she found the stare becoming hypnotic.

"Do you think it's rabid?" Brenda breathed.

"I don't know," she whispered hoarsely.

"Is Dylan safe out there?"

Vicki turned to peer out the passenger window again. The trees continued to twist as though there was a very high wind. But instead of bowing toward the car, they seemed to have turned around and were leaning toward Dylan.

He had walked a short distance across the open field of grass and stopped. It was obvious that he was staring at the cottage intently, though there was no sign of life there. Several moments passed and he'd barely moved a muscle.

She forced herself to turn her attention back to the dog, but it was gone. "Where'd it go?"

"I don't know." Brenda raised herself up and looked through the back window and then both sides. "It just disappeared."

They watched and waited but it seemed to have vanished. Finally, Vicki opened her car door. "I'll be right back," she said.

As she made her way across the field toward Dylan, she wrapped the thick sweater around her to keep the chill of the wind off her. But she was surprised and disconcerted to find that there was no wind at all.

As she came from behind Dylan, he made no move to turn around as if he was oblivious to her presence there. She was nearly beside him when she cocked her head and peered at his profile to find him teary-eyed.

"Dylan, are you alright?"

He turned toward her, his eyes widening momentarily as he noticed her. Then he reached his long arm out to her and pulled her to him so quickly that she almost stumbled on the uneven ground. He caught her easily and wrapped her into his arms, burying his face in her long hair. "Don't leave me," he whispered hoarsely, his lips brushing the hair against her ear. "Don't ever leave me."

She tried to pull back and look him in the eye, but he held her captive in his muscular arms, one hand intertwined in her hair as he held her to him. When she spoke, she found her lips brushing against his jean jacket. "I won't leave you. Now or ever."

"Promise me."

"I promise." His heartbeat was so strong that she could feel it through her clothing as he pressed closer to her. She began to feel as though they were the only two people in the universe; nothing mattered outside of this moment. He wanted her with him always and that was precisely where she wanted to be. She found herself rising on her tiptoes to whisper in his ear, "I have something to tell you."

"We have to go." His voice had changed and he abruptly loosened his hold on her. He brushed a lone tear from his cheek.

She felt her heart sink. Swallowing hard, she said, "Is this where you grew up?"

He reached for her hand as he turned away from the cottage, gently but firmly leading Vicki back to the car. "No. I grew up in the next village over, where we're headin'."

"So that house—?"

"I didn't grow up there."

"It's not your Mam's—?"

"No."

She wanted to ask whose house it was and why it had elicited such an emotional response but there was something about the way he brushed aside the tear from his cheek, the appearance of his narrowed eyes, the manner in which he avoided looking at her, and the tight grip of his hand around hers. He pulled her along until they reached the car, wrapping his arm around her as he walked her around the vehicle, depositing her gently into her seat before closing the door and returning to the driver's side.

"What was that all about?" Brenda asked.

"I'm clueless," Vicki answered as Dylan slid back into the car. He started the engine without glancing at the cottage again and pulled away. She nervously drew her sweater closer to her as a chill set in. But as they moved farther away from the bridge and the cottage, she realized the icy sensation she'd felt hadn't been from the weather—but from the young woman who had stared at her.

She glanced in the side mirror as the black and white dog moved into the center of the road behind them, watching them until they were out of sight.

10

It was only a short distance to the next village. The main street that wandered through the center of town was no more than three blocks long, making the village where they'd eaten earlier seem like a metropolis. In the distance, a gray stone building towered over them as if it kept sentry on the village below.

"What's that spooky monstrosity?" Brenda asked, pointing.

"The Catholic Church," Dylan said. He'd become quieter since leaving the tiny cottage and his speed had slowed considerably as they neared the village. He pulled diagonally into a parking spot at the far end of the main street and turned off the engine.

Vicki peered through the windshield at the hulking white building. *The Bog & Trotters Pub* was displayed across the double-wide doors.

"Thank God," Brenda said. "I'm starving."

"We'll not be eatin' here," Dylan said. His voice was abrupt as he rested his hands on top of the steering wheel and stared at the door. "Father Rowan agreed to meet me here. He's to give us the keys to the cottage where we'll be stayin'."

"We're not staying in a hotel?" Vicki asked. She leaned forward and smiled at Dylan but he didn't glance her way. Her heart skipped a beat; she'd much prefer to stay in a quaint cottage but hadn't voiced her opinion one way or another.

"No, Darlin'. It's a cottage we'll be stayin' in. It has all the creature comforts you could possibly want."

"Father Rowan—that's his church?" Vicki asked.

"Aye."

"Why not just drive there?" Brenda asked. "It can't be far."

"Twenty minute walk," Dylan said. His eyes never left the pub door. "But he won't be there. He's tendin' to folks in the village that need him." He opened the door. "Stay in the auto. I'll be retrievin' the keys and we'll be headed to the cottage and supper straight-away."

"I haven't been left in the car since high school," Brenda moaned, trying to stretch her legs but failing miserably.

"I said, stay here."

With that, he stepped out and closed the door behind him, plunging any objections they might have had into silence.

"They may as well have left me in prison," Brenda said.

"I don't know what's wrong with him."

"He said he didn't want to come back here." She propped her feet on either side of the driver's headrest. "We should have listened to him."

A rusting and beat-up truck pulled alongside them. Music was blaring and the three men inside alternated between banging their heads to the music and talking quite loudly. They seemed as if they'd already had quite a bit to drink but their destination was clear as they climbed out—or poured out, Vicki thought—and headed to the pub door. The largest man was so large that she marveled at how he ever fit into the small truck. His hair was red and unruly, his skin so freckled she could see it from the car, and his shoulders so wide he looked like a linebacker. The other two were smaller but had the same flaming red hair and fair, freckled skin. Though it was cold, they all wore short sleeves, revealing well-developed biceps. Their jeans were dirty as if they were accustomed to working in the fields.

"Oh, boy, do I know that type," Brenda said.

"Oh?"

"They're looking for trouble."

"I don't feel right," Vicki said.

"God, don't throw up in the car."

"It's not that. Something's not right inside that pub."

"Are you seeing it psychically?"

Vicki shook her head. "No. But Dylan needs me."

Brenda rummaged through her luggage. "Wait a sec," she said as Vicki opened the door and climbed out.

She popped her head back into the vehicle. "What?"

"I'm going with you." Brenda pushed the seat forward and climbed out. "And we're not going in alone." She shoved a pistol into Vicki's hand.

"But—"

"If he needs you, you need that."

She nodded. Taking a deep breath, she walked the few steps to the door and slowly opened it.

It took a moment for her eyes to adjust to the dim light. The pub was long and narrow. It wasn't quite the supper hour apparently, because it appeared largely empty, the rows of thick wood tables sitting idly. She stopped for a moment while Brenda caught up with her, glancing from table to table to try and locate Dylan. He wasn't in the room, she realized with a sinking heart.

Turning around, she realized a bar with stools was on the other side. She noticed Dylan's thick black hair as he sat with his back to them at the bar. There was no glass or bottle in front of him and he glanced at his watch as they started toward him.

"Well, if it isn't the murderer Mick Maguire," came a thundering, drunken voice.

Vicki stopped in her tracks as the three men from the truck surrounded Dylan.

"We should'a finished him off when we had the chance," a second one said.

They appeared even larger in the pub and Vicki suddenly felt very small. She sensed Brenda leave her side but she didn't turn around to follow her. Her eyes remained locked on the scene unfolding in front of her.

"We warned ya if ya ever crossed our paths again, we'd kick seven shades o' shite out o' ya," the largest man said, making his way in front of Dylan. He flexed his hands as if readying for a fight.

Dylan stood up, holding both his hands in the air. "I'm only here to see me grandmother afore she passes," he said. "I want no trouble with you."

The large man slammed a beefy fist into Dylan's jaw and Vicki involuntarily gasped. He reeled backward but one of the smaller men caught him, pulling his arms behind his back while ramming his knee into Dylan's lower back. His intent was clear: he was holding him for the other two to pummel.

The bartender backed slowly away from them without the slightest objection to a fight in his bar. Out of the corner of her eye, Vicki glimpsed the other patrons silently leaving.

The largest man grinned wickedly, showing yellowed, uneven teeth. His round, bulging eyes locked onto Dylan's exposed abdomen.

A gunshot rang out, whizzing so closely past the smaller man that he immediately dropped his hold on Dylan and grabbed his ear. The bullet continued into a whiskey bottle on the cabinet behind the bar, shattering it into a thousand pieces.

"Move away from him." Brenda's voice was even deeper and huskier than usual. "Or the next bullet goes right in the head."

"You don't know what you're doin'," the first man said, though he stepped back a couple of paces. "He murdered our sister. Everybody in town knows it. He should'a hung for it."

"If he stays alive, who's to say you're not the next mot he kills?" the third man said, though he, too, stepped back.

"She doesn't mean it," the man who had been holding Dylan announced. "She wouldn't protect a murderer."

"Maybe not," Vicki heard her own voice clear and strong. "But I'll kill you if you lay one more hand on him."

"Get over here, Dylan," Brenda ordered.

Dylan didn't answer but immediately strode across the room to join them. His face was ruddy and his eyes narrowed as he glared at Brenda and then at her pistol.

"So that's what they call ya now, 'eh, Bowsie?" the largest man sneered. "Had to change yer name to keep yer self-respect?"

Dylan's hands balled into fists and he turned around as if ready to charge across the room at him.

"He's baiting you," Vicki muttered, backing toward the door. "Don't fall for it, Dylan."

She was still backing up when the door abruptly opened and she ran into someone entering the pub. She gasped instinctively and hurled around, coming face to face with a priest's collar. Stunned, she looked upward. The door was still held ajar with the priest stranded between it and Vicki, the waning light illuminating part of his face. He was young; perhaps the same age as Dylan. His hair was light brown with golden highlights and it was long, brushing past his collar. It might have covered his ears but he had it combed behind them, revealing long sideburns that might have looked like a style from the past. But on him, it looked perfectly natural. He sported a mustache under a chiseled nose but his strong jaw was clean-shaven. His eyes were blue and sharp, taking in the scene unfolding in front of him. The slightest of frowns creased his brow.

The pub owner, who had remained conspicuously silent during the ordeal, moved from behind the far end of the bar.

"Any damages?" the priest asked.

"Aye. A whiskey bottle."

"I'll be back to cover it."

Dylan pushed by him, grabbing Vicki by the elbow and pulling her onto the sidewalk. The priest held the door for Brenda, who sauntered past him with a sly grin on her face.

"Nice to see you again, Mick," he said as he joined them.

Dylan tossed the car keys to him. "Drive."

The girls had scrambled into the back seat before the two men left the sidewalk. Vicki wanted to get away from the pub before the trio decided to take their fight into the street, and it felt as if Dylan was moving in slow motion.

He climbed into the passenger seat, his foul emotions emanating from him like lightning bolts, rapidly filling the small vehicle. The priest got in and started the engine. He backed out quickly and headed toward the opposite end of town.

"Ladies, this is Father Rowan," Dylan said. His voice was low and heavy as if he was gritting his teeth as he spoke.

"A Catholic priest," Brenda breathed to Vicki. "What a waste of a good man."

"Pleased to meet you," he said, "I'm sure."

"And these two delinquents in the back seat," Dylan continued, his voice rising, "are my girlfriend Vicki and her good-for-nothin' sister Brenda."

"You're welcome for saving your life," Brenda retorted.

"And I'm wonderin'," Father Rowan said evenly, "why it is that you didn't kick the shite out o' the three o' 'em. I've seen you do it a'fore. And w' two men tryin' to hold you back to boot."

"Shut up," Dylan said.

"America toned you down then?"

"Just shut up or—"

"Or what? You'll beat the h'ail out o' a priest? And me, with me collar on, too." He cocked his head toward Dylan. "It's not such a novel idea, you know. It's been done a'fore. Ooh, that's right. But you'd be knowin' that, wouldn't you? On account o' it was always you who saved me."

Dylan groaned and spun around in the seat. Turning his attention to Brenda, he said, "Give me the gun."

"I will not."

"I swear to God I will climb in that back seat and thrash your arse if I've got to take it from you."

"That sounds like fun."

Dylan made a sound akin to a roar, his sudden movement rocking the small car. But instead of coming across the seat as Vicki feared, he ranted, "Do you know how much trouble you've just gotten us into? Do you understand that guns are illegal in Ireland?"

"Gee, I don't remember reading that in the travel brochure."

"I'll be damned if I spend the rest o' me life in an Irish prison on account o' *you!*"

"Here," Vicki said, shoving her pistol into Dylan's hand. "Take this one. I don't want it. Now will you all just stop it? I don't need dysfunction."

He slipped the gun under the seat and glared at Brenda. "This isn't America. You don't 'ave the right to bear arms here.

Just carryin' a weapon like this could get you hard prison time. And it won't be like federal prison in the States, either. There'll be no one to rescue you here!"

"He's right, Brenda." Vicki sighed. "Just give him the gun. I can't go to prison."

With an audible exhale, Brenda handed him the gun. "Fine. Next time, they can whip you bloody. See if I come to your rescue."

They drove in silence for a minute before Father Rowan said, "I like you, Miss Vicki."

"Miss Vicki," Brenda smiled. "Feel free to call me Mistress Brenda."

"You've a cool head," he continued unabated, "somethin' Mick here has always needed. His two never were."

Brenda and Vicki exchanged glances.

"Are you two like, *brothers?*" Brenda asked.

"Aye."

"No!"

"She said 'like' brothers," Father Rowan said.

"Like doesn't mean like to Americans like like does to the Irish."

"Huh?" Brenda and Vicki both said.

"Please," Dylan said, "will everyone just be quiet? Just for a moment. We're on hallowed ground now."

Vicki peered between the seats to the church beyond. They were at the edge of town, the giant structure perched atop a gently rising hill. Father Rowan drove around it, following the narrow road about a mile farther. A small house came into view and he continued along the meandering road, finally pulling onto a dirt path.

The house was made of white-washed stone; it was rectangular, at least three times wider than it was deep. A mottled white picket fence surrounded it, leaving barely five feet of neglected garden between the home and the fence line. Trellises were strategically placed between the windows on either side of the front door, though the plants had withered so the walls appeared bare but for skeletal stretches of shrunken vines. The door and window trim were painted a medium shade of blue that had faded in spots, reminding Vicki of the Carolina blue skies speckled with clouds. The roof was steeply pitched with chimneys at each end.

It was beautiful, she thought. The perfect place to stay. Nothing else mattered now. The memory of the three men at the pub couldn't touch this idyllic location. The paint-chipped wooden bench beside the front door would suit her perfectly as she drew her sketches; that is, if she could get her focus off the beautiful view.

She felt as though she'd stepped into yesteryear. A small pond just down the incline from the house beckoned to her, the waters rolling gently in the slight breeze. The village was at least a mile away—far enough to make them feel secluded yet close enough if they needed something there.

Yes, she thought, this was going to be the perfect vacation.

11

Vicki put the finishing touches on the hastily drawn picture and laid it on the kitchen table. She worked quickly with one eye on Dylan and Father Rowan as they talked just outside the window, anxious to get the sketches from her dream faxed off to Sam.

It was clear that Dylan had been in this house before but he hadn't offered any details. It was a charming place. The front door opened into the living room and to the right was an eat-in kitchen. A fireplace separated the two rooms; Father Rowan had come by earlier in the day and started a cozy fire which warmed both rooms and provided a soothing ambiance. A dining table that could easily seat eight people was positioned near the fireplace, providing further warmth during meals. Which, Vicki thought as she glanced up again, she hoped would be soon.

On the other side of the living room was a short hallway leading to a small bedroom, which Brenda immediately claimed as hers, and a larger bedroom at the end of the hall. Between the two rooms was one bathroom with a claw-foot tub.

The bedroom consisted of a double bed which looked very small compared to the king-sized bed she'd left behind, two small nightstands and a free-standing closet. And it was perfect. She'd set her luggage at the end of the bed, not even bothering to unpack her clothes. There would be plenty of time for that after she worked on her drawings.

Dylan and Father Rowan had spoken quietly as they remained at the front door before venturing outside. Now she watched them with curiosity.

Seeing them side by side, she knew they were close in age. She'd expected the priest to be an older man with white hair; staid and distinguished. But she could easily picture Father Rowan in the same clothing as Dylan—jeans, a flannel shirt and jean jacket. His hair was slightly longer than Dylan's and his physique was something any warm-blooded woman would crave.

And they obviously knew each other quite well.

They laughed at times and at other times were pensive. They looked out across the fields and pastures, commenting perhaps on how much things had changed—or not changed at all. She was dying to overhear their conversation but the walls were thick.

She was finishing a second sketch when Brenda came out of the bathroom and wandered down the hall toward her while combing her hair, still damp from her shower. She joined her at the table as the men entered the house. Vicki closed her sketchbook and placed it face-down on the table atop the finished drawings.

"Is everything satisfactory?" Father Rowan asked.

Brenda smiled slyly. "Oh, I'd say so."

"Thomas—ah, Father Rowan," Dylan said, "has stocked the cupboards for us."

"Thomas," Brenda whispered.

Father Rowan brushed past them to the refrigerator, where he removed a casserole dish. "Shepherd's Pie," he said, smiling. He had a broad smile that displayed pearly white teeth. "M' mum made it h'self just this mornin'." He turned toward Dylan. "She remembered it's your favorite, Mick. She cooked it with lamb, just as you like it."

"So," Vicki said, "you two grew up together?"

Dylan pulled out a chair and sat down, motioning for Father Rowan to join him. "We've known each other nearly our whole lives. Haven't we?"

"Aye," he said, setting the oven before sliding the casserole dish inside it. He grabbed a loaf of bread that appeared homemade and set it on the table. "Mick was at our house so often, m' mum said she thought she'd bore twins."

"So you two are the same age?"

"A month apart, I think?" Father Rowan placed a jar of butter on the table along with a butter knife and four small plates.

"Aye," Dylan said, breaking the bread. "Thomas is the elder and he never let me forget it."

"You were always one fer gettin' y'self into scrapes. You needed an older brother."

"Interesting butter," Brenda said. "Why do I think it's homemade?"

"Near about. 'Twas made right outside the village here. You must get Mick to take you about."

"We'll be doin' a bit o' sightseein' in the mornin'," Dylan said. "Vicki wants to see where I used to work."

He almost snorted. "The bogs? That'll take all o' five minutes."

"They're that small?" Vicki asked.

"They're that borin'. But would you believe, Mick, tourist buses come through here now? Aye. And they take the folks through the bogs."

"Is that so?" Dylan answered. "They can't take the bus through there; they'd sink."

"Ooh, no. They take the horses from Aengus' stables. He's got a thrivin' business now."

"Aengus w' a thrivin' business! Will wonders ne'er cease?"

"So," Brenda said, "what exactly did you do when you lived here, Dylan?"

His face grew pink as he appeared to consider his answer. "I worked for a time for Bord na Mona."

"What's that?"

"It's a company, if you must know."

"Do you know what peat harvestin' is?" Father Rowan asked pleasantly.

Brenda and Vicki shook their heads. Dylan got up and opened the refrigerator. "Ah," he said, pulling out a few bottles of Guinness. He passed them around the table as the priest continued.

"You've seen turf farmin' in the States, 'eh?"

"Yes."

"I suppose it's similar to that. Only the peat in the bogs— which we 'ave instead o' turf—is used for fuel." He reached into a metal bucket beside the fireplace and pulled out a briquette. "In America, you use wood in your fireplaces?"

Vicki nodded.

"We're on an island here, in case you haven't noticed," Thomas said. "And most o' the forests have been cut down o'er the centuries. So we use the peat; make 'em into these briquettes. You notice they're smokeless."

"I hadn't noticed," Vicki mused. "But you're right."

"Well, Mick here, he operated some o' the heavy equipment that harvested the peat."

"You're borin' the panties off 'em," Dylan said, taking a healthy swig of beer. "Anyway, that's a life I left behind."

"But I thought you were a butcher—in a butcher shop," Vicki said softly.

"Ah," Father Rowan said before Dylan could answer, "that was when he left the village here and moved to the outskirts o' Dublin."

"You went from farming peat to being a butcher?" Brenda asked. "I don't get the connection."

"There is no connection," Dylan answered abruptly. "That was the whole point."

Brenda and Vicki exchanged glances. "But—"

"There's no 'buts' about it," Dylan said irritably. "I don't care to go into it, if it's all the same to you." He turned to Father Rowan. "And I'll thank you not to bring it up again."

He shrugged and sipped his beer. After an awkward silence, he asked, "So, you're goin' touristin' tomorrow?"

"Aye," Dylan said grudgingly. "Vicki wants to see the bogs. Don't you, Darlin'?"

"Yes. And maybe check out some shops in the village, have lunch in a pub or café…" She cocked her head and looked at Dylan. His jaw was still red though he'd paid no attention to it.

He was going to have a bruise, she thought, and not even a five o'clock shadow would be able to hide it.

"If you're worried about those blokes at the pub tonight," Father Rowan said, his eyes narrowing, "Don't be."

"No pistol totin' women tomorrow," Dylan said, eying them both. "I'll not spend me life in an Irish prison."

"Do you think the police will come here and question us?" Vicki asked.

Father Rowan chuckled. "No. I'd bet a year's wages on it." The women looked at him quizzically while Dylan paid an inordinate amount of attention to the beer he swirled around in the bottle. "Those blokes are in constant trouble. Fact is the real ring-leader, their oldest brother, is sittin' in an Irish prison at the moment."

"*Their brother?*" Brenda asked. "They were brothers?"

He looked at Dylan with a slight frown, as if waiting for him to answer. When he remained silent, he said, "Aye. Four brothers." His voice had become quieter. "Perhaps I've said too much."

"Perhaps?" Dylan said sarcastically.

Vicki looked from one to the other. "You knew them," she stated.

"The whole village knows 'em," Dylan said. He stood up abruptly, nearly knocking his chair over. "Supper must be warmed by now. And I'll not spend this trip discussin' a bunch o' wasters."

Father Rowan stood. "I'll be takin' m' leave, ladies," he said.

"Don't go," Dylan said.

"I must pay Paddy at the pub and get back to the church."

Dylan waved his hand. "They can wait. The church will still be standin' centuries after you're gone, and Paddy knows you'll be around directly."

"Well, I suppose…"

"Please stay," Brenda urged. They all nodded their agreement.

"Then I'll make m'self useful," he said, opening the cabinet and pulling out plates.

As Vicki watched the two men cooking and setting the table, she felt as though she'd lived there all her life. She knew nothing more about the country than she had before she left America, but there was something comforting about the cottage, about seeing the men side by side like blood brothers, hearing the crackle and pop of the fireplace and watching the sun disappear on the distant horizon… It was as if she'd come home.

12

An odd mix of fresh forage, ammonia and horses tickled Vicki's nose as the horses were led out of the stable. Dylan followed close behind, chatting amicably with the stable owner.

"So, you went to America, did ya now, Mick?" The man was small and wiry, his face leathery. When he glanced at them, his eyes shone a vivid green.

"Aye," Dylan said. "And I've brought me girlfriend and her sister to Ireland to meet me Mam and show them around a bit."

"How is Bonnie doin' these days?"

"I'm told she'll be up to seein' us this afternoon. 'ave you seen her lately?"

"Oh, maybe a month ago. Then she took to her bed and has been there ever since…" He saddled up the first horse while Dylan worked on a second one. "Let 'er know I asked after 'er, will you, Mick?"

"Aye. Be pleased to, Aengus."

Brenda pulled Vicki to the side. "Are you sure you should be doing this?"

"Dylan knows I've never ridden before. He promised he would get me a very gentle horse."

Brenda eyed the horses. "You're pregnant, Vicki," she said through clenched teeth.

"Tell me something I don't know."

"What if you fall?"

"I won't. I'll hang on tight."

"Dylan," Brenda said, turning away from Vicki, "are you sure you don't want Vicki riding with you on your horse?"

He glanced up with narrowed eyes that said, *Don't question me,* and Brenda chewed her lip.

"Not to worry," Aengus said. "I've picked a horse for beginners, I 'ave." He gently slapped the hindquarters of a blond mare. "This 'ere is Abigail. She'll be thirty years old next month, she will. You can kick 'er all day long and she'll ne'er do more than a steady walk." He chuckled. "You're not in a hurry, are ya, Mick?"

Dylan smiled. "No. Just doin' the touristy thing, ya know. Speakin' o' which, Father Rowan tells me you've a thrivin' business 'ere now."

"Aye," he said, his eyes widening. "Would ya believe I make good money sendin' these horses through the bogs each day? They come in buses now, Mick, and they stand at the edge o' the bogs and ooh and aah like they're lookin' at the queen."

Dylan chuckled. "Is that so?"

"Aye. And you're about the only one I'd allow me horses with, Mick, without a guide. I know you'd be knowin' those bogs like the back o' yer hand, you do."

"Aye. Been ridin' 'em since I was a tyke."

"Aye," Aengus said, patting the rump of a light brown horse. He eyed Brenda. "So you're an expert at horse ridin', 'eh?"

"Wouldn't say I'm an expert," Brenda said, sauntering to the horse and taking the reins. "But I was raised around them."

His eyes narrowed. "How is it then that you're sisters and that one doesn't know 'ow to ride?" He nodded his head toward Vicki.

"Our parents died when we were young," Vicki said, joining them. "She got adopted to one family and I went to another."

He clucked. "Ah, a shame that is, separatin' tykes." He clucked again.

Brenda easily climbed onto her horse and clicked her heels for a brief jog around the perimeter of the building.

Dylan led the blond mare to a tree stump. Her back was swayed and she moved slowly, as if she was reluctant to move at all. He helped Vicki climb onto the stump and then hoisted her onto the horse.

She had never been seated on a horse before and her first thought was how high it felt; much higher than she thought it would. It seemed now like the ground was a long way down and she realized why Brenda had been so concerned. If she fell off the horse, especially if the horse trampled her… She closed her eyes. She didn't want to think about it.

"Are you alright, Darlin'?" Dylan asked.

She looked down to find him watching her curiously. "Fine. This will be fun."

"You got your camera?"

"Yes."

He turned toward Aengus, who was watching them. "She has to take pictures o' everythin'," he laughed.

"Well, they are tourists, after all," Aengus answered.

"Stay right where you're at," Dylan said, "and I'll be joinin' you in a moment."

Vicki watched as he mounted a black steed. He looked perfectly at ease atop the horse and as Brenda joined them, her cheeks flush with the wind, she realized how mismatched she was to this venture. But Dylan had discussed it with Sam and now she went over the plan in her mind once more.

It had been the reason for her tagging along, she reminded herself. She was a tourist. And they would do what tourists do: take pictures and explore the country. It had been the reason for Dylan selecting this establishment to rent the horses instead of simply borrowing one or two from one of the villagers he knew well. If anyone asked questions, Aengus could inform them of their intent. And no one would question a tourist taking photographs but they would certainly wonder about Dylan doing it, having grown up here.

Dylan rode to her and instructed her on the proper hold on the reins. "I've known Abigail here for just about me whole life," he said. "You won't have to do anythin'. Once I start to move off, she'll follow straight-away."

"And what if she doesn't?"

"She will."

And she did. Brenda and Dylan rode ahead at a steady walk while Abigail crept along behind them at a snail's pace. But she was steady and they were soon out of sight of the stables and heading into the bogs.

Dylan turned his horse around to join Vicki. He had his cell phone in his hand and studied the screen. "The longitude and latitude you gave Sam for the castle," he said, "is just a few miles northwest o' here. We'll be there shortly. Are you doin' okay now?"

Vicki nodded though she was getting very nervous about sitting atop the horse. She longed to do as Brenda was doing: galloping a short distance, turning on a dime, circling back toward them—and having fun. She was beginning to feel like a wet blanket.

But Dylan didn't seem to notice. Once they were on their way, he pointed at the flat land around them. "This is known as a raised bog," he said. "Would you like me to tell you about it?"

"Sure," Brenda answered. "Why not?"

"Well," Dylan's voice took on an excited quality, as if he was beginning to relish his role as tour guide. "I'd say perhaps five to seven thousand years a'fore Christ was born, all o' this area here that ya see a'fore you was forest. And there were craters everywhere; they say it was from ice meltin' or some such, and the craters formed lakes all around the little patches o' forest."

Vicki looked out over the flat land. She couldn't picture it as forests and lakes; it appeared nearly completely deforested and while there were patches of water, they seemed more like rain deposits than lakes.

"So," he continued, "along the edges o' the lake was vegetation, as lakes 'ave. And over thousands o' years, the vegetation broke down until it filled up the ends o' the lakes and then a little more and a little more. Until the lakes were completely filled, you see." His eyes were wide and wondrous.

Vicki smiled, despite her discomfort.

"Well, you see, all that vegetation," he continued, "formed the peat. That's what it is. Aye." He waved his hand. "And they say, they do, that once there were trees that formed in the lakes but as they filled up, why, the peat just swallowed up the trees."

"Are you saying," Brenda said, "that there could be trees buried beneath us?"

"Completely."

"Whole trees?"

"Whole trees. Aye. That's what they say. They do."

They rode along in silence for a moment before he pointed. "You see, the bog at one time formed a dome and that's how it was able to swallow the trees the way it did. But now, they've been farmin' the peat. Takin' off the top layers. Like you do in America with turf farms, as Father Rowan spoke last evenin'." He turned to each of them with wide eyes. "And you know, once they started cuttin' away the layers, all sorts o' thin's 'ave been found."

"Like what?" Vicki asked.

He turned in a slightly different direction and Abigail automatically turned to stay with the other horses. "Well, for one thin', and this is quite fascinatin', mummies have been found here datin' back thousands o' years."

"Mummies?"

"Perfectly preserved in the peat. They found one that they thought could 'ave been an Irish lord, a king o' a fiefdom. Another one, a young woman, looked to 'ave been sacrificed."

"Like Satan worship?"

He shrugged. "There were pagan religions here, you must understand," he said in a hushed voice. "And if you were to find bones risin' up out o' the bogs, why then, you must bury 'em immediately. Otherwise, their souls will become restless. And then it would be no good at'al." He stopped and checked the GPS app on his phone. "Over there."

When they began again, they seemed to be heading for a clump of trees. The ground rose higher there, as if the peat hadn't been stripped away as much as the surrounding terrain.

"There are those who say there's treasure in the bogs," he went on. "I know a few mates who 'ave spent nearly their whole entire lives diggin' in the bogs for treasure swallowed by the peat."

"Did they ever find any?" Brenda asked.

"Oh, no. It's like lookin' for the pot o' gold at the end o' the rainbow. And you see," Dylan said, turning in his saddle, "there's not a thin' for miles and miles. This is the latitude and longitude you gave to Sam. So when the satellites would've focused on this area here, they'd 'ave seen nothin' but the bogs.'"

Vicki's skin grew hot and clammy as they approached the knoll and her chest began to feel as if it was being squeezed.

"Those trees there," he said as they drew near, "encompass maybe an acre. Perhaps not that much," he added, squinting. "And other than that one clump, which is most likely why the peat wasn't harvested there... Are you alright, Vicki?"

"Fine. Just listening."

"You're sure? Not afraid o' the horse, are you?"

"No. Abigail is very gentle."

Brenda and Dylan moved slightly ahead of her and their voices grew faint. The trees, Vicki thought, were drawing her in. She didn't want to move along the peat as Brenda and Dylan were doing. She wanted to aim straight for the trees. Yet, she could easily see between them and around them and knew no castle stood there.

Brenda disappeared over the knoll and Dylan followed at an easy pace. But as she continued staring into the grove, Abigail suddenly changed direction. The old horse charged the trees like a bull after a red cape. Vicki leaned into her back, grabbing both the reins and her mane in both fists. She called out to Dylan but the wind seemed to suck her voice from her, rendering her words nothing more than whispers. Then just as she thought Abigail was going to rush headlong into the wide trunk of the nearest tree, she abruptly made a ninety degree turn, kicking her back legs with a vengeance. All Vicki could see now was gray skies and the tops of the trees.

And then complete darkness.

13

The air had changed. Vicki tried to adjust to the darkness as she ran her hands along her body. She was standing up and she didn't recall the horse having thrown her. Yet, she was standing on solid, even ground.

The skies had disappeared; gone was the grayish cast and the scattered clouds overhead. She peered upward but could see nothing.

The odor that seemed to permeate everything was strange and yet, strangely familiar. It was acrid, musty and damp. She tried to take a deep breath but the air felt heavy, as if she was standing in an enclosed area. It was dramatically different from the open, crisp breeze as though—she shuddered at the thought—she'd been plunged into a crypt.

Vicki cautiously spread her hands beyond her body and tried to touch something solid, reaching for anything that could identify where she was. She shuffled her feet along the ground, expecting to bump into tree roots or feel the sponge-like texture of the bogs. But as she moved, she thought she detected stones beneath her. They were laid evenly and though some protruded upward slightly more than the others, she knew she wasn't standing on a haphazard jumble of rocks. There was a floor beneath her.

She fought a rising panic as she sniffed the air once more. Of course it was familiar, she thought. But how could she have arrived here? Had she been thrown from the horse after all? Was she lying unconscious on the ground above while her spirit moved through the dungeons?

As her eyes adjusted, she made out the sconces along the walls. Those closest to her were unlit but further down the meandering hallway were flickering lights; they were very dim and nearly imperceptible but she had no doubt now where she was.

She continued to feel her way along the wall. It was darker and more fetid than she recalled from her previous missions here. Then she realized she smelled human waste—and decay.

The wall gave way beneath her hand and as she jerked it backward in surprise, her knuckle raked across a piece of metal. She gasped and then reached for the metal, this time with intent. Yes, she thought. It was a bar from the cell doors.

She moved closer to it, clutching it while peering beside it into the darkness. Then she grasped at another bar and then another, making her way along the wall while still attempting to see inside.

The bars were rusted and they tore at her hands, embedding pieces inside her palm. She recoiled, shaking off the bits of metal, and then more cautiously reached for them again.

It was useless, she thought. Everything was enveloped in pitch blackness.

She sighed heavily and leaned her head toward the bars when a man's face appeared inches from hers.

He was imprisoned on the other side. It was so dark that she thought her eyes were deceiving her. But then he moved slightly and she saw his chiseled face streaked with grime. Light brown strands of matted and greasy hair fell unchecked across his forehead and an unkempt beard was knotty with the same grime that smeared his cheekbones.

His eyes were light colored, wide and unblinking as he stared at her.

"Can you see me?" Her voice was barely more than a croak.

"You're American." His voice was deep and dry and the words came slowly, as if he'd grown unaccustomed to speech.

"CIA," she heard herself saying.

He sucked in his breath and then his eyes raked over her body. She felt very small and useless; if he could not get out of this cell himself, how could she possibly think she could save him?

"Are there others?" he asked, as if thinking the same thing.

"Two. Maybe more."

He looked beyond her, his eyes skirting the perimeter. "Where—?"

"I don't know how I got here," she said. She reached through the bars and touched his face. "Can you feel me?"

It was obvious before he answered that he could feel her palm against his skin. A myriad of emotions flitted across his eyes—a basic need to recoil from the sudden touch of another human being followed by the need to draw her closer.

"Yes. I can feel you," he said. "I'm just in a bit of shock."

She opened her mouth but the sound of voices reached their ears and he hissed, "Quiet."

As the voices drew nearer, she realized if this wasn't one of her dreams—if this was real and she had somehow fallen into this other realm, she could be attacked, raped or imprisoned. And Dylan and Brenda didn't know where she was. *She* didn't know.

"Bolt cutters," he said.

She looked back at him.

"These bars are iron. But the locks can be broken with bolt cutters. There's only one way in and one way out."

"The stairs."

"The way you got here," he said.

Men were speaking, their voices drawing closer. Her heart began to pound wildly and her temples hurt. She had to run—but where?

"Over there," he said. "In the cell. Pull the door closed and go to the back. They'll pass right by you."

The hall wound tightly and as she took a quick step backward, she stopped abruptly and lifted her camera. The shot came fast and bright, capturing his astonished, stained face and disheveled appearance.

"What the devil was that?"

She realized too late it had been a mistake. The flash had alerted them to her presence and now their footsteps were coming swiftly toward her. She turned to look at Stephen Anders but he was retreating into the inky depths of his cell.

As she started to turn toward the opposite cell, the temporary safe haven seemed beyond her reach. And as she started to move toward it, she felt the heavy grip of a man's hand on her shoulder, pulling her toward him.

14

"Where the 'ail have you been?" Dylan demanded.

The sun felt bright and she squinted in a vain attempt to adjust to its intensity. Dylan stared at her with the same astonishment as Stephen had. She looked beyond him at Abigail, standing perfectly still.

Brenda was mounted on her horse but immediately slipped off as she rushed toward her. "Did she throw you?" she asked, inspecting her for signs of a fall.

"No," Vicki managed to say.

"You just took a fancy to jump off 'er and go for a walk?" Dylan demanded. His eyes flashed with growing ire.

"No," Vicki said firmly.

"We've been looking all over for you," Brenda said. "We've been worried sick."

"I couldn't have been gone for more than five minutes," she heard herself saying. "Maybe ten."

Dylan's jaw dropped. "You've been gone the better part o' an hour!"

"I was with him." The words rushed out.

"Who?"

"*Him*. Stephen Anders. He's here."

"Where?"

Her eyes wandered around them. There was the same clump of trees, the same expanse of bogs. There was no castle. *There was no castle.*

She grabbed her camera. "I took a picture of him."

"Let me see that." Dylan took the camera from her and pushed the button to view the last picture. There was nothing but a black frame.

"I'm telling you, he's there," she insisted.

Dylan and Brenda both stared at her as if she'd lost her mind.

"How did I get here?" Vicki asked.

"You rode a horse," Dylan said.

"No. I mean, after I disappeared, how did I get *here?*"

"We've been looking for you," Brenda said. "Abigail came over the rise but you weren't on her. We thought you'd fallen off so we backtracked. But we couldn't find you. We'd searched this area at least once—you can see there's not much to search—and then suddenly, there you were."

Dylan's face grew white. "We're gettin' out o' here."

"No. Wait," Vicki insisted. "Latitude and longitude."

He stared at her as if she'd grown two heads.

"*Latitude and longitude.*"

He pulled out his cell phone and peered at the GPS.

"Send it to Sam," she said. "Everything. Right down to the decimal degree. *Do it.*"

He tapped the screen and chose to send the coordinates to Sam via text message. "There's nothin' here, Vicki."

"But there *is* something here. And we need bolt cutters."

"What?" Brenda asked.

Dylan waved his hand. "To cut what? A limb from a tree? You fell from your horse, Vicki, and you hit yer head. I'm takin' you home."

"Then why didn't you find me when you were looking for me?" she demanded. "Why wasn't I lying on the ground unconscious? You said you searched this whole area." She turned around so they could examine her clothing. "I didn't fall. I have no grass stains on me or dirt—or peat. The ground is damp; don't you think my clothes would be, too?"

"Can you lead her horse back?" Dylan asked Brenda, grabbing Vicki's elbow and leading her to his horse.

"Sure thing," Brenda said. With a worried glance at Vicki, she returned to her own horse, mounted it and then trotted to Abigail. The docile mare allowed her to grasp her reins and as Brenda clucked to lead her closer to Dylan's steed, she moved like an old woman with creaky bones.

Dylan arranged the saddle and blanket on the steed's back. "If you were there, Vicki, you were there in your mind. Not your body. You went into a trance-like state—that thin' you do—and you fell off your horse." He nodded his head toward Abigail. "Look at 'er. She can barely move. She couldn't 'ave tossed you."

Dylan mounted the steed and then beckoned Vicki to come closer. "Put your foot in the stirrup there," he instructed. When she did as he ordered, he said, "Now haul y'self up."

As she grasped the horn, pain radiated through her palm and into her arm. But Dylan had already clenched his own hand around her arm and was helping to pull her upward. She clumsily swung her leg over the horse, settling in front of him. Her palm hurt so badly that she fought back tears.

As she settled into him, he wrapped his arms around her and brushed the horse with his inner legs. With a simple cluck, the steed moved forward.

"You had me worried half to death," he whispered in her ear. "I cannot lose you here, Vicki. Are you understandin' me? I cannot lose you."

With his strong arms around her and his confidence in riding obvious, Vicki released her grip on the horn. She turned her wrist and stared at her palm. Lodged in the skin were embedded pieces of rusty metal.

15

Dylan set the laptop on the kitchen table and pulled out a chair for Vicki and one for Brenda, who seemed reluctant to leave the window.

"What is it?" Vicki asked.

Brenda turned around with a slight frown. "It's that dog again."

"What dog is that?" Dylan asked.

"A big dog. I saw him on the drive here, saw him again at the edge of the bogs. Now he's on that hill over there, shifting from side to side."

"Where?" Dylan joined her at the window.

"Over—well, that's odd. He was just there."

He shrugged. "A stray, most likely."

"I think he's rabid."

"Why do you say that?"

"I don't know." She made her way to the table and sat down. "What's on the screen?" she asked, leaning forward to see more clearly.

"I thought I'd check in on the fish room a'fore I called Sam," Dylan said, settling into a chair between them.

"What's he doing?" Vicki asked.

They all stared at the screen for a moment. "Oh," Dylan said, pressing the volume button.

"Why didn't they tell me angels eat their own eggs?" Sam was complaining as he scurried from one tank to another. He passed Benita going in the opposite direction. They passed each other several times, each with loaded nets in their hands.

"I've never seen Sam move so fast," Vicki said.

"But what's he doin'?" Dylan asked, his brows furrowing.

"Don't you dare tell them some of the eggs were eaten, do you hear me?" Sam said between oaths.

"They're taking the parents out of the tanks," Vicki said, her face growing pale.

"Oh, no."

"If you breathe a word of this to anybody, I'll have you deported!" Sam said as he scuttled back down one aisle and Benita hurried up the next.

"Yeah, yeah, yeah," the Mexican woman said.

"Is he havin' Bennie help him?" Dylan said incredulously.

Dylan pulled out his cell phone and dialed Sam's number. The phone rang once and they watched as Sam ignored it. When it rang a second time, he cursed. But on the third ring, he reached into his pocket. Seeing it was Dylan's number, he rested against one of the tank shelves and brushed hair obviously damp from perspiration off his forehead.

"So, what'ya up to?" Dylan asked when he answered.

"Paperwork," Sam growled. "I'm up to my ears in it. You know how the agency is."

"Ooh," Dylan said. "So, I caught you at your office, did I?"

"Yeah, I'll be here all night. You got news for me?"

The three watched as Benita continued scampering up and down the fish aisles, moving adult angels from one tank to another.

"So, aye. I do," Dylan said finally. "I have an interestin' situation for you."

"Well, don't take all day. I've got a lot of work to do here."

"I see," Dylan said. Vicki stifled a laugh and he shook his head in warning. "Okay. I've got a longitude and latitude for you."

Sam looked around for a piece of paper. Finally, he grabbed one of the record-keeping charts that hung from the end of the tank. "Shoot."

Dylan recited the coordinates Vicki provided earlier and watched as he wrote them. "Now, here's where it gets interestin'." He relayed what had happened to them and waited for Sam's response.

"You're saying," Sam said, "that Vicki claims she was there and spoke to Stephen Anders?"

"Aye. In the flesh."

"But she was—" he glanced at Benita as she crossed to the opposite side of the room. He turned his back to the woman. "She was on a psychic mission right? This isn't the first time that she's thought someone could see her."

"I think this time might be different," Dylan said. Over Sam's objections, he said, "She injured herself against the cell bars."

"She might have injured herself but it wasn't at Anders' cell."

"Then explain this to me. I just finished tweezin' metal slivers out o' her palm and doctorin' her up."

"What?"

"You heard me."

"But how—?"

"I don't know how it was possible. But it happened. And Anders instructed her to bring bolt cutters. He said there's only one way in and one way out. It's down the stairs Vicki drew for you."

"Yeah," Sam said thoughtfully. "I got her faxes earlier today, also. Tell her she did a good job."

"I'll do it. But, what do we do now? Obviously, I can't follow Alice through the lookin' glass. So how are we supposed to get to this man and get him out o' there?"

Sam didn't answer immediately and they watched the computer screen as he stroked his chin. "We have some new technology," he said thoughtfully. "We've not had much of an opportunity to use it yet. But this might be just the right mission for it." He looked for Benita, who was mopping her forehead of perspiration. Apparently satisfied that she wasn't listening, Sam continued, "It's called Ground Penetrating Radar System, or

GPRS. We just placed some devices on our satellites. The way it works is, it uses the latest technology in sonar, very much like submarines have had for decades—but this is used to penetrate the ground. It then draws two and three dimensional images."

"Well, that sounds perfect," Dylan said, glancing at Vicki. She nodded her approval.

"Mind you, I don't know if it will work in this case. Or if it will find what we're looking for. But it's worth a shot… Once we get the images from the satellite, I'll send them to our computer animation team."

"Sounds like cartoons," Dylan said.

"They're gamers. You know, those three-dimensional games kids play, where everything looks so real? They send GI Joes through the rooms, encountering all the enemies and obstacles?"

"I've never played 'em m'self."

"Well, it's amazing technology. The same computer skills are applied to the ground penetrated images. So what we arrive at is a three-dimensional computer model where we can walk you through room by room—that is, if we're able to find anything."

"How soon can you get this done?"

Sam looked around the fish room. "Well, I'm in the middle of a very important project right now," he said. "National security and all that."

"I see," Dylan said. "But a man's life is in danger."

Sam glanced at his watch. "You're about five hours ahead of us," he said as if thinking out loud. "I can make a few calls. If they're able to do it in the next few hours… If they can do it in the dark," he interrupted himself, "then I might be calling you in the middle of the night."

"I'll be ready."

"If—and this is a big if, mind you," Sam said, "we're able to confirm Vicki's psychic images, then you'll be called upon to extract him within the next 24 hours. Got it?"

"Got it. I'll do what it takes to complete the mission."

"I'll be in touch," Sam said.

"Oh, a'fore you go, do you think you'll be able to check on the fish today?"

"I'm a very busy man," Sam said. "I was there this morning. Everything's fine."

"Ooh. No losses?"

"Nah. I told you I'd take care of everything."

"Ooh. Well, in case I neglected to tell you, don't worry if you happen to have any angelfish lay eggs and then eat 'em."

Sam stood up straighter. "What?"

"And if the eggs hatch and the parents eat 'em, don't worry about that, either."

"You think you might have remembered to tell me that before now?"

"Well, it was in the book I left you, you know. It's just that the male doesn't always fertilize every single egg the female lays. So he eats the unfertilized ones."

Sam looked across the room at Benita, still scurrying between tanks with loaded nets.

"And when the fish hatch, if any are so weak they wouldn't survive anyway, the parents eat 'em to give the others a better chance at livin'."

"Listen," Sam said gruffly. "This is all totally fascinating, but I've got items of national security on my desk. I don't have time for all this talk about something not even large enough to be bait."

"Sorry," Dylan said, suppressing a smile. "I'll let you go then."

"I'll be in touch."

"Fine." Dylan clicked off the phone and the three watched Sam on the screen.

He turned to look at Benita for a few seconds and then said, "Forget it. Put everything back where it was."

"What?" the Mexican woman nearly shrieked.

"Turns out, it's okay if they eat their eggs. They're only eating the ones that aren't fertilized."

Benita marched up the aisle to stand in front of him. Her face was ruddy and sweating from her exertions.

"So, do you remember where each angel's original tank was?"

Benita swore something they couldn't understand and threw her towel at Sam. "You do it," she said, stomping toward the door. "You're loco!"

16

Bonnie O'Sullivan's home was located only a mile on the other side of the church. It was a tiny brownstone bungalow with harvest gold trim and door. From the looks of the imperfect window glass and the home's condition, it appeared to be at least two hundred years old but Dylan informed them it was much older.

The gate at the front hung precariously on the hinges and Dylan hesitated as he opened it, no doubt thinking of the work he'd done at Aunt Laurel's home while his grandmother's rented bungalow, the only home she'd known since marriage, lay in disrepair. His face was crestfallen as he approached the house. He didn't knock but quietly slid the door open and called out for his grandmother.

"She's restin'," came a hushed voice. Dylan entered, followed by Vicki and then Brenda.

"Mum Rowan," Dylan said as a heavyset woman waddled into the room.

"Mick," she said, smiling broadly, "how are ya doin' w' y'self, boy?" She wrapped her arms around him and hugged him close as tears formed in her eyes. "You're a sight for sore eyes, you are."

"I've brought me girlfriend from America," Dylan said. He pulled back from the older woman, though it was clear she didn't want to let him go. He wrapped one arm around Vicki's shoulders and edged her forward. "This is Mrs. Rowan, Father Rowan's mum. She's been Mam's neighbor for as long as I can remember. And me second mum. Mostly, me only mum."

"Aye, Mick," she said, dabbing at the corner of her eye. "I always felt as if you were as true a son as me Thomas."

He waved for Brenda to come forward. "And this is Vicki's sister, Brenda."

"You must have a set and a cup o' tea," Mrs. Rowan said. "I made some fresh scones for ya, as well."

"May I help you?" Vicki asked.

"Oh, no, child, I've got it all prepared for ya, I do. T'will only take me a moment." As she waddled back through the door she'd come through, Vicki glanced around the room for a place to sit.

Her eyes landed on a television set that appeared to have been manufactured in the 1950's. It had a small screen but was set into a large mahogany cabinet. The channel dial with perhaps a dozen channel numbers further accentuated its age.

As she made her way toward it Dylan said, his face reddening, "The telly is black and white. But Mam wanted it because she said it was a good piece o' furniture."

But it wasn't the television set that had gained her attention. It was the plethora of photographs that set atop it that drew her interest; they were of all sizes and in various style frames, none of them matching or even complementary to each other.

There was a young boy with thick black hair and wide eyes standing with his arms around a woman barely larger than himself with white hair pulled into a bun. Beside it was the boy slightly older, gangly with pants just a bit too short and a shirt that appeared too large, hugging the same woman, who hadn't appeared to have aged at all. Another showed the boy with a reddish-brown dog of dubious parentage, his arms around its neck.

The boy grew older from one photograph to the next; in most of them, he had his arms around the woman and her arms were around him. His smile grew from tentative to boisterous to mischievous to loving. His height grew from a lanky boy to an awkward teenager to a man with broad shoulders and wide chest. But even when he clearly towered over the woman, he almost always had his cheek pressed against hers, even if he had to lean down to reach her.

Then the photographs changed.

Vicki picked up one and stared at it. The look in Dylan's eyes haunted her; they were sunken, the spirit gone. He looked lost. He stared into the distance and not at the camera at all, though the same woman hugged him. The smile that had appeared so broad in all the others was replaced with sullenness. His shoulders sagged and even in later pictures with his cheek pressed against the woman's, the spark was gone.

"This woman?" Vicki asked as Dylan joined her.

"M' Mam."

"And—?"

"Ah, here we are," Mrs. Rowan said as she entered the room carrying a tray.

Brenda jumped up from the sofa to help her but she shooed her away, clearly relishing her role as hostess.

Vicki reluctantly set the photograph back on the television. Each one was dust-free, as if someone had taken great pains to keep it that way.

Dylan led her to the sofa and the three sat down as Mrs. Rowan poured them cups of tea. When they were settled in with a tiny china plate of scones and their drinks cooling on the coffee table, Mrs. Rowan took a deep breath.

"So. I know you'll be askin' after your Mam," she said. Her eyes glistened. "She's been in and out the last few days. At times, she seems lucid and asks if her Mickey has arrived from America. At other times, she thinks you're a tyke yet and asks if you're out playin' with Flann."

Vicki stole a sideways glance at Dylan.

"Me dog," he said quietly. "She's been long gone."

"Aye," Mrs. Rowan said, "I suppose she passed when you were a teenager, didn't she?"

"Aye."

"But you must eat," she urged. She waited until they dutifully took bites of their scones before continuing. "At t'other times she thinks your Pap is in the room with 'er and she's speakin' to him. Once she said to me, Jean, she said, don't ya see me Arlen there in the corner? He sees you. Says you've put on a bit o' weight."

Vicki looked at Dylan as she sipped her tea. His eyes were downcast and his face strangely pink. As he blinked, the tiniest of tears appeared at the outer edge of his eye. Brenda was being uncharacteristically subdued as she nibbled on her scone.

"I don't know what she'll be like when you go in to see her," she continued, her voice softening. "I hope you've not made a trip for nothin', Mick. She may not open her eyes. And if she does, she might not recognize ya."

At that, he set his plate on the table and shielded his eyes with his hand.

"Are you okay?" Vicki asked quietly. He didn't answer and she rubbed his shoulder in what she hoped was a comforting gesture. She turned to Mrs. Rowan. "So, his grandmother's condition—?"

"She's not long for this world, child. She's got one foot here and one foot in the afterlife and it won't be long a'fore the other foot follows."

"But she isn't in a hospital."

Mrs. Rowan chuckled wryly. "Hospitals are for the sick, child. Bonnie O'Sullivan isn't sick. She's just dyin'."

Before Vicki could answer, Dylan stood up. "I want to see her." His voice was firm but he avoided looking at them.

Vicki rose to her feet at the same time as Mrs. Rowan.

"I'll stay here," Brenda murmured. "If you need me, let me know."

Vicki nodded.

Mrs. Rowan led the way down a very short hallway. They passed a door on the right that Vicki suspected had been Dylan's; it consisted of a twin-sized bed that was covered in a dark red and blue plaid quilt, a dresser and small chest in heavy, dark wood, and a laundry basket filled with a variety of toys. They passed it too quickly and Vicki longed to go back, to enter the room and to piece together the past that Dylan had left behind.

At the end of the hall was a tiny bathroom and she assumed there had just been the one bath shared between the two bedrooms. They stopped at the open door on the left. Mrs. Rowan stepped to the side and motioned for them to enter. Then she took her leave as they approached the bed.

It was a teeny room that was crammed full with only a double bed and a dresser. There were scant possessions; a mirror and hairbrush lay on the dresser beside two more photographs of Dylan and his grandmother. There were no other people in any of the pictures and Vicki wanted to ask what had happened to his mother; why she didn't appear in any of the photographs; and why there were no pictures of his grandfather.

Two chairs had been pulled into the room. They were situated beside the bed, obviously brought in for visitors.

Vicki quietly sat in the chair farthest from the head of the bed as Dylan leaned forward and gently tapped his grandmother's shoulder.

"Mam," he said with a strange mixture of excitement and sorrow, "It's me, Mick. I've come from America to see me best girl."

The woman stirred, slowly at first. Her eyes opened and settled on the wall opposite her.

"I've come a long way to talk to ya, Mam," Dylan chided gently. "Are ya gonna sleep the visit away?"

"Mickey," she said suddenly.

"Aye," he said, a broad smile spreading across his face.

She turned around to examine him. "Me Mickey," she said, drawing her hands up to his face. He leaned in farther and kissed her on both cheeks. She didn't seem to want him out of her grasp but when her hands slipped tiredly, he sat carefully on the mattress beside her and drew her hands into his lap.

She stared at him with intensely blue eyes. Her face was completely unlined and if it wasn't for the translucent tone, she might have been forty years old. Her hair was very long, very thin and as white as snow. She grasped his hands with long, slender fingers that clearly showed her blue veins. "Now wouldn't you be just the bee's knees for these old eyes o' mine? You always would be knowin' how to buck up this old gal's spirits."

He reached across her narrow bed to retrieve the brush from the dresser. "You remember how I always loved to brush your hair?" he asked as he began brushing the long strands. He worked slowly, smoothing the hairs as he brushed so he didn't pull on her scalp.

"And who might you be?" she asked suddenly.

When Vicki looked into her eyes, she fought a sudden impulse to rush into her arms and hold her. But before she could answer, Dylan spoke. His voice was full of barely contained excitement. "I brought me girlfriend all the way from America to meet ya," he said.

"Your girlfriend," she said, smiling. Her entire face beamed when she smiled; her eyes became the same half-moon shape as Dylan's and her nose crinkled. Lines that hadn't been visible before now stretched from the outer corners of her eyes, further accentuating her good humor.

"I'm Vicki," she said, leaning forward in her chair to rest her hand on the old woman's arm.

"You're the reason his smile is back," she said.

Vicki glanced at Dylan, who was watching his grandmother with a gentle smile.

"Mickey is a good boy," she said. "He's always been a good boy. Don't be allowin' him to tell you otherwise."

Dylan chuckled. "Mam always was an enabler."

"He's been the light o' m' life, m' sun and m' moon and m' stars," Bonnie O'Sullivan continued. "The best thin' that ever happened to this old soul."

Dylan stopped brushing her hair long enough to softly squeeze her hand.

"You have the gift," she went on, still eying Vicki.

"Oh, Mam, don't…"

"Excuse me?" Vicki laughed.

"It's in your eyes."

"I'm told they're an unusual color."

"Tisn't that, child. You know what I'll be talkin' about." She pointed one long finger at Vicki's eyes. "The veil is thin in Ireland."

"The veil?"

"Mam, cut it out," Dylan chided. "I've other news to tell ya."

"And you've news to tell Mickey, haven't ya?" she said to Vicki.

"Excuse me?" The smile faded from her lips as she stared into the old woman's eyes. She knew. She clearly knew. Yet this wasn't the place or the time she would have chosen to tell him.

"It's alright, darlin'," she said. "You and I, we'll have many a conversation. And Mickey here, he'll be thrilled with the news, he will."

Dylan cocked his head, his brows knit. As Vicki looked from one to the other, she knew Dylan was under the impression that she was speaking nonsense. Then he said, "I've news to tell ya, Mam. I'm a landowner."

"No."

"'Tis true. You can ask Vicki here. I went to America and I became a landowner. I did."

"So quickly?"

"Aye. And it's a big house, Mam." He squeezed her hand and ran his fingers through her long hair. "The whole o' this house wouldn't even equal the first floor. And there are three floors in all."

"Why so large?"

"It's meant for a big family, I suppose. But it's just Vicki and me. Come to America with me, Mam. I'll set you up like a queen."

She chuckled tiredly. "Now what would I be doin' in America, Mickey? Every soul I've ever known is right here. Why, when Arlen comes back to visit me, he won't know where to look."

He hesitated, clearly perplexed by this reasoning. "You'd have everythin' you could ever possibly want for."

"But I have all I'd be wantin' right here, child. I have you. And that's all I ever wanted."

"Vicki's sister came with us, too, Mam. She's sittin' in the parlor."

"Then I shall visit her on my way out." She took Vicki's hand and placed it on the bed beside her and then gently placed Dylan's hand atop Vicki's. She placed both her hands on top of theirs. "Listen to her, Mickey. She won't steer ya wrong."

Dylan stole a glance at Vicki and smiled. "I know she won't."

"And Mickey here, he'll take care o' you. He's a gentle soul. Always has been. But if he senses you need protection, he'll be there. He'll do whate'er it takes to keep ya safe."

"Oh, Mam, don't go there," Dylan said softly. His eyes were sad and dark.

She nodded. "Oh, Arlen," she said suddenly. "Have ya come to take me on a walk through the meadows again?"

Dylan glanced at Vicki and shook his head slightly. She understood. She was just thankful they hadn't walked in the room to find her comatose, unable to register that Dylan had come so far to see her. And it had been far, she was convinced of that; it had been further emotionally than it ever had been physically.

Mrs. O'Sullivan sighed.

They waited a moment for her to speak but she didn't.

"Are ya goin' to sleep now, Mam?" Dylan asked after a long moment. He leaned toward her, looking at her face. "Mam?"

With the movement of their hands, Mrs. O'Sullivan's slipped off the top, landing on the sheet beside her.

"Mam!" Dylan jumped up, placing his hand on her pulse.

Vicki felt her chest begin to constrict. I have to stay strong, she thought, for Dylan's sake. Don't cry. *Don't cry.*

But even as she choked back her own tears, Dylan began to sob quietly. "Mam," he cried. "Mam!" He sat down heavily in the chair and buried his face in his hands. His shoulders shook and he moaned as though his heart was breaking in two.

Vicki sat for a moment, stunned that she could have passed away so quickly. She almost expected her to turn around and ask what he was crying about. But as she stared at the woman, she knew in her heart that she was gone.

It was a private moment, one between Dylan and his grandmother. Silently, she stood and stepped around his chair. She would go into the parlor and inform Brenda and Mrs. Rowan. And then she'd wait for Dylan to join them, when he was ready.

But as she stepped toward the door, he reached out suddenly and grabbed her, pulling her to him. He buried his face against her belly and sobbed so forlornly, so hopelessly, that she wanted to do anything to ease his pain. But she found herself simply running a hand through his hair, allowing him to bury his face against her, while her other hand massaged his shoulder. It felt tight now and tense and as she looked up, her eyes landed on the photographs on the dresser. Dylan and his Mam; she was the woman who had reared him when his father had abandoned him and his mother… God only knew where his mother was. And what that young boy in the pictures had experienced. This tiny woman beside them had been the only real family he'd ever known. And now she was gone.

She heard a slight rustling sound and she half-turned to look toward the door. Father Rowan stood in the doorway. His eyes moved from the bed to Dylan to Vicki. He made the sign of the cross and backed away, brushing a tear from his eye. If they had been like brothers, Vicki thought, would he have thought of Mrs. O'Sullivan as his Mam as well?

His mother moved into the doorway as he backed away. Her chin trembled and she placed a handkerchief over her mouth and choked back the tears as she stepped quietly down the hallway.

More than thirty minutes passed before Dylan released his hold on her. Her clothing was soaked but she didn't care. Her own tears had run unchecked down her cheeks and as his body shook with his grief, hers shook for the pain she wished he didn't feel.

At last he became quieter and then a short time later, he released her and tried to dry his cheeks. She reached for a box of tissue from the dresser and he took it from her wordlessly, as if any attempt at speaking would cause him to begin weeping again.

She remained standing at his side, running her hand over his back.

He quietly rose and straightened the bedcovers around his grandmother, tucking her in as if she was only sleeping. Father Rowan appeared in the doorway with his mother and Brenda.

Seeing that his tears had ceased they entered the room and stood around the bed.

"Has anyone notified m' mum that Mam was…" His voice faded away as if he couldn't bring himself to finish the sentence.

"We don't know where she is, Mick," Mrs. Rowan said in a hushed voice.

He made a sound that might have been meant as a chuckle but it came out as a painful snort.

"The whole village has been prayin' for her, Mick," Father Rowen said. "I'll start the calls within the hour."

"Would you like tradition honored, Mick?" asked Mrs. Rowan.

His eyes grew wide and then he seemed to realize that he was her only relative in the absence of his mother—her daughter. "I don't know if Mam ever ventured more than fifty kilometers from this house," he said thoughtfully. "Do ya know o' anyone outside o' the village who needs to be notified?"

"Just your mother, Mick, and as we said, no one knows where she is…"

"Then the funeral will be tomorrow."

There was a collective gasp.

"Notify everyone," he said, his voice growing firmer. "The wake begins within the hour. It'll last only through the night. In the mornin' we'll carry the casket—" his voice choked on the last word, but he cleared his throat and continued "—to the church. The funeral will be at the gravesite. It's what Mam would've wanted."

"But the coffin—" Mrs. Rowan began.

"I'll take care o' everythin'," Father Rowan said. "I've got a phone tree now, Mick. It's all electronic. Everyone will know within the hour. I'll take care o' the casket and tomorrow, she'll be buried. I'll do everythin' the State requires—death certificate…" His voice faded as he seemed to realize how clinical his words sounded in the small room.

Mrs. Rowan threw a sheet over the dresser mirror and pulled the curtains closed. "Tradition, you know," she said.

17

If it weren't for the body of Bonnie O'Sullivan on display in the parlor, Vicki might have felt as if she was attending a cocktail party.

More than three dozen people were crammed into the tiny bungalow. They were crowded into the kitchen, where Mrs. Rowan was busy removing trays from the oven filled with sweetmeats. They were arriving on the front stoop bearing dishes of stew and potatoes and a variety of appetizers. They spilled onto the front lawn, where stout beer beckoned them from ice-filled chests. And they surrounded Mrs. O'Sullivan, remarking on the excellent job the women had done in preparing her for the wake.

All of the mirrors in the home had been covered and all the curtains drawn in keeping with tradition. Her body was not in view of the front door, lest her spirit escape when the door was opened. And at some point before the funeral, at some predetermined time that Vicki didn't quite comprehend, everyone would stand back, allowing clear access from the body to the closest window. Then a designated person would open the window and allow Bonnie O'Sullivan's soul to pass out of the house and into the next realm.

No one spoke in hushed tones. They were boisterous, laughing, imbibing and telling one story after another of the deceased woman. The funnier the story, the more it was enjoyed as it became clear to Vicki that the villagers were not mourning her passing but celebrating her life.

Only Dylan sat gloomily in a corner of the parlor, dutifully standing to receive one neighbor after another and sitting quietly in between. Though he didn't ask anything of them, Vicki and Brenda decided to join him, one on each side of him. In this way, they could provide a buffer of sorts between him and the increasingly raucous crowd.

But he seemed not to notice them. He appeared instead to be lost in his own world. He sipped his beer quietly, retreating farther and farther into himself as the evening wore on.

"Some wakes," remarked Mrs. O'Brien, a lady who lived in the village, "would be goin' on for six days or more. 'Tal depends on how far friends and family must travel, you know. This will be the shortest wake I'll ever have attended in the whole of my entire life."

The group nearest Vicki laughed loudly apparently from a story one of the villagers told.

"And do ya remember the time," an older man said with great gusto, "that Mick was picked up by the authorities and put in jail?"

"Ooh," the crowd said in unison, smiling broadly. Some gave sideways glances toward Dylan, who pretended not to hear the discussion.

The man rubbed a bulbous red nose. "Aye, and he must 'ave been all o' fourteen years old. Painted graffiti all o'er the village. Some say the ground shook clear to Dublin when Bonnie got the call. She took out o' the house here and walked all the way to town with her arms folded. Ne'er said a word. Walked the five kilometers to the jail. Went right in, snatched up the cell keys and marched right back to the place where they were keepin' young Mick. Unlocked the door and grabbed 'im by the ears. They say Mick was beggin' the jailors to lock 'im up again!"

After the laughter died down, Vicki stole a look at Dylan. He was shifting in his chair and looking down at his beer but the slightest of smiles tugged at the corner of his mouth.

"She walked him all the way home by his ear," a buxom woman took up the story, "an' Mick here was already approachin' six foot and the top o' Bonnie's head hardly reached his chest. He was bent down by his ear for five full kilometers, beggin' her the whole time to let him go."

They all looked at Dylan as they laughed again.

"Next day, he was seen all o'er town, paintin'," a third joined in. "The village ne'er looked so good. After he painted o'er all his graffiti, Bonnie had him continue paintin' 'til there was nothin' left to paint!"

Dylan stood up abruptly and turned back to Vicki, who rose. "I need a bit o' fresh air," he whispered.

"I'll just get my sweater," Vicki said.

"No. I need to be alone." He looked in her eyes for the briefest of moments before averting his gaze. "Stay as long as you want. You know how to get home?"

Vicki hesitated. "Of course."

"Father Rowan will be here if you need an escort."

"We'll be fine."

He set his beer bottle on the table and walked toward the door, where the priest was chatting with a few villagers. He whispered something near his ear and he turned to look at Vicki and Brenda, nodding his head. With that, Dylan slipped through the door.

Vicki felt as if her breath had escaped her when he left the home. There was no reason for her to remain in this room filled with strangers. And as she glanced down at Brenda, who was watching her quizzically, she knew there was even less reason for her sister to remain here. As for herself, she belonged with Dylan.

She sat down in the seat he had occupied.

"What's happening?" Brenda asked in a low voice.

"He's going for a walk," Vicki answered. "He said he needed to be alone."

"You want to leave?" Brenda asked.

She nodded. "But we'll give him a few minutes first so it doesn't look like we're following him."

The group burst into laughter again, as if no one else had noticed that Dylan had taken his leave.

"Oh, that's when the trouble started," a man with a ruddy face and red nose said. "When he met up with the Hoolihans."

"The Hooligans, is what we always called 'em," another man with wire-rimmed glasses said. He was tall and thin and looked to be at least a hundred years old. "That family was ne'er worth their salt. Generation after generation o' law breakers."

"Why on earth a good boy like Mick Maguire would take up with the likes o' them," a woman said, shaking her head. She glanced at Bonnie's body. "Oh, he gave 'er many a sleepless night after that."

"In and out o' Children's Court after that. The four brothers and Mick."

They shook their heads in unison.

"And then," the ruddy-faced man said, "he took up with 'er.'"

"Shhh," the woman closest to him cautioned. She nodded toward Vicki and Brenda.

Vicki waited for them to continue but the group began to disburse self-consciously. She stole a glance at Brenda.

"Time to go," Brenda said as if reading her mind. They both rose and made their way to the door under the watchful eye of the villagers.

"Would you care for a ride home?" Father Rowan asked as they approached the front door.

Vicki shook her head. "It's just a couple of miles," she said. "We'd enjoy the walk."

"Phone me if you need anythin' at all," he said.

Vicki hugged him. "Thank you. You've been a great friend."

As she made her way through the door, she felt as if Brenda had lagged behind her. She turned to see her planting a kiss on Father Rowan's cheek. Then she sighed heavily, shook her head and joined her sister.

"What unpardonable sin could he have committed," Brenda said when the two were out of earshot, "that would prevent a man like that from having sex for an entire lifetime." She shivered as if a chill had gone up her spine.

Vicki was silent. She was too busy trying to connect the dots of a child born in America to Irish immigrants. A toddler whose father abandoned them, stranding them in a strange country. A mother who returned to her mother's home long enough to dump her child before taking off again.

She remembered a conversation she and Dylan had soon after they'd met. He'd been telling Vicki about his childhood. He described his mother as an alcoholic; apparently there had been a time when the two of them lived together. He would arrive home from school to find her gone. A latchkey child is what he'd be called today, she thought as she wrapped her arms around herself to try and stave off the cold. He'd been alone every evening except, as he'd told her, when he really needed his mother he would make his way to the pubs, where she could always be found.

It was clear now that at some point in his young life, his grandmother had taken him in. It was also clear that they loved each other very much and Vicki was certain that Bonnie O'Sullivan had provided him with a good home.

What was the pull of the Hoolihans, she wondered, those bad eggs that Dylan had fallen in with? Was the graffiti just the beginning of living a life outside the law? Why would he leave the love and security of Bonnie's home to be out on the streets committing offenses against his neighbors?

They had each greeted him warmly when they arrived, she thought. It was as though they really liked him. No doubt some had owned the buildings he'd spray-painted but they'd been pleased with the resulting amends when he painted the town.

But no one mentioned his mother.

Brenda had fallen silent. There was a full moon but plenty of clouds, which resulted in strange, shadowy shapes forming as the clouds made their way between the moon and the earth. They undulated, sometimes appearing like people ready to jump them as they approached or follow them as they moved past.

As they neared the church, Vicki noticed that Brenda visibly stiffened. She followed her gaze to the cemetery just beyond the church courtyard. Perched at the top of the hill, some of the stones were tall, casting long shadows across the ground as they seemed to peer over the stone wall nearer the bottom of the rise. Others were leaning, giving the impression that whoever— or whatever—was underneath was trying to get out. They appeared haphazardly placed, which in turn made them look as if they were people gathering to watch them move past.

Once past the church and cresting the hill, they could see the lights to their cottage. They chose the direct route, walking across the meadow in lieu of taking the winding road.

When they reached a halfway point between the church and the cottage in an area that was completely open and devoid of trees, Brenda pointed to the horizon.

"There's that dog again," she said.

Vicki looked toward a small rise behind the house, where the shadow of a large dog was silhouetted against the moonlight. The head was hung low as if it was watching them. The weight shifted from one leg to the other, moving back and forth, the tail low and bushy, as it watched them approach the house.

She felt her feet moving faster over the uneven terrain, hoping she didn't trip over some unseen obstacle in her path. Her heartbeat quickened and her breath grew shallow.

"Get behind me," Brenda said. "If the dog charges, I'll try to draw him away from you. Whatever happens to me don't stop. Just get to the house and get inside."

"You don't think—?"

"I don't know. But he's spooking me. It's like he's always there, always watching."

She expected Dylan to be in the house when they finally reached the door and slipped inside. But though she drew an initial sigh of relief that they'd arrived safely, her mood was soon sullied by the fact that he wasn't there. And by all appearances, he hadn't been home even for a brief time.

As the clock ticked the hours away, Brenda took a shower and finally went to bed. And though Vicki tried to relax, she found herself feeling like a wind-up toy that was wound too tight. She longed to get in the car and drive to the village pub, to see if he was there drinking and becoming more sullen as the night wore on. She wondered if he was linking up with the Hoolihans and committing crimes as the neighbors were gathered in his grandmother's home.

Then just as quickly, she chided herself. He'd been a teenager then. He was an adult now, a "landowner" he'd called himself proudly to his Mam. He was responsible—not only for himself but for her now, too. He was walking by himself, she thought. Or maybe he'd found a place to sit somewhere that was quiet, where he could reflect on the events that seemed to be unfolding too quickly.

As she readied for bed, her mind went in circles; one minute, she was convinced he was at the pub getting beaten by those men with whom he'd had the run-in before. The next minute, she pictured him sitting in the courtyard of the church, thinking or perhaps praying.

Her mind continued in circles until she fell into an uneasy sleep.

18

Vicki was awakened from a fitful, shallow slumber by a phone ringing. She stirred; for a brief moment, she imagined she was back home in Lumberton and Sam was phoning with another mission. But when she opened her eyes, she found Dylan lying on his side in the narrow bed next to her, watching her with intent eyes.

"What—?" she began groggily.

"Sam," he said, turning over to answer his cell phone. "Aye." He listened for a moment and then said, "Hold on. I'm putting you on speakerphone."

He rolled onto his back. He was completely nude and as Vicki awakened more fully, she had trouble concentrating on the phone call. He ran one hand through his hair as Sam's voice crackled through the speakerphone. "Just heard back from our guys. The sonar worked. Here's what we're looking at: there's some sort of ruin underneath the surface there. Looks like it might go pretty deep—I won't know exactly how deep until the computer specialists do their bit."

Dylan met Vicki's eyes. "So, there *is* somethin' underground, 'ey?" he mused.

"That's not all. We also ran the infrared component. It picked up some movement."

"Stephen Anders," Vicki said.

"They'll try sharpening the image over the next few hours. That's the assumption we're going on right now but we need more definitive evidence before we send a team in."

"A team?" Dylan asked.

"I've got two operatives en route. Here's the plan. You listening?"

"We're both listening," Vicki said.

"I'll be in contact within twelve hours. I'll walk you through the plan on a secured network in 3-D. But we're looking at you going in, Dylan, in roughly 24 hours, along with the two reinforcements I'm sending."

"That would be midnight here," he said slowly.

"You've got to go in under cover of darkness. Once you're underground, it's no big deal. But that area doesn't have any natural cover—those few trees there aren't sufficient."

"Aye. It's very flat there; a person could be seen for a couple o' kilometers at least, especially if one had binoculars."

"So we'll post one man at the entrance as a lookout. You and the other operative will go in and extract Anders. I'll have a safe house for you tomorrow."

"A safe house?" Vicki asked.

"We have—shall I say, 'cooperation' among some of the citizens in Ireland. The plan will be for you to extract Anders and get him to the safe house, where he'll remain until we're ready to helicopter him out."

"And how long will that take?" Dylan asked.

"If all goes according to plan, no more than 48 hours."

"And me and Brenda?" Vicki asked.

"You're to stay put. After Dylan gets Anders to the safe house, he can join you back at your rental. They'll know what to do with Anders—immediate medical care, etcetera."

"So, after he's delivered, me job here is over?"

"That's the plan."

Dylan shrugged. "Sounds simple enough."

"There's something you ought to know, Sam," Vicki spoke up.

"Yeah?"

She glanced at Dylan, who knit his brows. "Dylan's grandmother passed away this afternoon. There's a wake going on overnight and she's to be buried tomorrow."

"What time?"

"Noon," Dylan said.

There was a moment of silence on the other end of the line. Then, "Do you want to delay this mission?"

"No," Dylan said immediately. "I want to go in tomorrow night and get 'im out, just as you said. I want to leave Ireland as soon as possible."

Vicki cocked her head and tried to catch Dylan's eye but he avoided looking at her. She had hoped for a few days of real sight-seeing before they returned home and now she felt her heart sink. She wished she understood why he hated being here so much. His grandmother had clearly loved him and the villagers she'd met—other than the three goons at the pub—seemed to bear no ill will toward him.

"You sure?" Sam asked.

"Positive."

"Once we start the wheels turning…"

"I understand. I'll be ready."

"I'll call within twelve hours."

"Okay then," Dylan said. He clicked off the phone and returned it to the nightstand.

"I was hoping to stay a few days," Vicki said. "We don't have to stay here in the village if you don't want to. If the memories…" She allowed her voice to trail off while she gauged his response.

He wrapped his arm around her and pulled her to him, where she nuzzled her cheek against his broad chest. "I suppose you know by now there are painful memories for me here."

"Yes," she whispered. "Mind if I ask where you've been?"

"Not at'al. I was sittin' in the church sanctuary. Thinkin'. Seemed like old times, actually. I spent many hours in that sanctuary, thinkin'. For all the good it did me."

She wished she'd known he was there. She might not have been uneasy as Brenda and she walked home. And she might not have worried so much about him before drifting off to a restless sleep. "I'm sorry your mother wasn't here."

He sighed and twisted his hand through her hair, kneading it gently. He focused his eyes on the long strands of strawberry blond, but it was obvious his mind was elsewhere. "We moved here from America when I was about three years old. We had a tiny place—one room, really—in the village. That didn't last long; me mum drank any earnin's she had and couldn't hold onto a job."

He rested his other arm across her back and absent-mindedly stroked her shoulder. His fingers were soothing and they penetrated into the muscle, relaxing her further. There had always been something about his touch that she couldn't resist.

"Thin's went from bad to worse. And one day, Mam showed up at the flat. I was there, maybe all o' four years old. God only knows where me mum was."

"She left you alone when you were four years old?"

"Thin's weren't much better when she was there," he said quietly. "She was usually passed out. Anyway, Mam took me to her place. The room she set up for me was once me mum's room. For a time, me mum would pass through and sleep on the couch there in the parlor. The visits got fewer and further between. Until one day…" He stopped speaking and Vicki waited quietly for him to continue.

After a long moment, he rolled them both onto their sides. "Will you go outside w' me, Darlin'? I used to enjoy lookin' at the stars. They're very pretty here."

"I'll get dressed."

"No need."

She looked at him with wide eyes. It wasn't lost on her that he was completely nude and she had been sleeping in only her lace panties. "But—"

He slipped out of the bed and grabbed a blanket. "Wrap this around you," he said.

She slid out of bed and dutifully wrapped the blanket around her. Then before she could take a step toward the door, he reached down, sliding his arm under her knees and lifting her into his arms.

As he walked down the hall with her, Brenda's bedroom door opened behind them. "What's up?" she said.

Vicki caught a glimpse of her sister over Dylan's shoulder. Brenda's eyes had traveled to Dylan's nude backside, an amused smile inching across her face. "Never mind," Brenda said, "I think I know."

"Go back to bed," Dylan said without altering his stride. He opened the door and as he stepped outside he said over his shoulder, "And no peekin'!"

Vicki clutched the soft blanket against her skin as the cold air hit them. "What are you doing?" she giggled. When Dylan didn't answer, she wrapped her arms around his neck. The ground was uneven as he carried her across the lawn toward the pond, but he was as sure-footed as if he was walking on smooth concrete. The cold air didn't seem to register with him, but goose bumps were forming along her skin. "It's freezing out here!" she breathed.

He chuckled. "No, it's not, Darlin'. It might be fifty degrees, if that. And I promise you, once you're in the water, you won't be cold."

"No! You can't be serious!"

When he reached the water's edge, he set her on the ground long enough to strip her of the blanket, which he tossed on the ground. Then despite her growing protestations, he scooped her into his arms again and waded into the pond. As she felt the water against her backside, she squealed and buried her face against his neck. "Don't drop me in here!" she begged.

He threw his head back and laughed. "I'm goin' to do a lot more than that," he said as he waded in above his waist.

As they neared the middle of the pond, she pleaded, "Please don't drop me. It's freezing!"

He stopped and looked at her, a broad smile across his face. "What are you doing?" she asked. "Are you insane?"

He raised one brow. "Perhaps I am, at that. But it's high time you learned to live life to its fullest."

He shifted his arms so she was half-floating in the water. "It's warmer under the surface than it is above," he whispered. His voice had grown husky. "In the deepest part o' this pond, it's under five feet. So when we go under, your feet can still be touchin' the ground."

"Don't put me down," she warned, her voice growing serious. "Don't—"

Before she could continue, he ducked them both under the water's surface. Seconds later, she re-emerged to find him grinning from ear to ear.

"I didn't lie to you, now did I?" he said. He let her slip from his arms. As her feet found the bottom, he continued, "It's warmer now, isn't it?"

"I ought to brain you," she said in mock anger. She leaned back, allowing the water to soak her long hair. As she pulled her head above the water once more, she finger-combed it away from her face.

He stepped toward her as a lock of water-soaked hair fell across his forehead. His eyes had turned to vivid green in the light of the moon. With the initial shock wearing off and her body warming under the surface of the water, she pressed herself against his chest. As his arms wrapped around her gently, she tilted her head back and draped her arms around his neck.

His lips were full and soft as they brushed against hers. He looked into her eyes and smiled, causing his laugh lines to crinkle and his irises to sparkle. He had an uncanny ability to live in the moment, she thought as she parted her lips. This gift was infectious, and as his lips found hers once more, she felt her heart grow lighter. She felt weightless as he held her, his strong hands rubbing against her back and through her hair while his chest pressed against hers. She didn't ever want this moment to end.

His kisses grew more passionate and his arms tightened around her until she had to pull back slightly to catch her breath. Her heartbeat had quickened and now as she remained pressed against Dylan, she could feel his heart beating faster as well. He looked down at her, his long lashes shading his eyes. His lips were slightly parted and he was breathing more heavily, his lips slightly upturned in a sly smile.

They stood in the center of the pond for a long time, simply holding each other and feeling the water lap against them in the gentle breeze.

"Lean back," he said in a soothing voice. "And I'll catch you in me arms."

She couldn't imagine trusting anyone as much as she trusted him. She turned perpendicular to him and started to lean back. True to his word, he caught her in one muscular arm and helped her float along the water's surface as her long hair billowed out across the water's surface, glowing almost golden in the moonlight.

She watched his face; his eyes appeared so placid, so kind. He kept one arm beneath her, steadying her. His biceps were so large and so powerful that she felt completely safe; and yet as strapping as he was, there was a tenderness about him that made him completely irresistible.

Dylan glanced at the sky. "The stars are beautiful tonight, aren't they?" he said. His voice was hushed. "You can make out the plough—what you call the big dipper." He nodded toward the stars.

She gazed at the night sky but then turned back to him. "I'd rather look at you."

"Would you, now?"

"Do you remember telling me how I should visit Ireland, and how beautiful it is?"

"I do. It was the day we first met."

"I never in a million years dreamed I would be here one day, and I'd be lucky enough to be here with you."

He set her on her feet and wrapped his arms more tightly around her, pulling her closer to him. Her toes felt massaged by the soft earth and she found herself finding his much larger feet and rubbing against them.

"It's a magical place," she said. Her voice had grown low and silky.

He rubbed his cheek against hers. His hair was soft and she found herself kissing his five o'clock shadow and running her lips lightly over his before his lips parted and he began to kiss her with a passion that grew in intensity. The air was still now and she felt as though they were the only living creatures within miles. She ran her hands through his hair, feeling the locks as they curled against his neck.

When he pulled back from her, she moaned in protest and tried to tug him back toward her.

He smiled. "You're gorgeous under the moonlight."

"Kiss me."

"I'll do more than that."

She felt his hands under the water, easily removing her panties from around her hips. "What are you doing?" she laughed.

"What do ya think I'm doin'?"

She picked up her feet one at a time and stepped out of them. But before she could reach down to grab them he had her in his arms again. "My panties—"

"If it doesn't wash to shore in the mornin', we'll go to the shops."

He lifted her into his arms as she wrapped her legs around him. His lips were upon her once more, bruising her lips and exploring her with a hunger that grew more insistent.

Just as she felt breathless and weak, he gently released her so her upper torso was floating. And there in the moonlight in the warmth of the water, his hands and his body alternated between the gentle caresses of a devoted lover and the fervent passion of unbridled bliss, until she felt nearly delirious.

He scooped her back into his arms and carried her to shore. She shivered in the cold night air as it struck against her wet skin.

He set her on the ground and they acted as one, bundling into the blanket as they dropped to the ground. She giggled as Dylan rolled them over until she felt like the stuffing in a loose burrito.

She pressed her body against his, allowing the warmth they shared to chase away the chill. His skin smelled fresh and musky, a combination of the pond water intermingled with his own perspiration and the faintest aroma of the cologne she loved so much. He drove her crazy and she was certain he knew it.

As his lips found hers again, she felt lost in this moment. Whatever had happened earlier in the day and whatever might happen tomorrow no longer mattered. It was just this one moment in time. As she opened her eyes and found his opening, the irises large and dark, she knew she would carry this memory with her forever.

They made love in the close confines of the blanket, the stars and the moon imprinted on her mind as he ran his lips along her neck and collarbone. And when they were both spent, they remained locked in each other's arms, their breath labored. He grew heavy atop her as if his strength was sapped before he reluctantly rolled onto his back. She curled against his side, one leg thrown over his midsection.

They watched the sky for a time as Dylan pointed out constellations and individual stars and then they grew quiet. She began to feel the march of time and the approach of dawn, which would come too soon. She ran her hand absent-mindedly across her tummy, feeling a slight roundness there.

"Dylan," she said, placing her hand on his cheek until he turned to look her in the eye, "there's something I need to tell you." She smiled, eliciting a wide grin from him. Her heart felt as if it was swelling with her news and she grew breathless again.

"What is it, Darlin'?" he whispered.

An odd sound echoed through the still night air. Before she could answer, he lifted his head in the direction of the sound. His expression abruptly changed as his brows knit and his jaw stiffened.

"What is it?" she asked, following his gaze. Across the broad, rolling landscape she watched as a light bobbed.

"Headlights," he said, his voice tense. "And from the sound o' the engine, I'll be knowin' who it is." He hurried to unwrap them from the blanket's confines. "And they're comin' here."

19

They were halfway to the cottage when the door opened and Brenda rushed out. Dylan's face grew crimson as she hurried down the path to hand him a pair of jeans and his boots. But her eyes weren't on his physique but on the rapidly approaching pickup.

"Get Vicki in the house," he said as he pulled on the jeans. "Whatever happens, don't come out. Are you understandin' me?"

Brenda nodded but hesitated while Dylan slipped into his boots.

"What are you waitin' for?" His voice grew impatient as he, too, watched the truck grow near.

Without a word, she slipped him a pistol. His eyes locked onto hers for the briefest of moments before he accepted it. "Thank you," he said.

"I'm calling the police," Vicki called back as she rushed toward the house.

"No," Dylan said in a hoarse stage whisper. "We can't have the authorities here. We can't risk callin' attention to ourselves—it could jeopardize the mission."

She stopped to stare back at him.

"Call Father Rowan," he said as Brenda and Vicki disappeared into the house. "He'll know what to do."

When the door slammed shut behind them, Vicki felt as if she'd walked into a tomb. With Dylan still outside, her life's energy had been sucked out with him and her hands shook as she grabbed the cell phone from the table. She scrolled through the caller i.d. before finding Father Rowan's number. "Come on," she moaned, "come on!"

His voice mail picked up and she groaned. Brenda rushed to the window and Vicki followed as she waited impatiently for his outgoing message to end. "Come quick," she said. "Someone's shown up at the cottage—Dylan's in trouble."

She clicked the phone off as Brenda motioned for her to stand to the side. Then she parted the curtains.

Dylan had come around the back of the house while three men tumbled out of the pickup. They immediately converged at the truck bed, where they picked up pipes and headed toward the front door.

"So, Eoghan," Dylan called. His voice was loud and heavy as he moved further from the house, drawing the largest man's attention to him. "What're wantin' with me now?"

"What have they got in their hands?" Vicki whispered hoarsely.

"Lead pipes." Brenda's voice was husky and strong.

"You know what we be wantin'," the largest one shouted. "We're here to finish your sorry arse off; what we should'a done a long time ago."

The men began to separate. They looked like a pack of wolves, Vicki thought, as one moved to Dylan's left while the other moved to his right. The ringleader, Eoghan, stood his ground directly in front of him.

"He doesn't stand a chance with the three of them," Vicki gasped. "Not spread out like they are, not even with the gun."

"Killin' me won't bring 'er back," Dylan called. He continued backing away from the house.

"No, but it'll put you in h'ail that much sooner," one of the others shouted.

"Kill me and you'll spend your life in a prison cell, Aidan," Dylan said to him. "I'm not worth your freedom."

"Why should we spend our lives in prison for killin' a man?" the third shouted. "You didn't spend a day in the clink for killin' our sister!"

Vicki gasped. "My God!"

Brenda grabbed her shoulder, forcing her to look her in the face. She hadn't realized that her sister had disappeared from the window. But now as she stared at her amber eyes burning hot, she began to take in the pistols in each hand. "Slip on a coat and your shoes," she hissed. "Fast."

While she rushed to cover her naked body and slide on shoes, Brenda moved to the opposite side of the house and quietly opened the door. As Vicki joined her, she handed her a pistol with a 15-bullet clip. "You go that way," she pointed to the far end of the house. "Do what I do. And if we have to start shooting, empty the clip. But don't shoot me and don't shoot Dylan!"

Vicki moved quickly along the back of the house. When she reached the corner, she glanced at the opposite end, where Brenda was disappearing around the cottage. Her heart was thumping so wildly it felt like it was between her ears. She tried to steady her nerves as she continued down the side of the cottage and emerged behind the men.

Remaining in the shadows, she moved slowly now, willing her feet to remain completely silent as they brushed against moss and stone.

She could see Brenda moving behind their truck until she stopped at the edge of the hood, her face concealed by the driver's door left ajar. Only the glint of metal revealed her intent.

They were circling him now. Eoghan slapped the lead pipe against his own brawny palm as a sneer crossed his face. Dylan tried to move away from the detached garage but Aidan and the other man were closing in, blocking off his escape routes.

"Killin' me won't make you feel any better, Ciaran," he called out to the third man.

"Oh, I think it will," Ciaran retorted.

"And if it don't," Aidan joined in, "jumpin' the bones o' your women friends will!"

"They're not part o' this," Dylan shouted.

Vicki moved closer to the man farthest from Brenda. Her movement caught Dylan's eye and his jaw dropped before he could stop the instinctive reaction. In the split second that his attention was averted, Eoghan swung the lead pipe like a batter aiming for the outfield; gripped in both hands as he leveled it at Dylan's torso.

Vicki cried out but the sound of her voice was drowned out by Dylan's roar as he tried to grab the other end before it reached its target. It slipped from his hand but he slowed its trajectory as it glanced off his hip. He went down to one knee as the others moved in.

The guttural, frenzied growl of a beast split the night air as a large, furry shape hurled itself through the air to land on Eoghan's chest. The man was large, towering over Dylan, but he quickly found himself overpowered with the sharp claws and teeth of the creature as it tore into him.

Aidan turned his attention from Dylan to stare in disbelief at his brother as he was brought to his knees. Then he seemed to snap back. His eyes darted as he moved toward the creature.

The sound of a gunshot whizzed past Aidan's ear and he whirled around to face the direction of the truck. Brenda moved away from the vehicle, the pistol leveled at him. "Don't even think about it!" she shouted. Her usually husky voice had grown deeper and more vicious as she approached them.

"Drop it!" Vicki shouted in turn at Ciaran.

The man stood for a moment with the pipe in his hand as if trying to gauge her seriousness. In response, Vicki fired the pistol, aiming to shoot over his head. Ciaran dropped the lead pipe as he grabbed his arm. He pulled his hand away to reveal bright red blood before turning to stare at Vicki.

"Oops," she said.

The gunshots had done nothing to stop the animal from attacking Eoghan and now they all stared at the two rolling and tumbling across the ground. The beast seemed to be everywhere at once, its teeth gleaming as its lips curled back before sinking into the man again and again.

Dylan whistled and the beast instantly stopped. It backed away from Eoghan, who was in no shape to do more than groan and continue writhing on the ground.

Vicki was astounded. It was a dog; a large black and white border collie.

"If ya hurt me dog, I'll have to kill ya fer sure," Dylan shouted.

"Drop the pipe!" Brenda shouted. They turned to see Aidan raising the pipe over his shoulder. "Drop it or I'll turn you into a girl!"

Aidan stared into the barrel of the gun before he dropped the pipe.

"Kick them away from you," Brenda ordered. "All of you!"

"You gonna let a couple o' girls do your fightin' for ya, Mick?" Ciaran taunted.

"I think I will," Dylan said, helping to kick the pipes further from the men. "A couple o' girls seem to be kickin' your arses pretty well."

"Over there!" Brenda yelled, gesturing with the pistol toward an open area.

Ciaran stopped to help Eoghan to his feet. Then the three came to stand side by side.

"What're aimin' to do?" Aidan shouted at her. "You gonna mow us down like Bonnie and Clyde? And Bonnie?" he added, glancing toward Vicki.

"Take off your boots," Brenda shouted.

Vicki looked toward her sister but she was focused on the men. She glanced at Dylan but he was also staring at them. She moved closer to Brenda and Dylan as her sister gestured with the pistol as though she aimed to shoot again.

The three men grudgingly removed their boots.

"Toss 'em over there!" Brenda yelled. She sounded like a drill sergeant, Vicki thought, as if the only level her voice had was full throttle.

"Now take your clothes off!"

The men stared at her.

"You heard me!"

Vicki stole another glance at Dylan, who was trying to suppress a smile. She came to stand beside them, her gun still leveled in the direction of the men.

When they were completely naked, Brenda backed toward the truck. Then she quickly turned and shot into one of the rear tires.

Ciaran immediately started to shout but when he found himself looking at two barrels, he stopped.

"Get in the truck," Brenda ordered. "You'd better drive as fast as you can because when that tire's flat, you're walking."

Aidan helped Eoghan into the wide front seat before rushing around to the driver's door. Ciaran was already crammed in beside Eoghan before his brother had the engine started. "You haven't heard the last o' us!" Aidan shouted as he turned the truck around.

Brenda waited until they were headed down the curving dirt driveway before shooting a bullet into the other rear tire. They could hear the shouts of the men inside before Brenda waved her pistol in the air. "Drive!" she ordered.

They were barely out of sight when they heard a massive racket. Dylan chuckled. "Sounds like they're drivin' on the rims."

"You didn't even draw your gun," Vicki said.

"No need to," he laughed. "Bonnie," he said, turning to Brenda, "and Bonnie." He looked at Vicki before turning back to her sister. "Thank you. They'd 'ave killed me, even if I'd 'ave shot one."

Then he grew serious as a set of headlights came across the hill toward them. His eyes narrowed as he watched it and his hand went to the pistol in his waistband. "Father Rowan," he said, relaxing.

"I called him," Vicki said.

Dylan let out a sigh of relief and turned back to the dog, who was still sitting in the same spot. He was kneeling down in front of it, rubbing behind its ears and inspecting its blood-splattered fur as Father Rowan pulled in.

The priest took in the sight of the two girls with their pistols still in their hands before approaching Dylan. "What just happened? I passed the Hoolihans drivin' toward the village on two flats."

"They came to finish me off," Dylan said. "These two ladies stopped 'em—along with Shep."

"Is she hurt?" Father Rowan said, bending down to rub the dog under its chin.

"I don't think so," Dylan said. "It's Eoghan's blood on 'er."

"That's your dog?" Vicki asked.

"That's the dog I've been seeing," Brenda added. "I thought it was rabid."

Dylan chuckled. "She's not rabid. Best dog I ever had." He turned to Father Rowan. "I gave 'er to a sheep farmer a'fore I left Ireland. You know that."

The other man shook his head. "She didn't stay, Mick. Kept runnin' away. Kept goin' back to the old cottage like she was awaitin' for you."

Dylan shook his head and averted his gaze.

"When she finally got it into her 'ead that you weren't comin' back, she went to the graveyard beside the church. Laid there for days on end. I started feedin' her. She came and went as she pleased but at least I knew she wasn't starvin'."

"God bless 'er," Dylan said, stroking the dog. "I'd 'ave never done that to 'er. I thought—I thought she'd be okay with the farmer."

"She should'a been," Father Rowan said. "If she hadn't been missin' you so much."

Dylan stood up, his focus still on the dog.

Realizing she still held the gun in her hand, Vicki felt as if everything happening around her was surreal. There was the faintest of light on the distant horizon, a sign the day was just beginning. She felt completely drained. She looked at Brenda, who was still holding her gun as well; but now her mountain of copper hair began to swim in front of her. There was Father Rowan, looking down the long driveway as Dylan recalled the night's events. They shook their heads and Dylan's voice began to drone on.

Then he was turning in her direction with wide eyes. He said something she couldn't comprehend as her knees collapsed underneath her.

Then Brenda was shouting, "The gun!" as Dylan was deflecting her arm away from them. She sensed the pistol leave her grip as he caught her. She wanted to stand on her own two feet but she couldn't feel them anymore. The last thing she remembered before the world went black was Dylan's strong arms around her and his frantic voice calling her name.

20

Vicki opened her eyes to find Brenda standing at the open door to the bedroom. The room had a blue-gray tint to it as if nighttime was long gone but the sun hadn't truly made an appearance. She rubbed her eyes sleepily and rolled onto her back. "What time is it?"

"Ten o'clock."

"Are you serious?"

Brenda walked to the window and opened the shade. She stood for a moment, her eyes wandering, before turning back to Vicki. "Dylan's been worried sick about you."

"Where is he?" She sat up and flung her legs over the side of the bed then caught herself as the room began to spin. She put a hand to her mouth and closed her eyes.

"He's getting ready for a briefing from Sam." She joined Vicki at the bed and placed her hand on her sister's forehead. "Vicki, you have to tell him."

"I've tried—several times. Somehow, something always interrupts us."

She sighed. "He thinks it's the stress of this whole situation— jet lag, his grandmother dying, the men last night… He thinks it was a mistake to bring us here. And he wants to leave as soon as this mission is over."

Vicki reached for her robe and stood shakily. "I'll tell him today. This afternoon, after his grandmother's funeral."

Brenda nodded though she appeared unconvinced. "I don't think he got any sleep at all." She glanced toward the door. "He's in the kitchen, setting up the laptop."

Vicki slipped through the door and made her way down the hall as Brenda followed. She found Dylan logging onto a secure network at the kitchen table.

"Ah, there you are, Darlin'," he said, rising to kiss her on the forehead. "How are you feelin'?"

"Much better," she said.

"You didn't 'ave much at'al to eat yesterday, you know," he said. "It's no wonder you were so faint. And the stress o' ever'thin'…" He walked to the stove and lifted a skillet. "I've made a good, hearty traditional breakfast for you. Eggs, rashers…"

Vicki turned away and closed her eyes. "I'm still a bit queasy," she said.

"But a good breakfast will fix that, it will."

"Can I get some orange juice for now? And I'll eat after your call."

His brows knit and he looked at the skillet and then back at Vicki, who was peering at him out of the corner of her eye. "Do you not like my breakfasts anymore?"

"Of course I do," she said, trying not to breathe in the aroma of all the meats cooked together.

Brenda brushed past her as she approached the refrigerator. Taking out the orange juice and a couple of glasses from the cupboard, she poured the juice, handing one to Dylan and one to Vicki. Then she reached for a third glass for herself. "Orange juice is so refreshing," she mumbled unconvincingly.

"Aye," Dylan said, setting his skillet back on the stove.

"Oh, honey, don't be sad," Vicki said. "I just woke up. Once I've been up for a while I'll feel like eating."

"I'm worried about you," he said. He set his juice glass on the counter untouched.

"It's everything that's been going on," she said. "I'll be better after the funeral—and after this mission."

Brenda stole a glance at her as she pulled out a chair and sat down at the table.

"My apologies," Dylan said, "but this is a confidential call I'm about to 'ave here."

Brenda took a swig of juice before answering. "How many times am I gonna have to save your life before you'll trust me?"

"That's just it," Dylan said. "I'll never trust you."

A sly smile crossed her face. "Good call, Irish." She stood up and finished off her orange juice before retreating to her bedroom.

Vicki sat down in Brenda's vacated chair. "What's going on?"

"I'm waitin' for Sam's call." He glanced at his watch. "He's late. And in an hour or so, we'll be havin' to leave for Mam's services. Are you sure you feel up to goin'?"

"Of course I do."

"I wouldn't be a bit upset w' you if you decided to remain here."

"I wouldn't dream of it. My place is beside you."

He cocked his head. "It is, isn't it now?"

The screen flickered and Sam's face appeared. "Dylan?" he said.

"Aye. I'm here with Vicki."

He adjusted a few things and then said, "Okay. I've got you now. You two are alone, right?"

"That we are." Dylan glanced down the hall at Brenda's closed bedroom door.

Sam entered something on his keyboard as they watched. In seconds, his face was replaced with a three-dimensional rendering of the dungeons. It reminded Vicki of a doll house she had as a young girl; it was several stories tall and opened in the center, splitting one side from the other. Once opened, she was able to move her dolls from room to room and down the staircases. Each room had three walls once the house was opened but the fourth was gone so she had an obstructed view of the entire house.

Now she studied the computer graphics. It appeared as if the ground had been cut away so she could view the stairway that wound its way at least thirty feet deep before branching off into the three hallways she had encountered.

An 'x' magically appeared as Sam drew on it. It was placed at the far end of the grove of trees. "At the eastern edge of these trees," he said, "is the entrance to this place. We're assuming it's the remains of an ancient castle."

"Aye," Dylan said. "I believe that's a correct assumption. I was obviously wrong before. Some eejit really did build a castle in a bog."

"We're also assuming the entrance is covered most of the time," he continued without skipping a beat, "maybe with leaves or underbrush."

"Aye."

"Over here—" he widened the view to include the surrounding area "—is another, larger grove. It's exactly three quarters of a mile to the entrance from here." He drew another 'x.' "Now what you're going to do is meet up with two operatives tonight at precisely eleven o'clock. I'll give you the address in a moment.

"They'll take you to an intermediate location where you'll get three horses. You'll ride to this mark over here—the one three quarters of a mile from the entrance. Tie up the horses there and walk the rest of the way."

"Understood."

"One will stand guard at the entrance. You and the other operative will go underground." Sam appeared on the screen again, replacing the computer simulation. "From the time you meet the others to the time you reach the entrance, we'll have you under satellite surveillance. If anyone attempts to follow you, we'll know. We'll also know if anyone approaches while you're underground. But once you enter the stairway, you're on your own until you surface again."

"Understood," Dylan repeated.

The screen began to move, morphing into something akin to a computer game. Now the three-dimensional animation made it appear as if they were moving down the stairway together.

The walls were stone, just as Vicki remembered them; gray and bleak. Some of the details were missing, such as the sconces— but she was impressed with the level of detail they'd been able to provide from the satellite's sonar.

"When you reach this landing," Sam continued, stopping at the point where Vicki had deliberated on which path to take, "it really doesn't matter which way you go. The left and the right form a circle while the center hallway ends at the opposite side of that circle."

The hallways began to move as if they were venturing down the center one. The animation stopped just before the three hallways converged. "In this location here," Sam drew another "x", "we picked up movement. We're assuming this is the cell where Stephen Anders is being held."

Dylan studied the screen. "And once we've cut him out o' there, we go back the same way we came in."

"Vicki," Sam said, "did you tell me that Anders claimed there's only one way in and one way out?"

"That's right."

The screen began moving again. "We picked up something else just on the other side of the three hallways. It appears to be debris, maybe from the time the castle caved in. We weren't able to get a clear focus on it." They watched as Sam zoomed in on a hazy area. "I can try to get a better view. But Plan A is to bring him out the way you came in."

"And Plan B?" Dylan asked.

"Plan B you make up as you go along."

"Oh, that's just grand, I want you to know."

"When you meet the other operatives, you'll be given earpieces and night vision goggles. We'll be in constant communication. If anybody is already in the tunnels, we'll either scrap the mission or put you into a holding pattern, depending on how things are unfolding. If anybody approaches, you'll know it, either from us or from the lookout at the entrance."

"What do we do once we're out of the ruins with Anders?"

"You'll take him back to the stables, where a car will be waiting. The key will be over the doorway to the stables. You'll separate from the other two operatives—they'll take the car they drove there and you'll take the new one."

"And where am I to take 'im?"

"To a safe house. You know that area pretty good, right?"

"Aye."

"There's a church not far from where you're staying. It's a Catholic church…"

Dylan's and Vicki's eyes locked.

"You're to see the priest there. Go in through the side door; he'll be waiting for you."

"Do you have a name for this priest?"

"Thomas Rowan."

"Father Rowan?" Dylan asked. "Am I dreamin' this?"

"You know him?"

"Are you tellin' me that Father Thomas Rowan is a CIA operative?"

"No," Sam answered. "He is not. He's cooperating with us."

"Does he know who will be deliverin' Stephen Anders?"

"He won't know until you arrive."

Dylan shook his head. "He's likely to faint and fall back in it."

"What was that?" Sam asked.

"Nothin'. What else do I need to know?"

Sam replaced the computer graphics with two photographs. One was a man with jet black hair, thick like Dylan's and slightly longer. His eyes appeared hazel or light brown. "This is one of the members of your team," Sam said as he placed an 'x' under his picture. "His name's Perry."

"Do I get a last name?"

"No. And they don't, either."

"Got it."

Sam switched to the second photograph of a young man with blond hair and blue eyes. "This is Rich."

"These are the two who will be waitin' for me at eleven o'clock?"

"That's right." Sam switched back to his own face. "Ready to take down the address?"

"Ready." Dylan slid a piece of paper and pen toward him. But as Sam read off the address, he hesitated, his hand over the paper.

"You know that address?"

"Aye. It's one o' the pubs in the village."

"That a problem?"

"I'm not to go inside, you're tellin' me? I'll see 'em on the sidewalk?"

"They'll be coming out of the pub. If they are not on the sidewalk at precisely eleven o'clock, the mission is scrubbed."

"And what exactly does that mean, it's scrubbed?"

"It means I'll contact you before midnight with new instructions. When you see them, you're to say, 'There's a thunderstorm brewing.' Got it?"

"Got it."

"If the mission is scrubbed, they'll say, 'No, I think it'll blow over.' If the mission is on, they'll reply, 'Looks to be a bad one.' Understand?"

"Aye. And these two gents, when we part ways at the stables—?"

"They're no longer your concern. And you're no longer theirs."

"And when I deposit Anders with Father Rowan?"

"Your mission is over. Someone else is responsible for getting him out of Ireland."

"Another operative."

"That's right."

"What about me?" Vicki asked.

"What about you?" Sam retorted.

"What's my mission?"

"You don't have a mission. You've completed yours. You found Anders. So sit this one out. Dylan ought to be home with you by morning. Have a good night's sleep; go sight-seeing tomorrow. Tell me when you want to leave and I'll have an aircraft standing by."

There was a brief moment of silence. Then Sam's cell phone began to ring. "I've got to get this," he said. "Any questions?"

"None."

"Okay. Next time we speak, it'll be through your earpiece." He made a move as if disconnecting them but his finger didn't reach the right button or press hard enough and Dylan and Vicki found themselves listening to his conversation. Dylan made a move to disconnect just before Sam said, "I need an eight inch tall silver angelfish with black stripes. It's got to be a male."

Dylan withdrew his hand from the keyboard and looked at Vicki.

"How the hell do I know how to tell the difference between a male and a female?" Sam growled. "Find an expert in angelfish."

There was a slight hesitation. "This is a matter of national security. You've got twenty-four hours to get me that angelfish."

There was a sound as if Sam was clicking off his cell phone and Dylan immediately disconnected from the conference call. He turned to Vicki. "How long 'ave we been gone? Two days? Two an' a half? And he lost one of our fishies already?"

Vicki shook her head. "We're just gonna have to move on," she said sadly. "Don't dwell on it."

"How could he lose an adult angel in two an' a half days, I wonder?"

"I don't know but we have to get ready for Mam's funeral."

Dylan reluctantly rose from the table and closed the laptop. "And when we get home, we'll 'ave another funeral to attend to. An eight inch angel's." He shook his head. "It's all arseways. I knew it was all jacked up to leave 'im in charge o' the fish."

21

Vicki pulled her sweater so it hugged her neck as the wind picked up. The sky had turned to varied degrees of gray and tumultuous black clouds were forming in the distance. The ancient stone wall surrounding the cemetery mercifully blocked some of the wind but not enough to keep her from shivering. As she eyed the skies, she hoped the rainstorm would hold off until after the services.

She was thankful for the chairs that had been thoughtfully arranged for Dylan, Brenda and herself at the gravesite. Despite Dylan's protests, she refused to eat any breakfast. So she was unprepared for the Irish customs that soon followed. Now, as she huddled against the cold, she relived the morning's events in her head.

They had walked the two miles to Bonnie O'Sullivan's home. Once there, it seemed the entire village had gathered in the parlor. They were crushed shoulder to shoulder in every available inch— except from the body of his grandmother to the nearest window.

There was a two-foot path cleared from the casket to the window and all who stood nearest the empty floor were hushed, their eyes wide. In a brief but poignant ceremony, Mrs. Rowan raised the shade and opened the window, immediately stepping to the side so as not to block it.

All stood back. Vicki's eyes roamed the gathering as the bodies pressed away from the makeshift path. Their eyes were wide as they stared at the casket, as though they expected to see Bonnie's soul rise from her body and glide through the window.

It was totally silent for several moments. Vicki thought she was going to swoon from the clustered bodies and stale air as her eyes moved from one to another: the stooped old man with his cap held tightly in his hands, the women fighting back tears, the overweight man with the bulbous nose and pockmarked cheeks…

Her eyes landed on a tiny woman whose smile reached from one side of her frail but beaming face to the other. Her hair was long and white and though the air was perfectly still, the locks seemed to rise up around her as though caught by the wind. She wore a white gown with lace at the neck and delicate wrists. And as Vicki stared at her, she winked one sharp blue eye.

And then she vanished.

Vicki grabbed at Brenda.

"What?" her sister whispered hoarsely. She wrapped her arm around Vicki's waist as if to steady her.

Then a sharp wind rattled the window. The room's still air was broken by sudden forced laughter as all commented that Bonnie O'Sullivan's spirit had successfully left her body and was now supposedly on its way to wherever good souls go.

Some words were said then as everyone continued to stand. Then Dylan and Father Rowan closed the casket, sealing the small woman in her white gown inside. Several men wordlessly lifted the casket and began the procession to the church, about a mile away.

Dylan had avoided looking at her as he raised it; in fact, Vicki realized, he'd avoided looking at anyone. She wondered how tenuous his hold was on his emotions and marveled at how he was able to juggle a mission and his grandmother's death simultaneously. At least, she thought as her eyes scoured the people, the men from the previous night had not returned.

Brenda and Vicki were placed directly behind the casket. It was a dreadfully slow procession, taking them nearly an hour. A glance behind her confirmed that the entire village's occupants had to be behind them. She was terrified of fainting every step of the way. Or worse, going into dry heaves. But she thanked God with every footstep that she hadn't eaten those eggs.

Once in the cemetery, the men carried Mam to a designated spot beside the open grave. A kind, heavyset woman with gray hair and sparkling green eyes motioned for Vicki and Brenda to sit in chairs set directly in front of the casket. Dylan joined them and the services began.

The villagers were positioned behind them and in a large circle around the gravesite. Obviously, Bonnie O'Sullivan had been well thought of in these parts and Vicki couldn't help but wonder once more why Dylan had resisted returning to Ireland. Both Sam and Father Rowan had been right; she was certain if he had succeeded in avoiding the trip, he would have lived to regret it.

She glanced sideways at him. His face was expressionless, though his lips were set in a way that made her wonder if he was biting the inside of his mouth. His eyes were narrowed and he did not look at Father Rowan as the priest droned on. In fact, he didn't look at anyone but stared at a spot near the bottom of the casket.

Her eyes panned the villagers. A tall, thin lady watched Dylan for a moment before turning her head to look at the far corner of the cemetery. Then another woman followed suit and then a third. Vicki thought her eyes were playing tricks on her as she watched one after another look at Dylan and then toward the same spot.

She reached under her seat and pulled out her pocketbook as she slyly glanced toward the object of their attention. But all she saw were tombstones. In the farthest corner was a concrete bench; perhaps, she thought as she took out a tissue from her purse, they were wishing that they, too, had somewhere to sit.

"Are you alright?" Dylan whispered as he leaned toward her.

"I'm fine, thank you," she whispered back. She wanted to say more but he returned to staring at the bottom of the casket under the watchful eye of the villagers.

No, she thought as the services continued, it was more than a few people wanting to sit down. There was something in that far corner that they associated somehow with Dylan.

The words of Ciaran Hoolihan seemed to return full force: "You didn't spend a day in the clink for killin' our sister!"

She'd seen Dylan kill a man. But he'd done it to protect her. She couldn't imagine him killing a woman. She gently placed her hand on his knee. He immediately positioned his larger hand over hers and squeezed it, though his eyes didn't waver from the casket. Just the touch of his hand on hers made her feel connected to him. She almost reached her other hand to her belly to feel the life growing there but stopped herself. She felt her face reddening under the watchful eyes of so many and wished the services would end.

They droned on for another hour with Father Rowan seeming to relish his role as priest. Then finally it was over and Dylan stood. "I'll be back in a moment," he whispered, his lips brushing her ear as he moved past her.

"What happens now?" Brenda muttered under her breath. "I feel like I'm on display."

"Me, too," Vicki answered as she watched Dylan.

He put one hand on Father Rowan's shoulder and bent slightly to whisper in his ear. The priest looked at Vicki with slightly widened eyes and nodded. Dylan patted his shoulder and returned to the girls.

"I hope you don't mind," he said quietly, "but I told Father Rowan that you were ill, Vicki. I don't want to stay and it seemed like a good excuse."

Vicki's eyes met Brenda's. "Yes. Of course."

He reached for her hand and gently guided her past scores of people wishing to pay their respects. Even with their hasty departure, it took half an hour to move past the crowd of sympathizers and through the iron gates of the cemetery.

Dylan was uncharacteristically silent on the walk back to the house. He stared ahead but Vicki got the impression that his mind was far away. His mouth was turned down and at times she thought he was fighting back tears. She was caught between wanting to console him and wanting to get home and get something in her belly that wouldn't threaten to upset it.

When they finally walked into the house, she made a beeline for the orange juice while Dylan loosened his tie and slipped out of his dress shoes. He seemed unaware that she was watching him and she suddenly realized that she'd never seen him dressed so formally before. She'd become accustomed to seeing him in jeans and a simple shirt—or in the summertime, no shirt—and a pair of cowboy boots.

Now she found herself staring at his black shoes, dusty from the long walks of the day, to his dark trousers that accentuated his muscular thighs and rear view. He slipped off his suit jacket to reveal a pinstriped shirt that hugged his biceps and his chest.

"Are you feelin' alright?" he asked as he pulled off his tie and unbuttoned his shirt.

"Fine," she said. "Just hungry. There are several casseroles in the frig, if you'd like for me to heat up something for us?"

"You two go ahead," he said as he walked down the hall.

"If I were you," Brenda said under her breath, "I'd be half a step behind that man."

22

The afternoon hadn't gone quite as well as Vicki had hoped. Dylan had been unusually quiet and when she'd tried to comfort him, he appeared distracted. For the first time since they'd met, she began to worry that he'd lost interest in her, even though Brenda sought to assure her that it had more to do with having just attended his grandmother's funeral than their relationship. Though Vicki knew her sister was right, it still pained her to see the distant look in his eye.

Brenda heated a lamb casserole and Vicki had eaten like a starving woman. Though she was afraid it would make her nauseous again, it tasted so good and her stomach was so empty that she was having trouble pushing herself away from the table. Dylan hadn't joined them but sat on the small front porch and stared into the distance. He'd changed from his suit to his usual jeans and a flannel shirt and leather jacket. And she longed to be with him.

Finally, Vicki poured another glass of juice and headed to the bedroom. Her lids were heavy and her belly too full and now all she wanted was a short, restful nap.

She'd just climbed under the covers when Dylan joined her.

"I'm so glad you're here," she murmured, sitting up to kiss him as he leaned over the bed.

His lips were gentle and they lingered on hers as if he didn't want to stop. But after a moment, he pulled back and sat on the edge of the bed.

"Dylan," she said, cuddling up to him, "I have something to tell you." She wanted to erase that forlorn look in his eyes; she wanted to see them widen with astonishment and then crinkle as he smiled. She wanted to bring some joy to this day, to tell him that even though one soul was passing, another was forming inside her. And she wanted to show him that she was ecstatic that she was carrying his child.

"Can it wait?" he said gently but firmly.

"But I—"

"I need time to m'self." He said it abruptly and she pulled back to look him in the eye. "I'll be back in an hour or so, Darlin'. I just need to take a walk and clear me head. You understand, don't you?"

"Of course I understand." She swallowed hard and lay back against the pillows. "We can talk later."

"I need to clear me head before the mission t'night. I need to be in the right frame o' mind."

"Of course you do." She forced herself to smile. "And we'll have tomorrow. The mission will be over then and we'll have plenty of time to talk."

He stood up. "So I'll be back in about an hour."

She listened to his heavy boots on the hardwood floor as he walked down the hall. When the front door opened and closed, she felt like the life had been sucked out of the tiny cottage. It had always been that way with him, she realized. When they were together, she felt complete and when he was gone, she felt as though a piece of her was missing.

She lay on her side and stared out the window. It hadn't yet begun to rain but the clouds were thickening and tumbling overhead. Now there was no doubt there would be a storm this evening and perhaps a bad one.

Eventually, she drifted off to sleep to the sound of distant thunder.

She found herself striding across the meadow as the winds grew more intense. It whipped at her face, unchecked by the rolling grasses and occasional short trees and it rippled her jeans, penetrating deep inside to bite at her legs. Yet her stride didn't waver. She looked down at her feet as she easily traversed the soft dirt and jutting stones. But instead of seeing her petite black loafers, she stared instead at the pointed steel toes of aged brown cowboy boots.

Somewhere in the back of her mind, she knew she had somehow leapt from sleeping peacefully to viewing Dylan's movements. And somewhere in the depths of her soul, she knew she should turn her back and give him the privacy he craved.

But she couldn't. Or wouldn't. She wasn't sure which it was, only that she continued to feel his breath as he walked. She could sense his dark, solemn mood and the feeling that he must confront his past or he could never move forward.

He stopped at a crossroads while he observed the sky. Of course it would rain during his mission. It was always raining in Ireland. The fact that it hadn't thus far was an oddity. These were the skies he was accustomed to. He could feel the mist on his cheeks; could taste it on his lips.

He turned and gazed at the cottage he'd just left. His heart felt full for a moment as he thought of Vicki in his arms in a nice, warm bed. The cottage glowed from the lights within, casting radiant fingers across the lawn leading to the pond. There would be no full moon tonight, he thought. No skinny-dipping. Ah, well. He had his memories from the previous night and there would be other nights.

He turned again, facing the village. It was off in the distance, only perceptible by a faint glow on the horizon. Those would be the lights from the pubs as all the shops were closed by now. And he knew each of those pubs as well as he knew himself. He'd spent many a night there. Too many. And he regretted most of them.

He had a lot of regrets in his life, he realized. Looking back at the years behind him, it was nothing if not a long string of mistakes, bad decisions and stupid moves.

A quarter turn and he was facing Mam's house over the next knoll. It was quiet now and dark. Tomorrow afternoon he would have no choice but to go over there once more and clear things out. The landlord had Bonnie O'Sullivan as a tenant for at least sixty years but he'd be chomping at the bit to get another paying renter in there as quickly as possible.

It wouldn't take long; Mam didn't own that much. He'd go in with Father Rowan and his mum; they'd box up the photographs and scrapbooks and get them ready for the post, where they'd be mailed to him in America. And when he received them, he'd most likely stash them away in the attic somewhere. Maybe someday, ten or twenty years down the road—or more— he would haul them out and look at them.

Everything else would go to the auctioneer. It would be Old Mister Kilduff, a man he suspected was older than the village itself, who would come in and determine the starting bid on each object. People would come from miles around to buy off what they could and Dylan would be long gone by then. Mister Kilduff would get his take and send the rest by cheque to him in America. It was the way things worked. The way they always worked.

The sound of music and laughter reached his ears across the lonely knolls and meadows. He knew the source was Mrs. Rowan's home, although he could not see it from this vantage point. The celebration of Mam's life would go on through the night and into the morn. They'd be telling tall tales of her life, the entirety of it lived right there, a circumference of all of five miles.

How many times he'd stood at this crossroad, he thought. Of course, back then, the cottage he was renting now was leased by someone else: the Niven Sisters. They'd grown grapes and vegetables and knew where the best berries could be harvested and every week they'd be selling their jams and jellies at the market. He wondered how both of them could have passed in the short time since he'd left home. And he wondered who harvested the berries now, or if they were left to spoil.

No; when he'd stood at this juncture in the past, he'd been walking from Mam's house. He should've been walking the other direction to the Rowan house. But he hadn't. He'd turned and walked toward the village, the pubs... and her.

He made another quarter turn and faced the church. He wanted to go there and he never wanted to see it again. He wanted the sanctity of its presence and dreaded the condemnation of events past. He hated it and he loved it.

And he knew that was his destination.

The sound of voices and music grew faint as he approached the great stone walls. He had no idea how old this church was; he supposed it had been built in the 1600's, perhaps earlier. He didn't think it had ever expanded. For generations, the village population had remained the same. People died. More were born. Many moved away, ensuring there would be no growth. He had moved away once; he'd moved to the outskirts of Dublin, which had felt more foreign than anything he'd ever experienced. And somehow that move that he now realized was a mere sixty miles or so from this spot, had changed his life forever. Had he not gone there, he would never have been employed as a butcher, would never have learned his employer shared the same name as he, and he would never have immigrated to America masquerading as Aunt Laurel's nephew.

He opened the iron pedestrian gate and let himself into the cemetery adjacent to the church. The winds instantly subsided and a silence enveloped the church grounds. He stuck his hands in his pockets and wandered down the path to Mam's gravesite, where two men were placing flowers around the mounded, soft earth. Not far from them were the shovels and the equipment that had lowered Mam's casket into the ground. The tombstone hadn't yet been erected and by the time it was finished and Cam Cassidy had etched her name and dates of birth and death on it, Dylan would be back in America. He realized with a start that he might never see it.

One man nodded to him and he returned his silent greeting. As he stood there staring at the grave, the men quietly took their leave, allowing him time alone to grieve.

Once he knew he was completely alone, he turned away from Mam's grave and stared for a moment at the far corner. Then he made his way to the concrete bench he had paid for and delivered himself. It was under a massive oak tree that provided protection from the winds and the rains and the snow for the two graves beneath it.

He sat on the bench and took a jagged breath. It seemed like ages since he'd been there last and it seemed like it was yesterday.

As he looked at the tombstones erected in front of him, he allowed a tear to run unchecked down his cheek. His shoulders shook and his chest constricted with his pain and his sorrow. If he could turn back time, he would have done everything differently.

Somehow through his tears he saw the tombstones like watercolor Monets; the names and dates dancing across them like faeries tearing at his soul:

Alana Hoolihan Maguire read the first one; *August 25, 1990 – October 24, 2011.*

The second read simply:

Michael Kirwin Maguire, October 24, 2011.

23

Vicki nearly flew down the hall. She'd dressed so quickly she didn't even remember pulling on her slacks or slipping into her shoes. Now she hastily crammed her arms into an all-weather jacket without bothering to zip it.

"What's going on?" Brenda stood at the kitchen door, her face pale.

"I'm going for a walk."

"I thought you were sleeping."

"Don't follow me," she said as she opened the door.

"But—"

"This is between me and Dylan. *Don't follow me.*"

Brenda was at the front door before she could close it. Without another word, she started down the path toward the driveway. A yellow glow crept along the front lawn, broken only by her silhouette. But instead of turning onto the winding drive, she marched across the lawn in a straight line to the road. She'd nearly reached it when Brenda closed the door and the yellow light that had illuminated her way abruptly disappeared.

She found Dylan in the corner of the cemetery with his back to her. His shoulders were no longer shaking, his tears ended, and he remained perfectly still. He didn't appear to notice her presence until she walked around the concrete bench where he sat, still staring at the tombstones.

"Dylan," she said quietly. He didn't look at her and she added, "I know you wanted to be alone—"

He reached for her then, pulling her close to him. "I'm glad you're here." He rested his head against her belly and she stood for a long moment in silence as he wrapped his arms around her. She wove her fingers through his dark hair as she stood in silence. Her back was to the tombstones but she knew she didn't need to turn around to look at them. That would come soon enough.

It was barely five o'clock but the sky had grown dark and with the sun's departure went the last remnants of warmth. Finally, Dylan stirred, kissing her belly before looking up at her. "Sit down," he said quietly.

She sat beside him as he wrapped one arm around her and pulled her close.

"I'd known her just about me whole life," he said, gesturing toward the tombstone.

She gazed at the stones and read the words silently, noting the same names and dates she had seen in her dream.

"She was nothin' like 'er brothers," he went on. "It was as if faeries had delivered 'er to the wrong house. She was petite, like you. Blond hair, enormous blue eyes. Mam said she was fey and I thought they were both bonkers when they knew what would happen a'fore it happened."

Vicki remained silent and nestled against him. His jacket smelled strongly of aged leather and just the feel of his arm around her and his masculine scent was all she needed to feel that all was right with the world.

"I didn't go to their house to pal around with 'er brothers. I came to see 'er. But I got swept up in a family o' wrong-doers. And I'd do it all o'er again just to be near 'er." He looked at the clouds and took a long, deep breath. "And she told me she'd known 'er whole life that it was meant for us to be together. And I believed 'er. I wanted that, maybe more than she did."

He rubbed her shoulder absent-mindedly as he continued. "I dropped out o' school and went to work in the bogs with 'er brothers. We got married, Alana and I. Happiest day o' me life. And then I went and screwed it all up."

Vicki wanted to ask why he thought that but at the same time she wrestled with the presence of the woman buried in front of her. She felt as if her throat was constricting but she didn't know why.

"We rented the cottage down by the brook—"

"The one we passed on our drive in."

"Aye. The whole thin' might 'ave fit in Laurel Maguire's livin' room." He dabbed at his eyes though they remained dry. "And then I started thinkin'. She was all o' seventeen and I was just a bit older. And I thought, I'll be married to the same woman for the rest o' me life. If I live to be eighty, she'll always be right there. So what's the point in rushin' home after work each day? What's the harm in goin' to the pubs with 'er brothers and wanderin' home in the middle o' the night, half pissed?

"She was always there, always waitin'. Always wantin' to know if I'd cheated on 'er." He added almost as an afterthought, "Which I ne'er did, by the way. Ne'er even crossed me mind."

He paused and his chest rose and fell with several deep breaths before he continued. "Then one day she announced that she was goin' to have me child."

His arm was still wrapped around her and somehow the presence of the baby that grew within her loomed larger. She found herself nearly holding her breath waiting for him to continue. He hated children, she thought.

But his next words surprised her. "I was ecstatic. I'd never been so happy in all me life."

"You wanted a baby?"

"I wanted *my* baby. *Our* baby. I wanted to be a father. I didn't care if it was a boy or a girl. I was makin' plans to be the best father on the face o' this earth. She went to the midwife in the village, who confirmed the pregnancy—"

"She didn't go to a doctor?"

He pulled slightly away from her so he could look her in the eye. He smiled but it was filled with sadness. "We'd lost our village physician years before, when old Dr. Niall passed on. The closest doctor was twenty miles away in the next village. And the waitin' list was two years."

"Two years!"

"There's a sayin' in Ireland, Darlin', that when a man looks cross-eyed at ya, you'd better make an appointment. Cause if you wait till you're pregnant, it's too late to get in." He settled back. "Anyway, women—so they said—had been havin' babies throughout all o' time, with or without a doctor. And the midwives were just as efficient, even more so, they said."

A chill swept through the cemetery and Vicki shivered. He pulled her closer to him, warming her with his own body. "I straightened up me ways. No more visits to the pubs. No more drunkin' encounters. I did me work and I came straight home and tended to 'er. It was the happiest we'd ever been.

"Then on the twenty-second o' October, we'd been married three years by then, it started to rain. And she went into labor. I telephoned 'er mother—mine was God knows where—and I wanted to take 'er to the midwife straight away. But 'er mum came to the cottage and said it would be awhile yet; the labor pains were more than an hour apart. So we waited.

"I stayed right there with 'er. For twenty-four hours it rained and the labor pains grew more intense. I must 'ave phoned the midwife, Mrs. Gallaghan, two dozen times. I hated seein' her in such pain. I despised it. But it was nearly three kilometers to Mrs. Gallaghan's home. I had no auto—I walked to work each day—and she was clearly in no shape to walk. I thought o' carryin' 'er but her mum and her pup had moved in for the duration and they said I was crazy."

He stared at the tombstone for a long moment before continuing. "I know now I shouldn't 'ave listened. I should 'ave gathered 'er in me arms at the first sign o' labor and I should 'ave carried 'er into the village. But I didn't. I waited there and listened to 'er screams. And on the twenty-fourth, after she'd been in labor for nearly forty-eight hours, the flood walls broke." He swallowed. "The bridge by the cottage was washed away. We were surrounded by a moat that threatened to come up into the house but there was nowhere we could go. And I couldn't swim with 'er in me arms.

"I was frantic. She was screamin' non-stop and it went on hour after hour. This can't be right, I thought. Surely, every woman couldn't go through this h'ail.'"

After a moment, he continued. "I'd gone into our bedroom where she lay in a sea o' sweat and when she saw me, she reached for me. And when I bent down to hear 'er, she said, 'Mickey, if you don't get me out o' here, I'll die.' It seemed like it took forever but finally I got Thomas—Father Rowan now, but he wasn't a priest yet then—on the phone; the cell reception was so pitiful, it's a wonder we connected. But he understood enough to know that Alana was in deep trouble. It took him a few hours but he located a rowboat and he came to the house.

"And I announced to 'er parents that I was takin' 'er to the next village. To a proper doctor. The midwife had done nothin' but tell us to wait. And I was through waitin'. I thought I'd have to thrash 'er father to get past him, but once she was in me arms, they stood aside. But as I loaded 'er into the rowboat with the rains comin' down like a dam burstin' o'er us, 'er mother said to me that 'er death, were she to die, would be on my head."

He wiped at his eyes again and his arms squeezed Vicki tighter. "Father Rowan got us to the church and he helped load 'er into his auto. And we took off, with 'er screamin' every single minute, though I know she was tryin' hard not to."

He shook his head and stared into the sky. The clouds had succeeded in blotting out the moon and the stars. "The first bridge we came to between the two villages was washed away. I had no choice but to turn back and try a different route. And by the time I reached the second bridge and the water was rushin' o'er it, she was passed out beside me. And I thought, better that she be passed out because at least now she's feelin' no pain.

"I turned around yet again and tried a third route. And we'd gotten o'er the bridge and were on the straight-away to the village when she awakened and she begged me to stop right where I was.

"I didn't want to. Every second counted and I'd pushed that pedal to the floor to get 'er to a doctor as fast as I could. But she convinced me to stop.

"She asked me to hold 'er. And I did. Right there, in the middle o' the road, with nary another soul in sight. I held 'er. And she said to me, she wasn't goin' to make it. And she wanted me to know she loved me and she'd always love me."

He choked. "She died in me arms."

A silence enveloped them. Vicki wanted to say something to ease his pain but everything she thought of saying seemed pitifully inept. So she squeezed his hand and waited for him to continue.

Finally, he took a deep breath and said, "Our baby was still inside 'er. So I laid 'er out in the seat beside me and I continued to the next village. I found the doctor at his home and I carried Alana into his parlor. When he examined 'er, he found—" he stopped and swallowed hard "—our baby had breeched and the cord had gotten hopelessly wrapped around his neck. He'd died inside 'er. Her insides had kept pushin' but…"

He sobbed quietly and then continued, "I brought Alana and our son back to our village. To the mortuary there. Mam named him. She named him 'Michael' after the archangel and 'Kirwin' because in Gaelic it means 'little black-haired one.' She said he was a little black-haired angel. I was thankful that she named him because I—I was completely numb. I thought God had forsaken me.

"And when 'er brothers came off their drunk, they said I killed 'er. Her parents told the whole village I killed 'er. Until I began to think that I *had* killed 'er."

Vicki opened her mouth to protest but he said, "I went into a tailspin. I met trouble everywhere I went. Half the village ostracized me. The other half felt nothin' but pity for me. Damned child; father left him at three in a foreign country, to boot; mother was a whore and a drunk; now his wife and his child are dead.

"Only Father Rowan was there. I spent many a night sleepin' on the pews. I ne'er returned to that cottage. Ne'er went into it again. Me dog, Shep, she found me at the church. And we stayed there for months until Father Rowan convinced me to leave the village. To start fresh somewhere else, where nobody knew me. I could make a clean slate o' it, he said. There was a reason for everythin', he said.

"So I did. I moved closer to Dublin and I started earnin' money in fights. I liked fightin'. I could channel all the pain and all the hurt and all the anger into me fists—and me feet. I found I had a knack for kickboxin' and so I went down that road. Until I met a man in a pub one day who said he needed a butcher and he'd be willin' to train. So I took the job.

"And while I was there, I heard the others talkin' about Dylan Maguire, the owner. Same name as me, imagine that. And his aunt was dyin' in America and she was beggin' him to come and care for her. And he refused. Said he wouldn't leave his business for a woman he ne'er liked to begin with."

He cocked his head as if thinking. "And I thought to m'self, I thought, here's a man with a family. A family who's beggin' him to be with 'er. I had no one. No father. No mother. No wife. No child. Nothin'. And here he was, turnin' his back on his own flesh and blood. So I thought, maybe Father Rowan is right. Maybe I'm here for a reason, workin' in this butcher shop. Maybe I should go to America and take care o' this sweet old lady. Maybe she'll be me family."

He pulled away from her to look her in the eye. Her own eyes were flooded with tears that she'd managed to shed more or less silently as she listened to his story. "When Aunt Laurel died, I didn't know what to do. I couldn't come home. I had no home. I know I was wrong to stay and lie to ya, but I thought… I thought if I convinced m'self that I really was Dylan Maguire, all o' this would feel like it happened to somebody else."

He stood up and pulled her to her feet. He fished around in his pocket and she felt a sudden quickening of her heart. Not here, she thought, don't propose to me in a cemetery! But when he withdrew his hand, he held a dainty key on a chain.

"But I love you now," he said. "I needed to tell you about me past. You needed to know it. And if you'll still have me, I'd like to give you this." He gently swept her long hair to the side, fastened the chain around her neck and fingered the tiny key.

"It's an Irish tradition. This is called 'the key to me heart' and I want you to know that you'll always 'ave the key to me heart."

"I love you, Dylan," she said as his lips brushed against hers.

"I love you, Darlin'. I knew I was where I was meant to be, the first time I ever laid eyes on you."

The winds were growing in intensity and she knew that time had marched on. There was a nagging inside her to get back home so Dylan could undertake his assignment, even though every breath she took wanted to beg him not to leave tonight. They needed this night to heal, to bond.

"So," she said, "this hatred you have of children, this wanting never to be around one—"

"I'm scared to death o' children. If I ever made another woman pregnant again, I think it would kill me."

She drew back, a half-smile on her face to wittily retort. But when she saw the look in his eyes, so sad, so serious, she laid her head against his chest. Her words would wait for another day, another time.

He took a deep breath. "I've got to get you home," he said. "I've a mission to do and there'll be people waitin' on me."

24

They were still holding hands when they walked through the door to the cottage. Vicki thought she'd never felt so close to another human being in all her life, and at the same time she thought she'd never felt so utterly and completely alone.

The life that grew inside her was her own flesh and blood—and Dylan's, too. Yet she couldn't bring herself to tell him. And she was at a loss as to how she would ever break the news to him. At the same time, she wrestled with the knowledge that her belly would grow larger and rounder; and with that knowledge, she felt the clock ticking.

As he opened the door, a blast of wind whipped through, tearing the door out of his hands. They both turned instinctively to study the sky. The clouds had turned ominous and Vicki felt a chill creep up her spine and a feeling of dread wash over her.

"There you are," Brenda said. She stood in the kitchen doorway with her arms folded. "I was getting worried about you."

"I'll buck up the fire," Dylan said, wrestling the door closed and striding into the kitchen. But as he walked through the doorway, he stopped to stare at the kitchen table. His face grew pale and then his cheeks began to turn beet red.

"What is it?" Vicki asked, joining him.

Brenda followed them and stood back, her arms still folded.

On the kitchen table was Dylan's laptop. And on the screen was the three-dimensional model of the dungeons.

"What the—?" he began.

Vicki whirled around. "You know you're restricted from using a computer!"

She stood in silence.

"How," Dylan said, his face reddening even deeper, "did you know this was my mission?"

"This isn't exactly the Taj Mahal, Irish," she said, sauntering to the table. "My room is right on the other side of that wall. You think I couldn't hear every word?"

"But why did you do this?" Vicki asked.

"It's what I do."

"I'm not believin' this," Dylan sputtered.

"Listen. It worried me that Sam said there was one way in and one way out—or that Stephen Anders said it," Brenda said. She pulled out a chair and sat down in front of the computer. "That's a deathtrap. Think about it. The 'enemy' or whatever you want to call them, show up. All they have to do is block that entrance—a bomb, set it on fire, whatever—and the dungeons become one big grave."

Vicki pulled out a chair and shakily sat down beside her.

"You let me worry about that," Dylan said.

"Look, Irish. Sam said the satellite didn't get a good feed on this spot here." She moved her mouse over an area just outside the circular hallway. "But let me show you what I did." She pressed a few keys and while she held the mouse over the area, it began to spin. "See, people who don't want things to be seen on the Internet can blur that spot. Take a sex offender. He might get his kicks filming what he does but when he posts it on the net for bragging rights, he's blurred his own image. He thinks the feds can't track him down now."

"I don't see as how that's got anythin' to do w'—"

"But you can spin out the blur. See?" She stopped the area from spinning and the model began to take form.

"How did you do that?" Vicki asked.

"The how doesn't matter, Sis. It's the fact that I did it." She spoke matter-of-factly, without ego or pride. "What you've got here is a caved-in room."

"Well, that's helpful," Dylan said. He pulled off his jacket.

"But here's the thing," Brenda continued. "Assuming this was a medieval castle and these were the dungeons—do you think it's a correct assumption that only one entrance would be built to it?"

Before they could answer, she continued, moving the screen farther to one side, "Or, don't you think there would be a back staircase to it somewhere?" One spot at a time, she spun until she found another staircase.

"That's amazing," Dylan whispered.

"But here's what you need to know: it's been caved in sometime in the past. It's not completely impassible. But if you needed to—if the front entrance was blocked for whatever reason—you could climb over these rocks here and get to this back staircase."

"Are you sure about this?"

"The place is massive," Brenda continued. "Some of the stairs have fallen away. But it's a way out. And when you emerge, by my calculations, you'll be about a quarter of a mile from the first entrance."

Dylan's cell phone rang, startling them. "Sam," he said. "Aye?"

As Sam began to speak, he put the call on speakerphone.

"We have to scrub the mission," Sam was saying. "The system's been hacked. We're trying to determine now where the hacker is but we can't risk it tonight."

"I'll save you some time," Dylan said firmly. "I'm lookin' at the hacker now."

"You're—"

"Brenda Carnegie."

Sam swore.

"But hear me out. It's true, she hacked in without me knowledge and without Vicki's. We were together and she took advantage o' it. But she found a back exit, one we might be able to use if need be."

"Why?" Sam demanded.

"Why did I hack in?" Brenda asked.

"Why are you helping us?" Sam said.

She took a deep breath. "Vicki's my sister," she said. "And she loves Dylan. And I'll be damned if anything happens to him when I could have prevented it." She closed the laptop. "If you don't want to use my information, don't. If you want to send me back to prison, do. Either way, I'll know I did what I could."

There was a long silence. Then Dylan said, "So tell me what you want done, Sam." He eyed Brenda. "It's your call."

He was met with more silence.

"Sam?"

"No," Sam said finally. "Dylan, it's *your* call."

"Are you certain about that?"

"When you go in—*if* you go in—you're taking your life in your hands. And the lives of two other operatives. You see what she's done with the program. You decide what you're going to do."

Dylan looked at Brenda for a time, his eyes narrowed. He avoided Vicki's inquisitive look. Then he said, "I'm goin' in as planned."

"You're sure?" Sam asked.

"I'm sure. We'll use the back stairs only if the situation warrants it."

"You're not off the hook that easily, Brenda," Sam said, the firmness back in his voice. "By midnight, I want every step you took to break into this system. You got that? *Every step*. And if I don't have it by midnight, you're going back to prison."

"Piece of cake," she said, opening the laptop again.

25

Dylan lay on his back, basking in the warmth of soft flannel sheets and the smooth lines of Vicki's body. Her breathing was gentle and rhythmic in her sleep and she fit neatly under his arm as she curled against his side. He wished he could nap the way she did; she had the enviable ability to sleep at any time of the day or night. But then, he thought as he glanced at the clock, it was after nine o'clock and half the population that wasn't at the pubs would be tucked in for the night.

He took a deep breath, inhaling a fragrance that both relaxed and excited him. He loved the perfume of her long, strawberry blond tresses. There was something different about the water here and as it mixed with her shampoo, it had a slightly more floral scent than it had back home. He inhaled again; everything smelled differently here, he realized.

He knew that perhaps a week from now or a month from now, he would be glad he returned to Ireland. He had once believed he would never see this village again. In fact, when he left he vowed never to return. Yet, here he was. Another twist of fate the gods had thrown at him.

Mam deserved to see one of her own flesh and blood before passing, he thought. He was angry with his mother for not being here; angry that she'd left him but angrier that she'd left Mam.

His grandmother had deserved better. Maybe he didn't but she did. She'd always been there for him, even when he was hell bent on destroying his own life. She'd always loved him even when he didn't love himself. She'd always believed in him even when he'd lost all faith.

He wound his fingers through Vicki's long strands. He was glad Mam had met her; she would've liked Vicki, had she gotten the chance to know her. She had a kind heart and loving ways. And she pleased him more than anyone else ever had—even *her*.

Please forgive me, Alana, he thought. Forgive me for falling in love with another.

But he was worried about her. She hadn't been eating since they'd come here. She'd been a hearty eater of his cooking back home; he knew the bacon was different here—cut from a different part of the pig and healthier, he thought, than the American type. The eggs tasted different because they came direct from the O'Callahan's farm across the way. It should have been better. Yet, she wouldn't taste it. She turned away as if...

She seemed frailer to him somehow. She wasn't eating and yet when they made love, as they had this evening, she seemed softer, rounder.

When they'd first met, she was fragile. She fainted at the drop of a hat. She needed sleep at the oddest times of the day. But he understood now that her health had been compromised by her missions; by this wild ability to go somewhere else in her mind. But she seemed to have moved beyond that; she'd grown stronger somehow. But now—now, it was back; the fainting, the feebleness.

If he didn't know better, he might have thought...

He froze with her strands intertwined with his fingers.

No. She wouldn't keep something like that a secret from him. She couldn't.

He glanced across the room at the dresser. Nestled beneath his shirts in the top drawer was a tiny box. Ironically, he'd ordered it from Dublin while still in Lumberton, never believing they would be here together. And he'd brought it all this way, along with the necklace, to give to her here on these shores.

He could feel the chain beneath his fingers. He'd seen it as they'd made love. He'd felt it against his skin even as it rested against hers.

She was his future.

A vision of his mission rose before him like dawn arriving before he was ready to relinquish a hold on sleep. He despised these missions. If he'd been completely unencumbered, he might have relished them. World travel. Fighting. Work that could grow more exciting and more dangerous over the years…

But with her in his life, he felt like he was at the edge of a precipice. He was always worried what would happen to her if he didn't return. A single shot or wrong move could end their relationship—their future—in a literal heartbeat.

This was no way to think, he chastised himself. Especially right before a mission.

He replayed the events in his mind once more. It was simple enough. Meet two operatives in the village. Get horses from a local stable; the only one he knew was Aengus' and he wondered if that's where they'd go. Go to Point A and leave the horses. Continue to Point B on foot.

He remembered Vicki's mission all too well; the description of the stone stairwell, the odor, the feeling that she was being watched. The mold, the dampness, the evil that lurked below. He would descend with night vision goggles and an earpiece that would connect him to Sam and the other operatives. He'd help to get Stephen Anders freed and he'd get him back up those stairs and to Father Rowan.

He thought of Brenda hacking into the system while he talked with Vicki at the cemetery. He didn't know quite what to make of that. It was curious, he thought. When she had been ready to leave in Lumberton with Vicki's keys in her pocket, stolen money and his gun in her hand, he'd told her essentially the same thing she'd said to Sam this evening: they both loved Vicki and they would protect the other out of love for her.

It was a peculiar situation. Brenda was the opposite of Vicki. Yet, in many ways, she was the same as himself.

He sighed. It was time.

He gently extricated himself from Vicki, rolling her onto her side and away from him. She murmured something he couldn't quite comprehend and he bent down and raced his lips along her dainty ear before whispering, "I love you, Darlin'. I'll be back straight-away. And tomorrow, we'll go to the shops. We'll do the sightseein' you've been wantin' to do."

He hoped he would sleep like death warmed over when he got back. The funeral was over, the mission soon would be, and there would be nothing pressing against him as it was now. He didn't care if they slept till noon and made love until this time tomorrow evening. He didn't care what they did, as long as she was by his side.

He slipped out of bed and quickly dressed in black jeans and a dark marled turtleneck. It was strange when he thought of it; only a week ago, he was wearing short sleeves in North Carolina. Now he was donning wool. It would be cold on the bogs, though, with scant trees to block the wind. And with the storm coming in, the rains could make things difficult. He holstered his gun before slipping on a black jacket. Then he crammed a black knit cap and a pair of leather gloves into his pockets.

But then, he debated himself, the rains could keep the captors away from the ruins. The bogs were no place to be when it rained. The ground became sodden with the slightest bit of moisture and the ground felt anything but firm, anything but secure. It was said the bogs could swallow a cow and he believed it. It had swallowed up the dungeons, he thought. How many times he'd been in those bogs and never knew what lay beneath...

He quietly opened the door and slipped through to the hallway, pulling the door shut noiselessly. He held his boots in his hands until he was near the front door.

Brenda leaned away from the kitchen table to view him through the doorway. "Take care of yourself, Irish."

He slipped on his boots before answering. "I'll be back in about two hours," he said. "Will you be up then?"

She smiled and raised one brow coquettishly. "Why do you ask?"

He ignored the innuendo. "Take care o' Vicki, won't you?"

Her eyes widened and her smile faded. "Of course I'll take care of her. But you'll be back soon. And you can take care of her yourself."

"Aye." He had his hand on the doorknob. He hesitated a moment and glanced at Brenda once more. A voice inside him begged him not to go, pleaded with him to return to Vicki's side.

He opened the door and was gone.

26

Dylan parked the rental car in the village square before continuing on foot to the pub. It was six blocks away and there was plenty of parking directly in front of it. But if anyone recognized his automobile, they wouldn't know exactly which way he might have gone; there were pubs in all four directions. And this would give him an opportunity to approach the rendezvous point at any speed he chose. The last thing he needed to do was hang around in front of it.

His eyes scoured the street as he tried to remember all the things he'd been taught thus far; he memorized license plates, he watched the behavior of the villagers, he knew which drunk men wouldn't remember where they'd been this time tomorrow and which ones to keep his eye on. It was a quiet night, all things considered; most of the villagers were most likely leaving the Rowan house about now, having finished with their tall tales of Bonnie O'Sullivan—for now, at least.

The funeral seemed a lifetime ago. He pushed any remnant memories of it out of his mind as he stopped at a cross street and glanced in both directions. He should have brought a pack of cigarettes and some matches, he thought. Though he didn't smoke—he'd never smoked—it would have been an excuse for stopping longer, leisurely lighting a cigarette while watching for his contacts.

He was about twelve feet from the door of the pub when they walked out. They were laughing loudly and one slapped the other on the back in jest.

Dylan continued until he was almost bumping into them as they lingered for a moment in front of the pub. One acted shaky as he attempted to find his keys. If he hadn't known to expect them, he might have concluded they were tourists and more than slightly inebriated.

"There's a thunderstorm brewing," Dylan said as he started past them.

"Aye," said the one with the black hair. "Looks to be a bad one."

Dylan hesitated. "It does at that."

The blond-haired man found his keys and started past Dylan. "Around the corner. Blue Vauxhall."

Dylan didn't respond but kept strolling. He could feel the two behind him; they turned right at the corner but he continued straight. He walked to the alley and cut back through so he came from behind as they were getting into the car.

He was still settling into the back seat when the sedan took off. He glanced up to see the Hoolihan brothers rounding the corner. His eyes met Eoghan's for the briefest of moments before he turned his attention to the front seat.

"You know those guys?" one asked.

"The whole village knows 'em. They're troublemakers."

"They had their eyes on us the whole time."

"They were lookin' to roll you," Dylan answered. "One of their favorite pastimes."

The black-haired man stopped watching the side mirror as they left the brothers behind them. He turned and offered his hand. As Dylan shook it, he said, "Name's Perry. I'll be your watch."

"Dylan," he answered. He noticed the thick Irish brogue the man had used on the sidewalk was gone. He was unmistakably American.

"I'm Rich," the blond said. His accent had also changed; and as Dylan peered at his eyes in the rearview mirror, they no longer appeared to be the eyes of a man who'd imbibed too much. "I'll be going in with you."

Dylan nodded once and averted his eyes. It wasn't good to stare into the eyes of operatives for too long; it could be misconstrued as an attempt to assert dominance. It was one of the tidbits he'd learned in his classes. One never knew when a tidbit could save a life, he thought. Or a whole lot o' trouble.

The horses were waiting at the stables, saddled up and ready to go. All were black and Dylan recognized the steed he'd ridden the day before. They pulled the car behind the stables and Perry and Rich pulled three black bags from the trunk.

"Where's Aengus?" Dylan asked as he went through his bag. He spotted night vision goggles, earpieces, bolt cutters, rope, several knives, two pistols and ammunition. Brenda would love this, he thought.

Perry glanced at Rich. "Who?"

"Aengus. The man who runs the stables." He donned the earpiece and watched as the others followed suit. When they left the night vision goggles in the bags, he did the same, wrapping the bag handles around the saddle horn.

"Out," Rich said. "Last minute trip."

Dylan nodded and mounted his horse. He imagined the old man had been paid a pretty penny to saddle up these horses and leave them waiting, and even more for leaving town on an overnight trip. The thought occurred to him that Aengus would be shocked into the netherworld if he learned that one of the secretive men using his horses was none other than Mick Maguire.

"Testing," Perry said, cupping one hand over his earpiece.

"Read you loud and clear," came Sam's voice. "I need a check on the others."

Rich and then Dylan said a couple of words each and waited for Sam's acknowledgment. Then Sam said, "Some men followed you from the bar."

"Petty thieves," Perry responded, "village troublemakers."

"But they didn't follow us here, did they?" Dylan asked.

"Negative. You were gone before they were in their truck."

"They'll be lookin' for another tourist to jump," Dylan said, "unless they're passed out in the truck cab already."

"We'll be monitoring."

Dylan wondered who else Sam had monitoring their movements. But as they headed into the darkness under the roiling, restless clouds, it didn't matter. Just the thought that the satellites knew where they were and what they might encounter was comfort enough.

The bogs were no place to be during the witching hour.

Dylan had grown up with stories of the bogs at night. The ground percolated; it lived and it breathed. There had been many a time when he was harvesting peat in broad daylight that he'd heard a whisper at his ear or felt hot breath on his neck, only to find there was no one near. Now as he rode his horse in silence, he felt that presence tenfold; there were eyes watching them. The intermittent tuffs of heather swayed in the growing storm and he found himself watching them with narrowed eyes, waiting for the plants to morph into sinister creatures that claimed this land after the sun went down.

He knew there was a simple reason why animals were required in lieu of an all-terrain vehicle and he was glad Sam had taken this unique land into consideration when planning the mission. He could feel the hooves beneath him sinking into the spongy earth; a wheeled vehicle wouldn't have stood a chance, especially as they ventured from the area farmed for its peat to one far less stable.

A mist began; a slow, fine spray that he knew well. One moment the air was still and dry and the next, as though they'd passed through a curtain, the air swirled around them, the moist haze further inhibiting their ability to see. It was said many a man lost his internal compass in the Irish mist; it taunted as it grew into monstrous shapes, turning the landscape into something foreign and active.

With the moisture saturating the porous peat, the earth felt as if it leached and oozed under them. The horses picked their way with an exasperating lack of speed and no matter how hard they tried to spur them onward, they obstinately refused to quicken the pace.

Perry's horse whinnied, the sound echoing. It was another odd trait of the bogs, that ability for voices to bounce off every corner to return to the speaker like a chorus rising around them. It made it impossible to determine the source of a sound, threatening those lost in the bogs with near insanity, believing the spirits to be closing in around them.

Dylan's eyes narrowed as he searched the terrain in an attempt to silently determine the source of the horse's discomfort, but he could see only a few feet in front of him and even that was cast in a churning gray-black mist. He forced himself to think rationally, though his imagination clashed with the logic. There were no snakes in Ireland and he knew of scant animals who could survive in these bogs—at least those known to man.

"Tell me, Sam," he said in a voice that sounded low and hoarse, "can the satellites see through the cloud cover and the mist?"

"Affirmative."

It was clear from the silence that followed that Sam was not in a talkative mood and Dylan fell silent as well. The reassurance did nothing to quell a peculiar sensation that had begun to whirl around him and he struggled to explain the feeling that something otherworldly had begun to crawl up his spine.

As they continued on, the air began to change and he reminded himself that the oxygen in the bogs was thinner than elsewhere on the Emerald Isle, as if the very ground beneath their feet was sucking it in. The peat even swelled and constricted like a creature awakening and stirring and breathing.

Perry's horse was in front and as it stopped the others did, too. Then silently, as if the animals were communicating telepathically, they all backed up and traveled in a small semi-circle instead of moving straight ahead.

"What the—?" Rich started, glancing at Dylan.

"The land is pockmarked with bog holes," Dylan said. His own voice sounded strange to him and he swallowed before continuing. "You can see 'em durin' the day when the skies aren't too gray. But at night, they blend into the ground. The horses begin to feel their hooves sink and they stop and turn around. Otherwise, you could find y'self in ten feet o' muddy water—or more."

Neither man answered but he caught a glimpse of the whites of Rich's eyes growing larger. Aye, he thought. It was a dangerous thin' to be doin', goin' into the bogs at night.

There had been a time when he'd scoured these bogs looking for ancient oaks with which to make furniture; it was well known these swamplands had swallowed up the trees and anything built upon it. Bog oak was good and strong with beautiful veins. But he was just as likely to find skeletons or even mummies while he dug and it didn't take long before a perfectly preserved head that came up with his shovel convinced him to leave well enough alone.

But the Hoolihan brothers had fallen prey to the myth that gold and treasure was buried in the bogs. It was something he'd heard his entire life as well, but every sane man paid it no mind. If there was treasure, it would have been found a'fore now for sure. But the Hoolihans spent an inordinate amount of time looking for it, nonetheless, convinced they were right and everyone else was wrong.

Lightning flashed across the sky and a few seconds later, a low rumble of thunder shook the ground beneath their feet. The horses whinnied and turned completely around.

"What's that?" Perry asked as all three men fought to control their horses.

Dylan followed his gaze to the distant horizon. "Blue flames."

"Fire?"

"It's caused by the bog gasses. Methane. It's common durin' storms. When I was a tyke, the old-timers used to say they were faeries, cookin' their supper."

It felt as though it was taking far longer for them to reach their destination than it had in broad daylight with Brenda and Vicki. But that's the way it was at night, Dylan reminded himself.

During the witching hour and in the pre-dawn hours that followed, the terrain took on the feel of a vast, empty space in which compasses no longer functioned properly. It was said there were little folk who lived in the bogs, mischievous creatures who watched every movement and waited for the perfect opportunity to play havoc—or worse. Fooling with their compasses was just one of their tricks.

They were known as ballybogs or bog-a-boos, depending on who was telling the story. Some said they were the remains of the dead rising out of the bogs. Others said they were nasty creatures that were not related to humans at all.

"You're sure you know where this place is?" Perry asked uneasily.

He looked toward the horizon. "Aye."

The thunder and lightning grew and intensified and the mist began to turn to more solid precipitation, though it stopped short of becoming a rainstorm. It was well known that one had no business being in a bog when it rained. It often came fast and furious and often the peat was buried beneath ponds that could suck men into them in mere seconds. Dylan found himself wondering whether the water would pour into the castle remains. It would be a horrific way to die.

He turned in his saddle and peered behind him.

"What is it?" Rich asked.

Dylan shook his head. "Just feel eyes on me, tis all."

"I've been feeling that same way ever since we left," Perry said. He spoke in a stage whisper and his voice sounded strained and dry.

Rich stopped his horse and began to pull something out of his bag.

"Don't stop," Dylan cautioned as he went past him.

"My night vision goggles—"

"*Don't stop.* The horse could begin to sink. Keep movin'. Get anythin' you need while you're movin'."

"I don't like this place," Rich said but he allowed his horse to fall in line behind Dylan and Perry.

"Join the club," Dylan said.

The sky was ablaze now with lightning; it glowed blue over the bogs instead of the yellow or white he was accustomed to in the village. He couldn't imagine Stephen Anders being brought here in cuffs or shackles and being led down the ancient steps to a forgotten ruin. He must have felt as though he was being buried alive.

And maybe that was their intent.

He spotted the trees in the distance and pointed in that direction. Where trees continued to live, it meant the roots were in firm soil. As long as the horses remained under the trees they would not sink. But just a few yards beyond the longest branches could be quagmire.

They reached the first grove before he spotted the second. They tied up the horses, which were growing increasingly skittish. All three men then donned their night vision goggles.

"Operation Moor," Perry said.

Dylan heard Sam's voice in his ear. "Horses secured?"

"Aye." The Irish accent was back in Perry's voice.

"This way," Dylan said, starting out on foot toward a second grove of trees that rose out of the earth like skeletal remains, their branches swept outward like craggy hands ready to snatch anyone who passed near.

27

They found the door under a dense blanket of leaves. It was wood and looked to have been made recently; it was held in place simply by the ground around it.

"Be back directly," Dylan said to Perry as he slipped his feet into the hole. Touching something more solid than peat, he began to descend. He glanced upward as Perry and Rich exchanged glances, but Dylan couldn't determine their meaning with their eyes hidden behind the night vision goggles they donned.

He felt as if he was descending into a grave and he struggled against a sudden sense of claustrophobia. Narrow places had never bothered him before but this was different. If the air was thin above ground, it was even worse below and his breathing quickly became loud, laborious and rasping. And as his head completely disappeared from view, he knew the lifeline provided by Sam and the satellites were gone. They were on their own.

He hesitated as he grappled for the walls that Vicki had described in her mission while he tried to get his bearings. They were slimy; he could feel the slickness beneath his gloves. His heart sank as he realized if his feet slipped, he could not grab the stones on either side of him. Though they were of varying sizes and textures, there would be no firm hold.

As his eyes became adjusted, he realized the night vision goggles allowed him to see almost as if it was daylight but they also produced tunnel vision, which had been the reason for riding without them. Now he had to face one hand in order to see the stone beneath it; it was covered in thick, moldy moss. He turned in the other direction to view the other hand.

"It's very slick," he said. He looked at his feet. The stairs were not much better, though it appeared as if someone had come this way fairly recently. He couldn't imagine Vicki falling into this abyss during their morning ride and he fought to avert his thoughts from the surreal realization that she could see these walls in her mind.

He continued his descent as he heard Rich entering the stairs above him.

"I'm putting the door in place," Perry said. His voice came through Dylan's earpiece as a hoarse whisper. "Protection from the elements."

He could hear the door scraping against the dirt above them, and a chunk of peat and leaves fell across his shoulder. This *was* a grave, he thought.

The air burned his lungs as he continued into the void. There was no handrail and he felt himself groping with each foot, making certain he had planted each shoe securely on the narrow stones before moving the other one. As he moved ever deeper, a powerful stench began to pervade right through his clothing; it smelled as if something—or someone—was rotting. The stairwell reeked of something akin to urine, which grew stronger until he was nearly nauseous.

He held up his hand to signal to Rich that he was stopping and he reached his glove to his nose. He was right. It was the stink of mold; centuries of the stuff, growing unchecked like a malignant virus.

He moved down the stairs until he eventually began to pass sconces that had turned the stone black with soot. It was then that he realized the area in which he was just now entering had been underground when the castle was built; these were the dungeons Vicki had spoken of. They were the stuff of nightmares as a child after listening to ghost stories told in hushed tones; it was a place he never thought he would willingly go.

Sweat popped out across his brow, even though the air was deathly cold. He could hear his own breathing in the confined space; ragged, rasping and thunderous. It echoed in the stairwell until it sounded like dozens of people were whispering in his ears.

He heard a sudden movement above him. He jerked around to peer upward at Rich. "What is it?"

Rich was staring behind them. "Nothing," he said. "I thought I felt something fall on my neck."

Dylan hesitated for a brief moment before resuming. Aye, he thought. It was a place that could have a grown man imagining things. Vicki had told him that Stephen Anders had cried openly and he understood why. Confinement in this hell for any length of time could make a man see things, feel things, sense things that were better left in the netherworld.

He reached the antechamber and breathed a quick albeit temporary sigh of relief. As he waited for Rich to join him, he peered into each hallway. He could only see a few feet before the walls turned, just as the stairwell had been circular and confusing, interfering with his natural compass.

He wiped his brow on his jacket but the sweat popped up again just as quickly as before. His throat felt burned and parched. He remembered a canteen in his bag, but he didn't reach for it. He didn't know how long Anders might have been without food or water and it was best to conserve it.

"In the antechamber," he announced. His voice sounded foreign to him.

"The hall straight ahead is the shortest distance," Sam responded quietly.

Dylan thought of Sam sitting in front of his laptop, studying the three-dimensional model.

"Perry?" Rich said. "Status."

"All's clear."

Dylan nodded once to Rich, who returned his nod. They entered the hallway, which wound its way like a coiled snake. It was difficult to reconcile the straight hallway in the computer graphics with the one laid out before him now. His goggles illuminated cell bars, which appeared as an eerie shade of green. He peered at each cell door, searching for the telltale padlock that would announce Anders' presence.

He reached the end of the hallway and stopped, confused. He turned to face Rich, who was coming up behind him. They looked at each other wordlessly. Anders' cell should have been the last one on the left before the hall joined the other two in a three-way intersection but there had been no padlock.

He motioned for Rich to backtrack. He followed a few steps behind, until he was staring at a set of cell bars. There was no door and no padlock.

Peering into the cell, he fought the impulse to rip the night vision goggles off and shine a flashlight into the area. They created too much of a tunnel effect, he thought irritably.

But as he continued searching, his eyes landed on a shape in the far corner, curled into a ball so the head was completely invisible. It was disarming; it made the figure appear decapitated.

"Stephen Anders." He said it as a statement. His voice was firm and steady and in contrast to the rapid thudding of his heart.

The shoulders began to tremble.

"Show us your face," Rich ordered. The American accent was back and for the briefest of moments, Dylan wondered if he was American or Irish. He seemed to swing between the two accents effortlessly.

The head lifted to reveal grimy hair and a face streaked with dirt and tear tracks. The eyes shone eerily in the night vision goggles; wide, round and unearthly.

"We're here to get you out," Rich said.

"Where's the padlock?" Dylan asked, swinging the bag off his shoulder.

A man shouted and Dylan froze. The sudden noise had come not from inside the cell or even in the hallway beyond them. It had come through their earpieces. Instinctively, he placed his hand over his ear and cocked his head as if it would help him to hear more clearly.

"Perry," Rich said. "Status."

"We've got three individuals at the entrance," Sam said. "I don't know where they came from." His voice sounded incredulous.

As he listened, he was striving to understand what was transpiring above them. Because Perry didn't sound an alarm, could it have meant the intruders had come from behind? He, like them, was only able to see what was happening through the tunnel vision of the night vision goggles. But why didn't Sam see the men through the satellite technology?

The sounds of a scuffle were unmistakable. Now there were several shouts and the noise of a man's air expelling as if he'd been kicked in the gut. A single gunshot split the air. It was so loud in his earpiece that Dylan felt as if his eardrum could burst.

"Where's the padlock?" Dylan demanded.

"Perry! Perry!" Rich called urgently.

Stephen came to his feet unsteadily and pointed around the corner. The door was in the adjacent hallway.

As Dylan rushed around the corner, he grappled for his earpiece. "Can you see what's goin' on, Sam?" he said, his words coming fast and urgent. When he was met with silence, he turned to Rich. "Mute your device," he ordered.

28

Dylan wrestled with the bolt cutters. The padlock was larger than most, the shackles long and thick. When it finally gave way, it clattered to the ground, echoing in the close confines. Both Dylan and Rich burst into the cell, where they found Stephen manacled. The chains were a few inches short of allowing him to reach the bars in his cell. As the two men inspected it, Dylan wondered if they had the equipment needed to break it.

The metal was old, perhaps as ancient as the castle itself. The bands were meant for smaller men and as he examined Stephen's ankles, he realized the metal had cut deeply into the skin. It was rusty and coated with centuries of crud; and now as he stared at it, he realized Stephen could not walk far even after they freed him. He could barely stand on his bare feet; they had become dangerously infected, the ankles swollen and black, the blood dried like glue between the skin and the bands.

"We can't take these bands off," Dylan stated. "It'll rip the skin off him and possibly cause more damage."

"Cut the chain on that ankle," Rich said, helping Stephen sit on the frigid stone floor, "and I'll get this one."

They worked in tandem, grunting as they poured all their muscle into breaking a link on each ankle chain. Then finally

Dylan heard the pop of the chain as it fell away and a moment later, the other one was freed.

"I'll have to carry you," Dylan said.

"You can't get up those stairs carrying a man," Rich argued.

"I'll have to try," he said. "He can't walk on those feet." He wanted to say more but stopped himself. He didn't know whether Stephen knew exactly how dire his circumstances were. But from the stench and color of his skin, he had to know the tissue was rotting—and had been for some time.

"Just help to hold me up," Stephen said.

Dylan was doubtful but he helped him to his feet. With one arm around his torso, he half carried him out of the cell.

The sounds in their earpieces had continued, although his voice and Rich's continued to be muted. Now he heard one voice rise above the others. "It's not Mick Maguire."

Dylan's eyes met Rich's. *He* had been the intended target of the attack?

He stopped at the three-way intersection and listened as his mind raced. Perry had thick black hair and they'd come from behind. There wasn't enough difference in their height or body type to differentiate them in the dark. So whoever had come upon him had intended to kill *him* instead.

"The Hoolihans," he breathed. "They're at the entrance."

They heard the voices now in stereo—in their earpieces as well as an echo that originated from the stairwell a good distance away. In the dead calm of the dungeons, every word was magnified.

"There's a back exit," Dylan said suddenly, glancing around as he tried to get his bearings.

Rich looked doubtful. "I don't think—"

"It's down this tunnel and to the left. We can't go out the way we came in. We can't meet 'em on the stairs."

"There's only one way in and one way out," Stephen insisted.

"That's what you think." He started down the hallway, half carrying the injured man.

"Wait," Rich called out in a stage whisper. As Dylan stopped, he quickly came alongside him. "You're sure about this?"

"I'm staking me life on it. And yours and his, too."

"Then go. Your mission is to get Anders to the safe house. That's *all* you need to do." He turned the opposite way.

"Where are you goin'?"

"My mission's broader than yours. I'm meeting them in the antechamber. They won't be expecting me there. But I'll be ready and waiting."

Dylan nodded. There was no time to waste. As he started down the tunnel in search of the partially collapsed exit, he heard Rich's footsteps grow fainter as he rushed toward the antechamber.

He nearly missed the exit and even when he was certain he was looking at the alternate way out, he hesitated. Brenda had said that the exit had been partially caved in but he hadn't imagined crawling over and around rocks and rubble. Now as he studied it, it appeared as if they'd barely be able to squeeze between two boulders—on their hands and knees.

"This is it," he stated flatly.

"You can't be serious," Stephen answered.

He heard sounds of breathing in his ear and realized Rich had switched on his earpiece. *No doubt he wants us to hear what goes down,* he thought. "Get on the ground. You'll have to crawl through."

He saw a flash of questions mirrored in the man's eyes but he dropped to his knees and began to wriggle between the boulders. As Dylan watched, he worried about his own ability to get through. He had more heft to him than the other operative, who it appeared had been slowly starving to death. If he could barely squeeze through, it left it doubtful that Dylan could do the same.

He could hear the voices of the Hoolihan brothers but he couldn't make out their words. Rich's breathing was steady now. Dylan envisioned him at the edge of the hallway, waiting for the three of them to emerge into the antechamber, where he would be waiting with his weapon drawn.

He considered waiting and trying to get out the front entrance but as Stephen's ankles disappeared between the boulders, he heard his muffled voice announce, "I'm through."

Dylan bent to his knees and stuffed the black bag through. When he felt Stephen grasp it from the other side, he took a deep breath and began to edge into the crevice.

And that was all it was, he realized: a crevice. It was as if the stone had been double its size and had split as it tumbled into the dungeon. He tried to remain sideways with his arms outstretched above his head and his feet helping to push him along, afraid of angling just a bit too far to the left or right and becoming wedged permanently in between them.

He was nearly halfway when he heard shouts through his earpiece that were echoed in the distant hallway. Multiple shots were fired amid voices he knew well; but the problem, he realized with mounting consternation, was the shouting continued even after the shots. That meant the Hoolihans were not down.

He tried to move faster but the space was too difficult to maneuver. He fought the vision of the three brothers catching him with his legs hanging into the hallway and pulling him backward so they could take their revenge. Then he redoubled his efforts, attempting to propel himself farther with each push of his feet against the stone.

He'd barely popped his head into a dark, enclosed space when he heard the shouts drawing closer. He grasped the edge of the boulder and hauled himself through as the sound of voices continued down the hallway directly in front of the caved-in area.

He tried to catch his breath as he sat up and adjusted the night vision goggles, which were askew from his precipitous angling. The tiny space came alive in neon green as he examined it. Stephen was a few feet away, sitting on an unbalanced stone, his breathing labored. He looked even gaunter than he had in his cell, as if it had taken a superhuman effort for him to participate in his own rescue.

As his eyes continued around the room, he saw enough rubble to make it appear as if several floors of the castle had collapsed in that one space. It was a death chamber, he thought, trying to fight the panic that threatened to rise within him.

If nothing else, he reminded himself, they could remain where they were until the men left; then slither back through and attempt to escape through the front entrance.

The voices grew alternately louder and softer as the men rushed up and down the hallways searching for them. They began calling his name, taunting him and threatening him. He felt his ire rising and talked himself down; it was what they wanted, he thought; for him to come out with fists at the ready so they could mow him down. And they had guns now, he reminded himself. They had come prepared to finish him off.

A faint odor reached his nostrils and he met Stephen's eyes. Tallow, he thought. He supposed it made sense. Since they didn't have the advantage of night vision goggles and they might not have had the forethought to bring flashlights, they were using the sconces to their advantage. But as the voices continued, he realized they were gathering items they'd found in the cells—old rags, he surmised from the way they spoke.

And they were prepared to smoke him out.

He unmuted his device. "Sam?" he whispered. There was a crackling response as if the massive stone surrounding him was interfering with transmission. He tried again. "Sam? Rich? Perry?"

He came to his feet. The stone above him was only a few inches from his head. But it had stood thus for centuries, he reminded himself, and it would stand now. He moved around the room, running his fingers into crevices, gauging the space between boulders, trying to find someplace, somewhere, that he could push Stephen through to safety.

He muted his device once more. The air was growing thicker, the stench of a fire intensifying. It smelled of burning leaves, he thought; old wood and something else—something he didn't want to think about.

He found a gap that was barely more than another crevice but at least it was a vertical split that would allow them to pass through upright. He shone his flashlight into the cranny to view another room much like the one they were in.

He turned around to do a final check before deciding on this course of action. Stephen was still seated on the boulder, his head slumped to his chest. He needed medical attention and he needed it quickly, he thought. He noticed something in his narrow bit of peripheral vision and he turned his head to look back at the opening that they had pushed themselves through. The tiniest wisp of smoke was beginning to find its way into the room.

They were out of time.

He roused Stephen. "We're goin' through to the next room," he said, helping him to the gap. They had to turn sideways and inch through one at a time. As Dylan watched him move slowly past the stonework, he realized it was the walls themselves that were holding up the man. Without them, he wouldn't make it.

His belief was confirmed when Stephen reached the other side and collapsed onto the floor. Dylan could do nothing but painstakingly follow through the gap, kicking the black bag in front of him as he went. When he emerged, he found Stephen crumbled in a heap.

"Leave me," he said. "I'm slowing you down."

"You're the reason I'm here," Dylan said. "Whatever you've got stored up there—" he looked pointedly at his forehead "— is important enough for the agency to send at least three o' us to get you out o' here. And I won't be failin' in me mission, if I've got to carry you out."

Stephen nodded. "Do you have water?"

He opened the black bag, pulling out the canteen and offering it to him. "My apologies," he said quietly. "I should've offered it to you sooner."

The man was silent but drank like he was completely parched.

"How long 'as it been since you last ate or drank?"

He shook his head. "I've lost track of time."

"Are these the men who imprisoned you?" Dylan pressed.

Stephen shook his head. "My captors—were American."

Dylan felt his jaw drop before he forced himself to recover. "Do they come on a regular basis, you think? Like the same time every day, every week?"

"No. Sometimes I was there for days, I'm sure, sitting in the dark with nothing but rats and—ghosts. Other times, it seemed like they were there twice in a day."

Dylan nodded silently. He realized he'd heard no more sound from Rich since the Hoolihans had entered the dungeon. He didn't want to consider the possibility that he was dead. But if he was wounded, he told himself, he'd hoped he would at least hear him breathing.

He had no time for this, he thought. They had to get out of here. He had to get this man to the safe house.

He helped Stephen to his feet and started to clear debris off a boulder for him to sit. As he brushed away white colored sticks, he froze. "No," he breathed.

"What is it?"

He took a step back. "Fingers." He stared at the skeletal remains for a moment. He hated being in the presence of the dead. It gave him the unnerving sensation that spirits floated around him and he couldn't counter what he couldn't see. It was Mam's doing, he knew. She'd always talked about the dead as though only their bodies were lifeless but their spirits lived on through eternity in the very same space as before.

He forced himself to look beyond the boulder and recoiled instinctively as his eyes rested on a full skeleton propped against the stone. He was wearing a Nazi uniform; even as dusty as it was, he could clearly view the insignia. His heart sank. If the man was stuck in here that meant this was not the way out.

He moved around the boulder to view two more figures. One still had hair clinging to his skull, but the bone was crushed. Another had a leg pinned beneath rock. And the first one he'd seen he now realized had been trapped as well with a stone across his ankles.

What a way to die, he thought. The man with the head injury might have been mercifully rendered unconscious. But the other two—especially the one pinioned by the ankles—might have lived for days or even weeks.

"My God."

At the sound of Stephen's strained voice, he turned to look at him. He was seated on the boulder but staring at the three men. His face had gone completely pale and he looked as if he was close to fainting—or crying.

"What is it?" Dylan asked.

"I saw them," Stephen answered. His voice took on a disembodied tenor; not quite a whisper but also not a solid tone.

"You saw *them?*"

He nodded and swallowed hard. "Every night. It was the same thing, the same words, the same path they took."

"But how is that possible?" He'd spoken before he could stop himself and now he wished he could take back the question.

"It was as though they were reliving the same scene, night after night after night," he continued as though he hadn't heard him. As he continued to stare at them, his body began to tremble uncontrollably.

"They can't hurt you now," Dylan said forcefully, hoping he sounded convincing enough to stop the man from going into hysterics. He turned his back to Stephen. This was all the more reason to get out of here as quickly as possible.

But what, he wondered, would Nazi officers be doing in Ireland? It was well known that Ireland had just gained her independence before the war broke out. England had expected them to fight on their side but the island had been split in two; the Republic of Ireland had finally broken the yoke of the English and was not inclined to help them out as a great deal of hatred still existed. And Northern Ireland hadn't yet been able to free itself of the English monster. Sentiments there ran deep and ugly.

The Republic of Ireland had done the only thing she could do: she declared neutrality.

He had heard reports, mostly rumors or so he thought, of Nazi supporters. They were underground and as the thought crossed his mind, the irony didn't escape him that these men had died here. But what had they been doing here, in the ancient ruins of a medieval castle?

The clock was ticking, he reminded himself. And every second counted. He moved through the room, assessing their meager options. It was larger than the one they'd just left but the air was thin and foul. It carried the same odor he'd first smelled when he realized the Hoolihans were setting the dungeons on fire. They'd been burning bodies, he thought. Decomposing bodies.

Stephen continued to stare at the skeletons with wide, unblinking eyes and his trembling had increased. "They walked down the hall," he said. His voice had taken on a sinister tone; it was more than a whisper but less than normal speech, as if he was speaking to the spirits themselves. "Continuously. I never saw them come in. They only left by the same way each time. They always said exactly the same things. It reached the point where I'd memorized their conversation." He swallowed hard and tore his eyes away from the bodies to look at Dylan. "It was as though I was watching a scene from a movie, playing continuously." He held both hands to his head and his eyes grew wider.

Near starvation, possible sleep deprivation combined with the infection in both feet had played with the man's mind, Dylan told himself. But he knew as the thought crossed his mind that he wasn't even convincing himself.

"That's why we're gettin' you outta here," he said. His voice came fast and heavy. He'd meant for it to sound no-nonsense but it surprised even him.

He continued combing the debris for another exit. He didn't want to think about the wisps of smoke he'd seen wafting into the inner room; it could find its way through the same crevice they'd come through until they, too, could call this their grave. "I'll be damned if I stay here and die."

"We would be damned, wouldn't we?" Stephen said. "Damned through eternity under the earth's surface. Damned to spending every moment looking for a way out, never realizing we're already dead."

He tried to force himself to focus on the task at hand and let the man's words slip past him, unheeded. But a chill had begun to creep up his spine and he shivered involuntarily. As he continued around the room, he finally located a gap in the boulders about waist high; shining his flashlight through it, whatever was on the other side appeared darker than the space they currently occupied. He waggled the light in an attempt to see how long the gap was; the first piece appeared to be about six feet long before becoming larger; it looked as if they could come to their feet and move the rest of the way upright. The total length was perhaps fifteen feet.

As the light hit the wall on the opposite side, it appeared to come alive. It had seemed at first glance like it was solid black as though it was covered in a heavy layer of soot. But now as he stared at it in horror, it came apart with a cacophony that grew in intensity.

He stumbled backward as the screeching echoed and multiplied in an ear-piercing discord that rapidly surrounded them. His heart was pounding so strongly that he could feel it in his temples.

He continued moving backward until he bumped into Stephen's legs. "Bats."

"But—" Stephen turned to look at him in a brief moment of clarity. "They're not coming in here."

Dylan stared at him. What did it matter? He thought. They were between them and freedom. Then the realization hit him. Though his emotions implored him to retreat to the opposite side of the chamber, logic pleaded otherwise: where were they going?

He stepped back to the opening and shone his light again. Thousands of wings fluttered at once. Flyin' rats is what they are, he thought with a sick feeling in the pit of his stomach. But the sound receded and he could actually see parts of the wall now; they were leaving.

"There's a way out," he confirmed. He couldn't see it, he couldn't smell it, but he sensed it was there. It *had* to be there.

He didn't have to tell Stephen of their next move. The man was up, hobbling on swollen black and blue feet, his ankle restraints clinking.

"I'll go first," Dylan said. "Once I get through the first six feet, I don't know how far the drop is."

Instinct told him to go feet first. Logic said he needed to see where he was going, view the spot where he would drop. But instinct won out. He slipped his feet into the crevice and crawled backward on his stomach. His shoulders brushed both sides and he could feel the top of the aperture brushing against his back.

When his feet dangled at the far end, he glanced at Stephen's face and took a deep breath.

He sped up his movements, anxious to get this over with. As his waist dropped over the edge, he realized his feet had not yet touched ground. But there was nothing he could do to stop himself from sliding the rest of the way as Stephen stared at him in horror.

29

Vicki awakened to an undulating blue light in the corner of the bedroom. "Dylan?" she said sleepily, rising to her elbows to peer across the room.

She blinked and narrowed her eyes as she watched the light take shape. It seemed to pulse in cadence with her own heavy breath like a living, breathing being. She sat up and pulled the covers closer to her neck, suddenly aware of her nakedness. The room had been warm and the bed cozy but now it took on the frigid air of a winter night. She shivered uncontrollably as she watched a head form and then two appendages like arms growing out of the surreal blue light.

She threw off the covers and leapt from the bed, grabbing her bathrobe from the back of the chair. As she quickly wrapped it around her, she heard the soft sound of chuckling and she hesitated, her hands on the sash.

"I knew you could see me at the wake," came a gentle, melodious Irish accent.

"Mam?"

In the midst of the blue light, she began to make out long, flowing white hair. There were two dark spots like eyes but she couldn't be sure she was looking at the old woman's face.

"I gave 'em quite a show, didn't I now?" she chuckled. "But the veil has always been thin in Eire, wouldn't you know."

She wrapped her arms around herself but the movement did nothing to stop her shivering. "What does that mean, Mam?"

"It means, m'darlin', that to those who 'ave the gift o' fey, such as y'self, why, you can see us come and see us go." Her face began to take form until Vicki could make out her sweet smile.

"But—don't you want to go—?"

"In time, m'dear. In time. M'darlin' Mickey will need you a'fore this night is done."

"Is he in danger?" She stepped forward, her heart pounding.

"Take care o' y'self, child, and the baby that grows within you. Mickey will need you to be strong."

Before she could answer, the light flickered and faded. She rushed toward the corner, a myriad of questions on her lips, but the old woman was gone. As Vicki stood there alone, the air warmed around her and she was left wondering if she'd been dreaming.

The bedroom door stood slightly ajar, allowing a soft white glow into the room. It danced and swayed like fingers trying to crawl across the floor and up the bed to the opposite wall where Mam had appeared. As her eyes grew accustomed to the dim light, she realized the television set in the next room must have created the light show.

She looked at the pillow where she'd lain, her heart sinking as the realization hit her that Dylan wasn't there. If he had been, she'd never have risen; his legs would have been intertwined with hers, his arm across her torso protectively.

It seemed as if it had been only a few minutes earlier that he'd whispered he loved her. But as her eyes searched the room for the clock, the growing uneasiness in her gut told her he had been gone too long. *Mickey will need you a'fore this night is done,* she'd said. Or had she imagined it?

She slid her feet into the warmth of thick terry house slippers and then made her way down the hallway.

She found Brenda in the living room. Instead of watching television, she was working on the laptop; it must have been the shifting background of the website that had made its way into her room.

"What's up?" Brenda said, glancing up as she entered the room.

"Has Dylan been home?"

"No." She glanced at her watch. "It's still early yet."

"He said he'd be home in a couple of hours."

"Figuratively speaking, I'm sure." She peered at her sister curiously. "You didn't have a vision—?"

Vicki sat on the couch and pulled a throw over her, though the fireplace was still radiating warmth from the dying embers. "No. Just a feeling."

"Well, I'm sure he's okay."

"What are you doing on the computer?" Vicki asked.

Brenda cocked her head. "Sam said to send him the steps I used to hack into his system. Remember?"

"Oh. Yeah. You emailed him?"

"About an hour ago. I used Dylan's email address."

"How did you get the password? Oh, never mind," she said, waving her hand dismissively.

Brenda beamed like someone with a wicked secret.

"What do we do if something goes wrong?"

"Nothing's going to go wrong."

"I'm calling Sam." She found her cell phone on the coffee table and dialed Sam's number. After several rings, it went to voice mail. "Checking in, Sam," she said. "Haven't heard from Dylan and I was worried, is all." She disconnected and murmured, "He didn't answer."

"He's probably neck deep in the mission," Brenda said. She looked at her curiously. "You're sure you didn't dream something?"

"I'm getting dressed."

Brenda set the laptop on the table beside her. Her self-assured smile had transformed into a downturned mouth and furrowed brow. "Vicki, did you have a dream?"

"No," she said as she made her way back down the hall. "I just have this terrible feeling."

30

His feet landed on uneven ground, twisting his ankle and almost sending him careening into the jagged edge of fallen stone. He instinctively threw out his hand to break his fall but as it touched castle debris it slipped across a too-slick surface. His feet were skating as well and it was only the haphazard manner in which toppled stones were scattered that prevented him from sailing across the room.

When he abruptly came to a halt against a nearly serrated rock, he looked at the black stuff that coated his gloved hands. "I am goin' to be *so* ill," he groaned.

"Dylan!" The voice echoed through the confined area although it had been hoarsely whispered.

"Hold on," he called. "Don't start through until I give you the go-ahead." He slipped and slid back to the crevice. "Can you hear me, Stephen?"

"Yes."

"The room is covered in a thick layer o' bat guano. When you drop through, you'll fall about ten feet a'fore hittin' bottom. I'm standin' just underneath to help catch you."

The other man groaned. "Okay."

It seemed as if it took forever for Stephen's bare feet to stick through the crevice.

This is goin' to be so bad, Dylan thought, grateful for his own boots. He wiped his gloves on the wall and then held his arms out. "I'm ready."

Stephen waited a long moment before moving again. His labored breathing echoed in the close confines. Then his swollen feet began to wiggle and inch by inch his legs appeared. He spread them wide as his feet searched for the smallest crack in which to stick his toes. Dylan started to tell him not to bother but thought better of the idea. Watching him, he realized the man was accustomed to mountain climbing. But his toes were blackened and swollen and as he found an uneven surface to help hold him, he could almost feel the grimace that accompanied the involuntary moan.

He inched his torso back until he was able to hold onto the ledge with his fingers. It was only then that he dropped his feet from the wall. Dylan moved in quick to grasp him by both legs and help him to the ground.

"I wish I'd thought to bring some shoes," Dylan said apologetically.

"After what I've been through, this is nothing," Stephen answered.

Dylan turned his attention to the room. Most of the bats had passed through an opening near the ceiling, roughly twenty feet up. If he hadn't been wearing the night vision goggles, he might have missed the area entirely; now as he studied it, it was apparent that a slab of stone hung over it, no doubt shielding it from outside view.

A staircase had once descended from the opening—or rather, Dylan thought, from the castle that had once risen above them. There were perhaps half a dozen steps dangling from the opening shelf, ending in mid-air.

He began the distasteful task of scouring the room for anything that could be repositioned underneath the stairs to help them climb upwards. As he moved, he could feel the wind and hear it whistling into the cavernous room, along with the distant roll of thunder.

Everything was covered in a thick sheet of bat guano. Oddly, it didn't have the strong stench of livestock manure, which was a gift in itself. He couldn't imagine the men trapped inside with this—but then, as he considered it, he realized these bats most likely had not been here during the Second World War. He knew the castle hadn't been above ground, either; the bogs had long ago covered up the remains. But there had to have been a second cave-in, a collapse that had obviously caught the three Germans by surprise.

He tried to move a few of the smaller stones in an attempt to create a makeshift staircase but the combination of bog mud and guano had served as mortar between them, making them nearly impossible to move. He couldn't count on Stephen's assistance; the man was barely hanging on. Just the drop into this room had left him drained. He now sat on a flat rock covered in guano in an obvious attempt to stay off his grotesquely enlarged feet.

One partial wall was blackened and as Dylan approached it, he half expected bats to begin taking wing again. But as he neared it, he realized it was a tarp of some type. It covered something stacked underneath that was now partially buried by fallen debris.

He grabbed one edge of the tarp and tugged at it. It had obviously been in place for decades and the disintegrating material ripped more easily than paper. He almost abandoned his efforts; rotted material could serve no purpose for him. But something shiny caught his eye and he moved closer to take a better look.

He tore back the tarp to reveal an amber panel decorated with gold and mirrors.

"Look at this," he said to Stephen. He heard the man inhale from the other side of the room; even in the darkness, the gold shone. "Could this be the riches from the castle itself, I wonder?"

"No," Stephen said, hobbling over. "It's in perfect condition. Look at it. If it had been here during the initial collapse, it would be in ruins—all over the place." He reached through and tried to pull up one corner. "Look underneath. There are several of these panels stacked against the wall. It's obvious when this collapse occurred, probably decades or even centuries after the first one, it missed these panels entirely." He sounded lucid now and Dylan was grateful they had moved beyond the skeletons.

As he continued to pull the material away, more of the gleaming treasure was revealed. "They look like walls."

"They *are* walls," Stephen agreed.

"But who would make walls made of amber? Who *could* make walls like this? And gold leaf? I'm not an expert by any means, but this looks like pure gold to me."

"This design," Stephen murmured. "It's incredibly intricate."

That it was, Dylan thought. As he continued to move the material out of the way, he realized the leaf was just the beginning. There were dozens of cherubs in gold; ribbons, roses, and candelabras—all in gold. The amber was bound together, one small piece to another, in a completely solid and smooth design that might have been eight feet tall.

"I've never seen anythin' like it." He tried to envision walking into a room made entirely of amber, the complex gold figurines and embellishments jutting out as part of the wall itself and not temporarily affixed to it. "This has to be worth a fortune."

"You have a camera?" Stephen asked.

"Aye," Dylan said, pulling out his smartphone. "I don't know if I would've thought o' that." He took several pictures from different angles. When he was finished, he checked his GPS and made an electronic note of the coordinates. Once Stephen was safe and sound, he had no doubt that he'd return. His eyes moved from the treasure to the crevice leading to the skeletal remains. "Could this be part of Nazi plunder?" he mused.

"I think it's a fair assumption." Stephen seemed to be deep in thought and after a moment, Dylan snapped to the present.

"First thin's first. I've a mission—to get you to safety."

31

Vicki emerged from the bedroom fully clothed to find Brenda peering out the living room window. "What is it?"

"That dog," Brenda said, pointing.

Vicki stopped alongside her sister, squinting in an attempt to focus more clearly. The skies were nearly black with dense, tumultuous clouds; they hovered low to the ground almost as though gravity was pulling them in. The hulking walls of the church could barely be seen across the gently sloping meadows; they were visible only because dim yellow lights at the doors attempted to illuminate the immediate surroundings. The lack of other lighting or signs of life made her feel isolated and alone. For the first time since arriving in Ireland, she longed for the street lights along Elm Street and the close proximity of her neighbors back in Lumberton.

"He's along the ridge there," Brenda said.

"She," Vicki corrected. "I think Dylan called her 'Shep'."

"Well, *she* has been watching us all night. Every time I've looked outside, she's been right there."

"I wonder why she didn't follow Dylan?"

"He drove the car."

"Into the village? It doesn't seem like such a long way for that dog to wander."

"I wish I knew why she kept staring at this place."

"Maybe she's protecting us."

"From what?"

Vicki shrugged and turned away. "I wish Dylan was home."

Brenda continued staring outside for another moment before dropping the curtain back into place and joining her sister.

"I'm worried," Vicki said, tossing a few peat briquettes into the dying fire. The flames immediately took hold. She stood silently, warming her hands although the room was already quite temperate.

Brenda glanced at the clock. "It's early morning yet. It would take some time to get to the bogs and into the castle. Then he's got to get Stephen Anders to the church…" Her voice faded and she settled into a living room chair, pulling her feet underneath her.

"You're right. Even if everything goes according to plan, it's too early for him to be home. Right?" She turned to Brenda and raised one brow.

"That's exactly right," she reassured her.

"Then why do I have this feeling?"

"What feeling?"

"Like I need to be doing something. Like both of us need to get out of here and walk to the church. Wait for him there."

Brenda studied her for a moment before replying. "You don't want to blow his cover. And that's exactly what you'd be doing if you arrived at the church before he does."

"I know but Father Rowan would soon know anyway—"

"Dylan is the one who needs to tell him. There has to be a reason why Sam didn't inform Father Rowan who would be showing up on his doorstep, right?"

"But—"

"No buts. He obviously thought it should remain a secret."

Vicki paced to the kitchen, opened the refrigerator door only to close it, and then paced back to the living room.

Brenda abruptly rose and started down the hallway.

"Where are you going?"

"To get the guns."

"Why?"

She stopped and looked back at her. "Because you have a feeling. A bad feeling. And that can only mean one thing."

"What?"

"There's trouble brewing. And when it finds us, we're going to be ready."

32

There are times in a man's life when he has no choice but to ignore the pain. Dylan had done it many times himself. But now he was filled with respect and awe as he watched Stephen scale the rubble leading to freedom.

He knew it had to take a superhuman effort for him; he could barely stand unaided on solid ground. Now he witnessed the emaciated man raise each infected foot weighed further by the thick manacles that slashed through the skin to the tender nerves below. His enflamed and blackened toes fought to find a crevice, no matter how miniscule. Unable to feel in his extremities, it was left to Dylan to tell him exactly how far to raise each foot and then verify when his toes were placed in a secure location.

They each held their breath while a mere half inch of each foot was forced to support his body as he searched for finger holds. It was an excruciatingly slow process and before he grasped another minute crack with which he hauled himself upward an inch at a time, Dylan was certain he would fall backward into his waiting arms. Wrapped around one shoulder was the rope from the black bag, further weighing him down.

It should have been the other way around, Dylan thought, anger at himself growing. But it had been Stephen's insistence that he go first. Dylan had never climbed the sheer face of a cliff, which was what this wall resembled; but Stephen had, many times over. And it was apparent from the way he used every ounce of energy left within him that he was turning the tables to help save them both.

He reached the top and hesitated while he caught his breath. It was ragged and when he spoke, it was dry and rasping. "Bats are all over the place," he said. "This shelf is covered in guano so it's slippery. And it's raining."

"Lovely."

"I'm tying this rope off to the stone itself." His legs scraped the stones as he hauled himself onto the ground. He disappeared briefly only to reemerge a moment later. As he stuck his head over the side and peered down at Dylan, he half-smiled. "I made it," he said simply.

"You're a good man," Dylan said. "I don't know if I could've made that climb, especially wounded as you are."

"Freedom is a great motivator." He flung the rope down to Dylan, who caught it easily.

"You're sure it will hold?"

"It had better," he answered. "It's the only thing up here."

"Ooh." Dylan tied the rope around his waist and tested the knot. He didn't feel good about this, not good at'al, but he had no choice. He glanced upward at Stephen's face before securing the black bag over one shoulder. He took a deep breath and expelled it noisily. His hands were sweating and he removed the gloves and wiped his hands against his jeans but that did little to dry them. Then he groped the wall under Stephen's instructions until his fingers had a minuscule hold. Then he hauled himself upward, trying to remember the path the other man had taken.

His shoes felt slick and inept on the stones, the soles too smooth and now covered in slimy droppings that made his movements even more perilous. He tried not to think of the rope as the only sure thing that kept him from falling, hoping Stephen had more confidence in an ancient stone ledge than he did.

His boot slipped on a hold too tenuous and he hugged the wall as pebbles rained below. He made a mental note as though he might forget that this would be his only attempt at rock climbing. There was nothing even remotely fun about it.

The rope rubbed uncomfortably against his torso through the thick wool turtleneck and the leather jacket and he wished he hadn't tied it so tightly. He'd been concerned it wouldn't hold but now he felt its heat and coarseness.

The minutes crept past. Each time he found a toehold or a finger grip, he knew it would be his last. It made him marvel even more that Stephen had been able to scale the wall in his weakened condition.

"Dylan!" Stephen whispered hoarsely.

Dylan looked upward; he might have been a mere twelve inches from the top but it may as well have been twelve more feet. "Aye?"

"The ledge isn't going to hold."

"What?"

"It's been shifting as you've climbed. I thought it was embedded pretty well into the earth but…" His voice faded as he inspected the ledge.

Dylan forced his body against the wall until his cheek was pressed against the cold stone. It felt good against his skin; he was overheated and fatigued and the iciness helped in some strange way to calm him. "What might you suggest I'd be doin' at this point?" He called up.

"You can't untie the rope, I suppose?"

Dylan might have laughed if he'd had any sense of humor left in him. The truth was he was terrified to move; as long as he'd continued upward, concentrating on the next hold and the one after that, he'd been able to keep his fear in check. But now as he continued to press his body against the wall, he felt too large, too heavy and too clumsy. "No," he managed to say. "I'm thinkin' untyin' the rope isn't an option at the moment."

"I'm going to cut it."

A moment passed. He expected to feel the rope dropping off below him but it never happened.

"You have the knife, Dylan," Stephen said quietly.

Dylan pressed his cheek against the wall until it hurt. "Ooh," he groaned.

"Can you toss the bag up to me?"

He forced himself to look upward. Twelve inches. Maybe more. It was too far for him to throw his arms over the edge. He needed just one more finger hold; one more toehold. The rope dangled; there was slack to it.

"Tell me," he said, "why is the ledge movin' if there's slack?"

"When you're climbing, you're depending on the rope to hold you."

"And if I didn't?"

"You haven't fallen yet, have you?"

He processed this for a moment. "And if I started to fall now?"

"The ledge would come with you."

"Christ Almighty." He took a deep breath, exhaled sharply and inhaled once more. Then with a guttural groan, he forced one hand away from the stone as he sought frantically for another hold. He scrambled up the side of the wall, his boots slipping and sliding against the slick rock, until he had both arms over the side.

There was nothing but peat and the ledge and as he struggled to haul himself onto firm ground, he realized he had no choice but to depend on the ledge.

"It won't hold, Dylan," Stephen cautioned. He tried to grasp Dylan's arms.

"Let go o' me!" Dylan shouted.

"But—"

"I said let go o' me! If I fall, I'll take you down w'me, man. Get away from the ledge and get away from me!"

A wicked clap of thunder shocked the night air. A flash of blue light streaked across the black sky, momentarily lighting the ground beyond him.

He grasped the edge of the ledge and pulled with the entire weight of his body. As his torso cleared the opening, the stone teetered away from him and then toward him. He forced one knee over the edge as it shifted downward suddenly, pinning his remaining leg beneath it.

Stephen grasped the black bag, wrenching it away from him.

Dylan let out an involuntary grunt as he struggled against the ledge. Below him, the chasm felt wide and unyielding, the room beneath him a tomb waiting to accept his body. He felt like it welcomed him with open arms; it wanted him to fail, wanted him to fall into the same crypt that held the Nazi soldiers.

As he made one final push against the ledge to free his trapped leg, the skies opened, releasing a torrent that felt more like a river than rain. The peat seemed to turn to mud beneath his hands and he lost his precarious hold on the earth.

The ledge teetered once more and then slid along the back of his leg, scraping it and pinning it. He screamed out as he felt the rock break loose from the ground. As he grappled wildly for any hold, no matter how tenuous, Stephen lunged for him.

The ground released its hold on the stone as Stephen grabbed the rope. A roll of thunder rocked the earth and the stone crashed against the wall. Dylan steeled himself for the inevitable fall, for the rock to pull him downward like an anchor tied to his waist. But instead, he felt Stephen's hands underneath his arms, hauling him across the ground. Only a few feet of rope remained attached to him; the rest was plummeting downward with the ledge, sending up a plume of debris-laden dust.

The earth opened up and they both clambered across the peat even as it began to fall away beneath them. The ground shook so harshly that he thought an earthquake had begun. With a sinking feeling, he knew even as he struggled to get away from the widening chasm that he could not survive. He closed his eyes, mentally asking God to care for Vicki even as he continued to fight the inevitable.

Then all was still.

He opened his eyes to find his feet dangling over the precipice and he scrambled further away. "Stephen!" he yelled.

"In front of you!"

He turned to look away from the chasm, the relief of seeing Stephen's grimy face flooding over him.

When he emerged, he found Stephen lying prone on the ground. He followed suit, slipping out of the remnants of the rope and returning it to the black bag. "You saved m' life," he said. His voice sounded shaky. "And for that, I thank you."

"You saved mine. It was the least I could do to return the favor."

As he caught his breath, he studied their circumstances. The ledge had started another collapse like a game of dominoes. Once it had been dislodged from its precarious position, what appeared to have been a partial floor or ceiling had fallen to its final resting place below. Now there was a chasm roughly twenty feet square. But as the dust began to settle under the weight of the rain, Dylan realized that the wall against which the amber panels had been propped had also caved in. Now as he stared below, he realized the treasure was buried under a mountain of debris, all topped off with a thick layer of peat. The room they'd both stood in just a short time ago was gone.

He turned around and tried to get his bearings. The entrance was nearly a quarter of a mile away. With the rain bucketing down, he could barely see a thin plume of smoke making its exit from the stairs below.

"Have you seen any movement?" he asked, searching the terrain. He repositioned his night vision goggles.

"Seems like a guy at that entrance was moving but he didn't stand up."

He watched while he caught his breath but he couldn't determine whether Perry was really moving or he was witnessing an optical illusion. Then he noticed three horses tied up perhaps half a mile away; if he hadn't been wearing the night vision goggles, he would never have seen them. They were beneath another grove of trees in the opposite direction from where Perry, Rich and he had left their own horses.

He tried to figure out how the Hoolihan brothers had managed to approach Perry undetected. They'd clearly followed them to the stables and then to the bogs, staying far enough behind not to be seen nor heard. Then as Perry was left at the entrance, they'd circled in a wide arc, leaving their horses in the opposite direction from theirs and continued the rest of the way on foot.

But the satellites should surely have picked them up, he thought. Even if they'd come from behind, there was at least a quarter of a mile in every direction in which not even a bush was growing that could provide cover. And Sam had made it clear that neither darkness nor cloud cover nor rain would interfere with the satellites' ability.

His eyes roamed to the grove of trees in the other direction where their own three horses were still tied. Between their present location, the site of the first entrance and his horse, it formed almost a perfect triangle.

As he scrutinized the situation, he realized any course of action he chose would have consequences.

Finally, he opened the bag and handed Stephen a pistol along with extra ammunition. "Stay here."

Stephen didn't respond. They were both soaked to the bone from the storm. Dylan took one last look in each direction before he came abruptly to his feet. His intention was to run as fast as he could to their horses, but the rain had turned the ground into swampland that tried to suck him down. He felt clumsy and inept as he lumbered, nearly holding his breath in anticipation of the Hoolihan brothers emerging at any moment.

He reached the three black horses and untied the first one, then slapped him on the rump. The horse took off with a start, racing in the direction of the stables. The bogs were no place for a horse at night, he thought, and most decidedly not a place for them in a storm. If he had trouble traversing the bogs, he couldn't imagine how the weight of the horses could handle it any better.

He untied the other two, quickly mounting one while holding the other's reins. He hesitated briefly. He knew Stephen was coming to his feet in anticipation of rising fully and straddling the horse as quickly as possible.

This was a moment he might regret; the moment he could have turned the other way, rescued Stephen and been out of sight before the Hoolihans emerged.

But he could never live with himself unless he knew Perry's fate—and whether he could alter it.

He clicked his heels, taking both horses to the three in the opposite direction. Once there, he swiftly untied them and slapped them with his reins to spur them homeward. They were

more of Aengus' stock, he realized; no one else would have had
horses in the stables, ready for the picking.

Then he raced to the entrance of the dungeons, where he
dismounted quickly and rolled Perry over. He was lying in a pool
of blood. A cursory examination revealed a faint pulse and a
massive hole in his shoulder. He'd clearly been hit at close range
from behind with the exit out the front.

The voices of the brothers wafted upward through the
opening; they were coming up the stairs. For the briefest of
moments he considered standing at the entrance and shooting
each one as they emerged. But his mission was to get Stephen to
safety, he reminded himself; the man's life was in his hands.

He hauled the unconscious man up, the dead weight almost
too much to bear. Somehow he was able to get his body on the
horse as the seconds ticked past and the voices became louder.
He moved swiftly, ignoring the small voice that warned him that
the additional brusque movement could make a difference in
whether Perry lived or died, but he knew of no other way to get
him to safety. Rich would have to fend for himself. He had no
choice but to leave him.

With the Hoolihan brothers' voices now each easily
recognizable and discernible, he hastily mounted the steed behind
Perry and turned the horses toward Stephen. Then with a click
of the heel, he guided them swiftly to his charge.

Stephen had no sooner climbed atop the second horse than
the men emerged. The rain cast a gray cloak around them as
they blended into the storm and moved wordlessly away from
the Hoolihans. Behind them, Dylan heard their shouts but the
words themselves were lost in the growing squall.

As they hurried in the direction of the church, he had a
vision of the men's confusion, anger and frustration. They would
have noticed Perry was gone immediately; and then one of them
would have become aware that their horses were gone, also. They
might presume he was still alive and perhaps had risen while
they were underground, made his way to the horses and left
with them. Or they might guess that Dylan had escaped, angering
them further. He didn't know but he forced his mounting anger
back down. Now was not the time to confront them. There would

be another time and when it arrived he would not back down again.

He grew concerned with their painfully slow progress. He wanted to rush back at full gallop but the bogs had turned to mush, which threatened to sink the horses' hooves with each step. Their only recourse was to keep moving; to hesitate meant sinking into the quagmire. He glanced behind him frequently but did not see the brothers following him. In fact, he couldn't see anything at all.

Stephen slumped on his horse and Dylan pulled alongside him, afraid he would fall off his mount. The man nodded as if he understood Dylan's concern and waved him away. It had taken a superhuman effort for him to scale the wall, draining him of his remaining energy.

As Dylan fell in beside him, casting a constant eye in his direction, he wondered when he'd eaten last. He was gaunt and frail where his pictures had been robust. He chastised himself; he should have been on the same horse as Stephen, making sure he guided it to the stables and ensuring the man's safety. Instead, he was forced to constantly balance Perry in front of him lest the man slide off in either direction. A sack of potatoes straddling the horse would have been easier to steady.

But a man's life was worth the trouble, he reasoned, whether it was Stephen or Perry. He couldn't have lived with himself if he'd left the man there, wounded and fighting for his life. And now he struggled with the realization that he'd left Rich alone and with no means of escape.

Glancing behind him, he realized the horizon was ablaze in blue lights; a lightning strike had undoubtedly set the peat afire. If it traveled the same course as other storms, it would eventually move underground, travel a distance and then pop up somewhere else with an unexpected vertical flame.

He hated the bogs; he always had. And he loved them.

He loved the way they smelled, the bouquet of dirt and peat and of Mother Nature herself. And he hated the way they made the land unfit for habitation, unsuitable for any industry other than harvesting the peat itself. It was the land that kept the Irish poor for centuries. If it wasn't swamp, it was rock. Too difficult for most crops, too hazardous for homes.

And yet someone centuries ago had built a castle in quagmire, no less. And the land had risen up to claim it.

And someone else had found its remains and used it to hide untold millions in wealth.

And only he and Stephen knew how to find it again.

Somewhere behind them, the brothers would be forced to walk their way out of the bogs. It would be miles and they'd be lucky if they reached a road by dawn. He glanced upward at the roiling, tumbling clouds. Even in the dark, he knew this rain would keep up for days. It had been a rarity for the moisture not to make its mark on their first day in Ireland. Nature wouldn't make that mistake twice.

33

Vicki pulled back the drapes and peered outside. The skies appeared enraged, the black clouds tumbling and rolling over one another as though they were engaged in an epic battle. The rain descended in sheets that pelted the windows angrily as if determined to crack through the glass and slap her. Yet through the gloom she saw the silhouette of Shep along the ridge, standing still as a statue.

She held her cell phone in her hand, absent-mindedly shuffling it from one palm to the other. Sam still wasn't answering. And she dared not try Dylan for fear she would cause his phone to ring at an inopportune moment that could mean the difference between life and death. She thought of the men approaching in the tunnel just before she found herself back aboveground with Dylan and Brenda; the terror was still there, still palpable.

"Do you have rain gear?" Vicki asked as Brenda entered the room.

"I didn't exactly have time to shop," she said as she joined her. "But I think we both have boots and raincoats. Dylan drummed it into us that it would be raining the whole time."

"He did, didn't he?"

"What happened earlier today?"

"When?"

"When you left out of here like a bat out of hell. You two came back together and you didn't look like you'd been fighting."

"No. We weren't fighting." She let the drapes drop. "I need a glass of wine. And I'll tell you everything."

"No. You're pregnant, remember?" Brenda said. "But I'll whip up something virgin for us."

As she left for the kitchen, Vicki held back. Every ounce in her being screamed at her to go to Dylan. But she didn't know where he was. She didn't know if she could find him in broad daylight much less traverse the bogs on a night like this. She needed something to settle her nerves. And confiding in Brenda about Dylan's past could at the least help pass a little bit of time. Maybe by the time she was finished, he would be coming through the door. At least she hoped so.

Because if he wasn't, she'd have no choice but to go after him.

"Wow," Brenda said nearly an hour later. "No wonder he didn't want to come back here."

Vicki drained her virgin Peppermint Patty and stood up.

"So those guys used to be his brothers-in-law?" Brenda mused. "And he thought we were dysfunctional."

Vicki stared at the clock, watching the seconds tick toward three. Something was definitely wrong.

"You okay?" Brenda asked.

"Of course not."

"So what do you want to do?" She looked at the pistols laid out on the coffee table.

"We're walking to the church."

Her sister frowned. "In this storm?"

"If Dylan is okay, he'll be there. We'll stay out of his way but at least we'll know he's alright."

"And if he's not?"

"We tell Father Rowan that he left earlier in the evening to be by himself. And we're worried and we'd like to—I don't know, sit in the sanctuary or something."

Brenda snorted. "That line might work for you. He'd know I was lying."

"We can say I wanted to sit in the sanctuary. And you came with me. It's just a mile from here to the church but you could say you didn't like the thought of me out there by myself."

"That much is true." She stood and stretched.

Vicki found the raincoats in their luggage while Brenda located two pair of boots. She had hoped as the minutes ticked past that at any moment Dylan would walk through the door. But as the time grew closer to leaving, the fear within her was mounting.

As soon as they left the house, Shep joined them from the ridge and the skies seemed to open up with more rage. Inside the house they had been deaf to the storm's onslaught. But now that nothing but a pair of raincoats and boots protected them, the noise was nearly earsplitting. The thunder rolled in an elongated boom and the ground quaked beneath their feet. They slipped and slid along the lawn to the road; but once on the road, they were resigned to walking on the grass beside it. The road itself had turned to mud, the russet earth overflowing the tire ruts as it swept past them.

They hunkered down as if bending their heads against the rain's assault would somehow protect them. But of course it did nothing to lessen the torture and before they had reached the fork in the road, water had run unchecked down their faces, drenching their hair and sneaking into their collars to saturate their backs.

Brenda tried to say something but Vicki could not hear her for the storm's fury, although she knew her sister was shouting. They resigned themselves to hurrying as best they could without falling flat on their backs. Shep ventured a few yards ahead of them, only to stop and look back as if checking on her charges. She seemed to know instinctively that they were heading for the church, which now seemed an impossible distance from them.

It was a mistake to venture out, Vicki thought. And yet it felt right to do *something*. Relaying Dylan's past to her sister had helped to pass the time but not to quiet her fears. At least the storm gave her no choice but to concentrate on her own survival.

They turned toward the church and found themselves leaning against the wind. A hill that appeared gently rolling a few hours ago now felt daunting and steep and Vicki stopped repeatedly to try and catch her breath before pushing onward. Brenda was stronger but even she was holding one forearm against her forehead in an attempt to prevent the rain from further pounding her face. They both leaned sharply as they trudged onward.

When they reached the ridge, Vicki stopped. She turned around to peer behind her and found to her astonishment that the distant horizon, not visible while they were at the house, looked to be in flames. But they weren't the red flames she might have expected but blue ones that reached into the skies as if the earth was rising to battle the heavens.

A flash of lightning seared through the darkness like a pitchfork; its target was once more the distant horizon and as it struck a new wave of flames hurtled into the sky. Fear for herself and her vulnerability seemed miniscule compared to her fear and worry over Dylan's fate. Though she wasn't familiar with Ireland's geography, she knew enough to understand that those flames were in the direction of the bogs. And Dylan was somewhere between the distant horizon and safety.

She heard her sister's voice and turned to find her shouting at her to hurry. She turned her back on the flames and set her eyes on the church. The stone wall that rose around the adjacent cemetery seemed to taunt her and Dylan's words came rushing back to her; how it rained for days until the bridges were washed away, how Father Rowan had used a rowboat to help rescue Alana, and how he couldn't lose Vicki, most especially not in Ireland.

She felt Alana's fear and Dylan's anxiety merging with her own as she struggled to reach the safety of the church but the rains and the slippery ground beneath her seemed to be joining forces to prevent her from reaching her destiny. Shep rushed forward, her paws sure and steady, only to stop and bark at them as if trying to spur them to move more quickly.

She had never witnessed rains such as this. Not in the worst of rains in coastal North Carolina; not in any storm she'd ever encountered in Washington. This was a rain of vengeance and brutality.

Mam's words haunted her now: before this night is done, Mickey will need you.

The night would soon be done. And she'd be lucky if she managed to save herself. She couldn't imagine what benefit she could be to Dylan. At the thought of him, she felt the baby within her belly. She should never have ventured out in this storm. She realized only now that every decision she made would not affect her alone but also the child that grew within her.

When she at last was able to reach out and touch the stone walls of the ancient church, she almost cried with relief. It had taken more than an hour to walk one mile. And now every muscle in her body was screaming in a mix of exhaustion and pain.

Brenda reached the side door before her. She pounded on it but as Vicki arrived, she pushed the door open with a gust of wind and a torrent of rain. They found themselves standing on the threshold staring into Father Rowan's shocked face.

"What are you doin'?" he cried out. He pushed past them, sticking his head out the door and peering around as if expecting to see someone else there. Apparently satisfied they were alone, he leaned his weight against the door to wrestle it closed against the storm's onslaught. When he turned to look at them, he was soaked. His eyes were wide and his mouth slightly open as if he wanted to say something but the words wouldn't come.

"Dylan left last evening," Vicki said shakily, trying to catch her breath. She hadn't realized just how cold she'd gotten and she shivered uncontrollably.

"You can't stay here!" he blurted.

Brenda stepped in, wrapping her arm around her sister. "We're worried sick about Dylan. We thought he might have come here to speak to you—you being a priest and all."

A flash in Father Rowan's eyes signaled that he was coming to his senses. He brushed past them, gesturing them to follow. He led them down a long, straight hallway and into his office. A fire raged in the fireplace and Vicki sank to her knees in front of it.

"You're both soaked through," he said. His voice sounded incredulous. "Don't you have enough sense to stay out o' a storm?"

"Spoken like a man of God," Brenda answered.

He sat down heavily and stared at his lap as if he was at a loss for words. He looked at Brenda and then at Vicki, who couldn't stop trembling. "You walked from your cottage?" he finally asked.

"Yes," Vicki said. Her voice was tremulous. "And we wouldn't have done it if we hadn't been so worried."

"Well, he's not here," he said. "And he hasn't been here."

Brenda's eyes met Vicki's.

"So you see," he continued, "you came here for naught." He slapped his knee. "But you can take my auto and drive it home. I'll come after it tomorrow after the storm has passed."

"I don't want to go home," Vicki stated flatly.

"Well, you can't stay here."

"I feel safer here."

Father Rowan looked at her with wide eyes as if he was once again at a loss for words. Then, "God is with you, whether you're here or at home. And you have dry clothes at home. A warm bed. And Mick will know to look for you there. Not here."

Vicki's eyes met Brenda's. The room felt surreal; their arduous walk something out of a bizarre dream. The presence of her baby loomed large in her mind, as though it was growing as she sat there in front of the fire. She was dripping rainwater all over the floor but Father Rowan didn't seem to notice. He kept cocking his head and turning it toward the door, as if listening—listening, she knew, for Dylan to appear. But he didn't know it was Dylan he was waiting for. And for some strange reason, she couldn't bring herself to tell him.

The room began to spin; first slowly and then more rapidly. Brenda's face blurred into Father Rowan's. They were all listening for someone to come down that hallway. The fire was too hot and then she was too cold. She was trembling but sweat was popping onto her brow.

When Brenda asked, "Vicki, are you okay?" her voice sounded disembodied, huskier, slower.

She looked at the couch along the wall, the desk, the chair where Father Rowan sat. She looked at Brenda, on her knees beside her, warming her hands to the fire but studying Vicki.

She saw the painting on the wall of the Last Supper; the Celtic cross above the desk... And the wastebasket.

Before she realized what she was doing, she had hurled herself at the wastebasket and began to retch.

"Oh, dear God," Father Rowan breathed.

Brenda rushed to her aid, holding her hair out of her face. "Can you call a doctor?"

"A doctor?" he repeated.

"She's sick," Brenda said. "In case you haven't noticed."

"You want a doctor on account o' she's sick to her stomach?"

"That's right."

Vicki tried to look at her sister but Brenda avoided her eyes. But when she squeezed the back of her neck, Vicki understood she was to remain silent.

"We don't have a doctor in the village."

"Well, then, the next village."

He stared at her in silence.

"You know what a doctor is, right? You do have doctors in this country?" Brenda was growing agitated.

Father Rowan stood abruptly, exhaling sharply. "This is a rural area. In case you haven't noticed. If your sister needs a doctor, I suggest you take my automobile and I'll give you detailed directions for travel to Dublin. I'll check on your home in the mornin' and let Mick know where you are."

Vicki leaned back on her haunches.

"Fine," Brenda said. "I'll take her to Dublin. But at least allow her a few minutes in your bathroom to clean herself up."

He walked to the doorway and peered down the hallway toward the side door. "The facilities are on the other side o' my office, there," he said, pointing behind them.

Brenda assisted Vicki to her feet. "Are you okay to walk?"

She nodded.

She wrapped one arm around her and walked with her to the bathroom. Vicki stopped at the door and turned toward Father Rowan, but he was gone. "What are you doing?" she whispered. "I don't need a doctor."

"No," Brenda said, "but Dylan might."

"Oh."

"And if it takes hours for a doctor to get here, we may as well get him moving now. When Dylan gets here—and I said *when*, Vicki, not *if*—every minute might count."

34

Dylan found himself riding due east as the first rays of light began to emerge on the distant horizon. It was a mere sliver of golden yellow, and at first he thought his eyes were playing tricks on him. But as the light grew and morphed into orange and then red, he realized he'd spent all night navigating the bogs in the driving rainstorm.

The horses were spent. They trudged now, their hooves covered in mud and muck. Their heads were low, their beautiful manes now wet and stringy.

Perry had groaned several times on the ride but never fully regained consciousness. It was just as well, Dylan thought. As long as he was unconscious, he was unaware of pain and his dire circumstances.

Dylan sat directly behind him, both arms rigid on either side of him, helping to hold him upright and preventing him from falling. His arms ached now with a tension he hadn't felt since he'd ended his boxing career, what little of a career it was. His legs hurt as well, though he didn't know why; they'd done nothing but hang on either side of the horse's body as he allowed the steed to find its way out of the bogs. But then, he reasoned, they had also pressed against Perry's, helping to keep the man upright.

Stephen had slept most of the way and it had been a minor miracle that he hadn't fallen off his horse. At times he'd leaned so far backward that Dylan expected him to recline atop the horse's broad back. And at other times, he had slumped forward, his forehead touching the horse's mane.

Dylan had been left alone with his thoughts for much of the journey and now he was fighting exhaustion.

When they reached the edge of the bogs, he awakened Stephen and urged the horses forward. With dawn now on the horizon, they had to hurry. It wouldn't do for the villagers to find Mick Maguire on one of Aengus' horses accompanied by one man who'd been shot and another whose feet were in manacles. And instead of allowing the horses to find their way back to the stables, he'd turned them toward the outskirts of the village on a narrow dirt road to the church.

When he heard Sam's voice in his earpiece, the sudden sound jolted him.

"Aye?" he said.

"I've been monitoring you all night," Sam said. His voice sounded tired and monotone.

"Are you expectin' me gratitude?"

He thought he heard Sam chuckle. "You've got great instincts. I always knew you did."

"Oh?"

"I wouldn't have asked you to rescue Perry. Your mission was to get Stephen out of there. But I watched you take them both."

"I didn't get Rich."

"I know."

He rode in silence for a moment, his thoughts with Rich in the acrid dungeons as they filled with smoke.

"As soon as things began to go wrong," Sam said, "I dispatched another unit."

"So did they get him? Is he alive?"

"The nearest unit was in Germany. They couldn't navigate through the storm. They'll reach Ground Zero in about two hours."

So Rich will have lain in the tunnel all night without help, he thought. He may have been shot; he might be bleeding out… Perry moved and Dylan righted him once more. "Tell me, Sam, did you keep the satellites on Ground Zero?"

"Affirmative."

"No one left?"

"Rich didn't. Those three goons did."

"Those 'three goons' were after me, not Stephen. They're from me past. And they chose the worst possible time to rear their ugly heads."

"Stephen tell you they weren't his captors?"

"Aye. He said his captors were American."

"American?"

"Aye. And those three men you saw are the Hoolihan brothers. You may as well know they were once m' brothers-in-law. And I've got a score to settle w' 'em now."

"Do you have any idea how they could have followed you?"

"None. I was hopin' you'd tell me."

"I've reviewed the video several times. We were watching an area roughly a mile in diameter in minute detail. I could count the fingers on your hand; we were that close. Then we scaled outward to watch for anyone approaching from afar. And we saw absolutely nothing."

"You can't be sayin' they appeared out o' thin air."

"That's exactly what I'm saying."

"Are you jokin' me? I'm in no mood for jokes, I can tell ya that straight-away."

"We'll figure it out," Sam sighed. "I've got a team working on it."

"And did the Hoolihans disappear when they emerged from the dungeons, as well?" He felt irritated and he knew his voice reflected his sour mood.

"As a matter of fact, they did. Then they reappeared about a quarter of a mile away. Disappeared again. Reappeared again."

He could see the church up ahead. "Where are they now?"

"They've been at your cottage for the past two hours."

"What?"

"That's right. They've been sitting just beyond the ridge, watching the house."

"You're tellin' me that they walked out o' the bogs—when I had these horses—*and they beat me to m' cottage by two hours?*" He knew his voice was rising and though he instinctively knew he needed to remain as quiet as possible, his ire was growing to a dangerous level.

"That's precisely what I'm telling you."

"But Vicki and Brenda—"

"—are at the church."

"Since when?"

"Oh, several hours now. You think I wouldn't be watching the safe house, too?"

"Why would they 'ave gone to the church? Did the Hoolihans—"

"They were there long before the Hoolihans arrived at the cottage. When you get to the church, stay there. In roughly two hours, I'll have further instructions."

They turned off the road and began the climb to the side door. The sun was rising now as a bright red orb beaming through the remnants of the rain. As they passed the walls of the cemetery, the rain turned to mist. One might have thought the storm had passed but Dylan knew better. He knew what that bright red sky meant—and how very little time they had left.

35

He slid open the side door as Father Rowan came down the hallway. The look of shock was so great that Dylan thought the priest might faint. As he entered the hall with Perry in his arms, he said, "I'm the one you've been waitin' for."

"*What?*"

"This man's fightin' for his life. He's needin' medical attention."

"In here," Father Rowan stumbled over his words as he turned around and moved swiftly back up the hallway, past the door where Vicki and Brenda sat and into a room with a cot. He didn't appear to have noticed Stephen limping behind Dylan until Perry had been laid on the cot.

"You're hurt!" Vicki called out as she joined them.

"No, Darlin'," Dylan said. He'd been wet and miserable all night but now that Perry was separated from him, he realized it hadn't been only the rain he'd been feeling but also the man's loss of blood. He knelt beside him and felt his pulse; it was barely perceptible.

Behind him, he was scarcely aware of Stephen sitting heavily in the nearest chair. He glanced over his shoulder and pointed in his direction. "Father Rowan, that's the man I rescued. I don't know when he's eaten last. He needs food and water. And his ankles are infected."

"I'll get the food and water," Vicki said. "Where's your kitchen?"

"Second door on the left," Father Rowan said. His voice sounded dry and it cracked as he spoke. "There's soup on the stovetop warmin'."

"Let me see this guy," Brenda said, pushing her way into the room. She knelt beside Dylan and ripped Perry's shirt away from his shoulder.

"He may have a bullet in him," Dylan said. "I couldn't take the time to see if it passed clear through 'im."

"Who is this?" Father Rowan asked. His eyes were wide and questioning.

"Another operative."

"I might be able to get the bullet out," Brenda said. "And I can patch him up. But he's going to need blood. And from the looks of things, he's going to need a lot."

"You've done this a'fore?" Dylan asked dubiously.

"Christopher Sandige," she said, raising one brow. "And he lived through it."

"What do you need?" Dylan asked.

"I need gauze. And plenty of it. I need to assess where the bullet's at and whether it should be removed or left for a doctor." She looked pointedly at Father Rowan. "I need whiskey in case he comes to. Ice packs. I need two knife blades, one thin and one wide. And towels. This guy's bleeding everywhere. He's got a major artery cut, for sure."

"I'll get the knives," Dylan said, pulling the black bag off his shoulder and rifling through it. Father Rowan disappeared only to reappear a moment later with towels and a first aid kit. Then he disappeared again, reappearing with Vicki as he carried in a bottle of whiskey and several bags of frozen vegetables to use as ice packs.

"Do you have another cot?" Vicki asked, handing Stephen a bottle of water and pulling a table toward him on which to place the food.

Her question went unheeded as Brenda took the thin knife from Dylan. "I need heat," she said. She poured some of the whiskey onto the gauze and began cleaning the wound as she inspected it. She glanced at Dylan. "What are you doing?"

"Whate'er you tell me to do."

"Take the wide blade. There's a fireplace in the priest's office. Get the blade as hot as you can."

"Aye." He was on his feet and out the door before she could completely turn around.

She continued probing the wound, using the thin knife now with one hand while continuously wiping the blood with gauze held in the other hand. "There it is." She raised her voice. "How much longer, Dylan?"

"One minute."

Brenda studied the wound while she waited. "Get me some duct tape," she said suddenly.

"Duct tape?"

She looked at Father Rowan. "Duct tape."

Dylan returned to the room and handed Brenda the wide knife. "It'll burn you if you touch the blade."

"Good. Then it's hot enough." She turned back to Perry. "Get some more gauze out of that kit," she said. When Dylan had complied, she said, "Keep soaking up the blood for as long as it takes." She held the flat side of the blade over the wound.

"What're you doin'?"

She plunged the blade down, pushing it deep into the wound as Father Rowan returned. Perry's body convulsed and she ordered, "Hold him."

While Father Rowan held Perry, Dylan pulled back the gauze, wincing involuntarily as the man was burned. Brenda's mouth was set, her brow furrowed, but she didn't hesitate to keep it down.

"Christ," Dylan said, turning his head.

"You're killin' him," Father Rowan said, his lower lip trembling.

Brenda pulled back the knife. "Gauze."

Dylan returned to cleaning the blood. "It's stopped bleedin'."

"I've seared the artery shut. I think shrapnel is inside. It's deep and it's fragmented. It's too risky to get it out here." She glanced at Perry's eyes. "If he comes to, pour whiskey down him. In fact, pour a bit of whiskey on the wound. It's got to be sterilized to prevent infection."

As Dylan poured whiskey over the wound, she turned to Father Rowan. "Get me that roll of gauze over there."

He handed her the roll, his eyes still wide and incredulous.

"That's good," she said to Dylan. "Get one of those towels and clean any blood." She began unraveling the roll. When he'd finished cleaning the wound, she said, "Father, hold him so he's sitting up. I've got to close the exit wound on his back."

She began rolling the gauze tightly around him, stretching it from the front of his shoulder to the back and under his arm with each pass. She took her time, making sure the skin was pulled together and no longer gaping. "We don't want it too tight," she said as she pulled firmly on it, "or he'll lose this arm." When she was done, she motioned with a nod of her head. "Cut a piece of that duct tape and wrap it around the gauze. We don't know how long he'll be in this condition before we can get him proper medical care."

Dylan wrapped the duct tape securely around the gauze.

"Reminds me of you bandaging my leg," she said. "You did a good job. I hardly scarred at all."

Dylan glanced at her but said nothing.

"He's lost too much blood," Brenda said. "We've got to get him out of here. He needs a doctor right away."

"Sam," Dylan said, "are you listenin'?"

"It'll be one to two hours before we can get a helicopter to you," he said.

"Can't you do better than that?"

"I'm working on it."

"He's workin' on it," he relayed to Brenda. "He's already got another team in route. There's another man down in the bogs. They're goin' after him and he's sendin' a helicopter here."

"Vicki," she said, turning to her sister, "I need a bucket of water."

"Hot or cold?"

"Room temperature."

As she left the room, Brenda turned toward Stephen. He had downed one bottle of water and was working on another in between gulps of soup and fistfuls of bread. "Not so fast," she admonished. "You'll get yourself sick and then you'll be in worse shape." She moved to his side and began inspecting his ankles.

Father Rowan stared at Dylan. "Mick," he said in a hushed voice, "you're workin' for the American government now?"

"Aye."

"And the girls, too?"

"Just Vicki. Well," Dylan said as he watched Brenda, "I guess she is, too. Unofficially."

"Yeah," Brenda said over her shoulder. "I'm almost a felon. These two are my guards."

"She's not serious," Father Rowan said.

"I'm afraid she is."

Vicki returned with a bucket that sloshed water over the sides. "I sure hope this isn't a mop bucket."

"No." Father Rowan took it from her. "Where do you want it?"

"Between both these guys," Brenda said. "Dylan, clean off that guy's face. The water will cool him down. He's got to be running a fever. Keep one of those ice packs on the wound to keep the swelling down. Don't allow him to be completely prone. Make sure his airways stay clear. Listen to his breathing and monitor his pulse. You got a bp cuff around here?"

"A—?"

"Blood pressure cuff."

Father Rowan shook his head. "No. Are you a nurse?"

"Nope."

While Dylan cleaned Perry's face and propped his head up with several pillows, Brenda began cleaning Stephen's ankles as he ate. "This doesn't hurt?" she asked as she examined the metal cutting into black and swollen flesh.

"What do you think?" Stephen answered.

Brenda glanced at Dylan. "Ah, a kindred spirit."

Father Rowan knelt beside Dylan. "How did you do it?" he whispered.

"Do what?"

"Ya left 'ere a farmer. And now you're a spy?"

"I'm not a spy."

"What're ya then?"

Their eyes met. "I'm a ground operative."

"What the 'ail is that, a 'ground operative'?"

"Are ya cursin' at me, Father?"

"That smell," Brenda said, "is your flesh rotting."

"I figured as much," Stephen answered.

"He needs a cot. The closest doctor is in Dublin," Vicki said to Dylan.

"She said she needed a doctor," Father Rowan said, gesturing toward Vicki.

Dylan came to his feet. "You need a doctor?" His face grew pale. There were bags forming under his bloodshot eyes.

"No," Vicki said. She placed a hand on his cheek and gently stroked his five o'clock shadow. "We were asking for a doctor in case these guys needed one. I had a bad feeling."

"Are ya sayin' you were fakin'?" Father Rowan said.

"Yes."

"You can fake vomit?" he pressed.

"You threw up, Vicki?" Dylan's eyes grew wider.

"Nerves. Nothing more."

"Why didn't you tell me who you were?" Father Rowan interrupted.

Before Vicki could respond, Brenda said, "We honor the chain of command." She looked pointedly at Dylan.

Father Rowan continued to stare at Vicki. Her hair was still damp and hung in folds down her back. Her clothing had been soaked through and partially dried and she looked a mess. "On account o' you're ground operatives," he said in a monotone.

"No," Dylan corrected. "I'm a ground operative. *She's* a spy."

"And I'm a felon," Brenda chimed in. "Now that we have all the introductions out of the way, could somebody tell me what we're going to do with these men while we're waiting?"

Dylan took Vicki's hand from his cheek and squeezed it. With her hand still in his, he turned his attention to the priest. "It was the Hoolihans what shot 'im." He gestured toward Perry.

His jaw dropped. "The Hoolihans are fightin' the American government?"

"No. They came from behind and thought he was me."

"They were lookin' to kill ya, Mick?"

"That's the looks o' it, 'ey?"

"Do they know you work for the Americans?"

"No."

"Where were ya when this happened?"

Dylan glanced around the room. "I don't need to say that what's said in this room won't go any farther."

"Then why'd you say it?" quipped Brenda.

He turned back to the priest. "We were in the bogs. Stephen was being held captive underground."

"Underground?"

"Castle dungeons. Who'd 'ave thought somebody was dense enough to build a castle in the bogs?"

"Ooh," Father Rowan said, "There's more than that in the bogs, there is. Don't you know, they've found all sorts o' things there o' late, they have."

"Like what?"

"Well, you know how the Hoolihans got that map when they were tykes, and they were convinced there was treasure in the bogs."

"Aye. Everyone thought they were off their nuts."

"Well, it turned out there may 'ave been a village or two there, centuries ago. They started finding ruins underground, some o' which were connected, they said, via tunnels."

"Tunnels, you say?"

"Aye. And—"

"So that's how they did it."

"Did what?"

"They had horses—Aengus' horses—and I untied 'em and set 'em toward home. I started off on horse with these two. Left the Hoolihans to get back on foot. And don't you know, they beat me back 'ere? And I've been scratchin' me head, tryin' to sort it out."

"They're here? Where?"

"At the cottage."

"What cottage?" Vicki said.

"Our cottage. The one where we're stayin'."

"How do you know this, Mick?" Father Rowan asked.

"I know people. Anyway, could it 'ave been possible for 'em to 'ave walked through the tunnels and arrived a'fore I could?"

"Oh, I'm sure. For one thin', they would've been protected from the weather. And dependin' on exactly how the tunnels go, they might've had a more direct route."

"Did they find any treasure, then?"

"Oh, no. I'm sure the treasure is nothin' but a tall tale."

"Aye," Dylan said. "I suppose it must be."

"But they did find somethin' else."

Dylan waited for him to continue. The priest rubbed his chin and glanced at the girls and Stephen before motioning to him. "Come w' me."

36

They stood in the dim confines of the cellar. The air was damp and so frigid that Dylan felt as if he'd stepped into a freezer. The room was as old as the church—perhaps four hundred years old or more—and would have served as a wine cellar or for refrigeration long before electricity was invented. There were still sconces along the walls but now a set of wires were laid neatly along the stone at intervals, occasionally making their way to the ceiling and across the beams where naked bulbs now attempted to illuminate the area.

Heavy wood shelving ran the length of the room. They passed by a myriad of items ranging from mundane office supplies to those used during church services. As they headed into the far corner of the cellar where the air dipped even further and the bulbs no longer reached, Father Rowan picked up a flashlight on the corner shelf and turned it on.

As he shone his light on the corner shelves, Dylan's jaw dropped. He found himself staring at hundreds of weapons and boxes of ammunition. He stepped forward, gingerly picking up a rifle in his hands and ogling it. "Where the 'ail did you find this?" he managed to ask.

"I believe most o' these weapons date back to World War I," Father Rowan said, picking up another and running his palm along the smoothly polished stock. "You know where these came from, Mick?" Without waiting for an answer, he continued, "They're German. They're Deutsche Waffen und Munitionsfabriken."

"Don't tell me—"

"Aye. It's true. All the stories we heard growin' up about the gun-runnin' that took place in Ireland."

"Durin' the war," Dylan murmured as he inspected the weapons, "when Ireland was tryin' to throw the yoke Britain had around us—there were always stories o' how the Irish sided w' the Germans in an underground movement to amass weapons."

"Aye. And it's true. They told us in school that most o' the shipments had been intercepted by the Brits. And that none survived in Ireland."

"But you found these."

"I didn't. The Hoolihans did."

"What are ya sayin'?"

"I heard reports that the Hoolihans had weapons. You know as well as I that it's against the law to own weapons such as this. So one night they were drunk and chatterin' in the pub, you know how they were always talkin' out their arses, and they said they'd found a stash o' German weapons. Everyone there thought it was the Arthur Guinness talkin'. But I followed 'em, Mick. I followed 'em right to the stash. They were so clobbered they didn't e'en know I was there.

"I waited for 'em to leave, which didn't take long, on account o' dawn comin', and I nearly cleaned 'em out, Mick. I took every weapon I could carry. And most o' the ammunition, too."

"They never suspected you?"

"No. And when they tried to report their German weapons were missin' from the bogs, the whole village thought they'd gone bonkers. They thought the alcohol had finally eaten away all the brain cells."

Dylan stared at the rows of weapons, neatly arranged.

"But that's not all, Mick." Father Rowan brushed past him to the weapons closest to the corner. "These over here date to World War II. It was true, all the rumors we used to hear. The Nazis had been here, right here in Ireland."

"But, as I recall from me learnin', Ireland was already a sovereign country b' then. It's why they declared neutrality durin' the war—they didn't want to side w' with the Brits. But they didn't have the military to fight 'em, either."

"No. But Northern Ireland was sidin' with the Germans underground. They were buyin' weapons from the Nazis and they'd planned on leadin' a revolt to run the Brits out o' Ireland so the island could be reunited as one."

"But how come these weapons are here, and not in Northern Ireland?"

"I don't know, Mick," he answered in a hushed voice. "I don't know." He held out a rifle for Dylan to inspect. "But you can see, this one's newer than the others. This is World War II stock. I'm sure o' it."

"Aye," Dylan said. "And—could this type o' weapon be what the Hoolihans shot Perry with, ya think?"

"I think it's definitely possible. I mean, I stole what I could from 'em. But who knows, what they might've found at another place, another time. There's been rumors they have a stash at their house. They spend a lot o' time in the bogs. You know that, Mick. They've been lookin' for the pot o' gold for years. You know that y'self, Mick."

"But you didn't turn these weapons over to the authorities."

Father Rowan scoffed. "Of course not. Ya think I'm daft? One ne'er knows when weapons could come in handy."

"Ya missed your callin' when you went into the priesthood."

"It's the priesthood that keeps me above reproach."

"I suppose it is, at that." Dylan placed the weapon on the shelf with the gingerly fashion he might have used with a baby. "How is it that you're workin' with the Americans, Father?"

"I do what I can for the good o' humanity. It was just in this case, I was in the right place at the right time."

Dylan let this sink in. Then, "So. And now the Hoolihans are waitin' for me at the cottage. They've wounded an American operative. When this day is done, the woundin' might 'ave turned to killin', as bad off as Perry is. And there's still a man left in the castle dungeons, a man another unit has been dispatched to extract. Who knows if he's dead or alive?"

"What're plannin' to do now, Mick?"

"I'll be doin' the only thin' I can do. I'm bringin' the fight to them."

37

I need you to stand down on this one," Sam said.

Dylan paced Father Rowan's office, his face growing ruddy. Vicki had seen that look before; it had led to murder and now she fought to keep her heart rate steady. "He's right, Dylan," she said. Her voice sounded gritty and forced.

"This is *my* fight," he insisted. "I've known the Hoolihans me whole life. They've ne'er been nothin' but trouble. And I looked the other way because I was in love with their sister. I didn't even fight back when they very nearly killed me, on account o' I was tryin' to understand their anger at their sister's death."

"But it's gone beyond that," Sam countered. His face appeared tired and lined as the group watched him on Father Rowan's desktop computer. "They attacked one of ours—"

"On account o' they thought he was *me*. *I* was their target."

"Makes no difference. Look, we've got them on attempted murder."

"And precisely how 'ave you 'got them'?"

Sam rubbed his eyes. He'd clearly been up all night and just observing his actions made Vicki want to curl up in bed and sleep forever. "We'll pick them up."

"And do what? Have a trial here in Ireland? Tell how we were workin' a mission to rescue a captured operative? How's that gonna play out on international telly?"

"Listen to me, Dylan. Listen carefully." He waited until Dylan stopped pacing. "Two American tourists visited your village. After leaving the pub last evening, the Hoolihans kidnapped them. They took them to a remote area and they shot both of them, intending to kill them both. They took their passports, their identification, their money… everything they had. If one dies, it's murder. If both live, it's attempted murder and robbery."

"I don't know how you can pull this off. The trial—"

"A third man was with them. A third American. He didn't enter the pub; he was—window shopping, hell, I don't know. But this third man followed, saw what happened, and got to the American Embassy in Dublin. The consulate there calls higher-ups; the word comes down to the village, it doesn't flow upward. We'll control this. They'll stand trial with the third man testifying. The other two will have brain injuries and won't remember a thing. We'll convict them based on the testimony of the third man, a direct eye-witness. If they need more, we'll supply more."

"And how will you get the Hoolihans to begin with? Call the local law and ask 'em to go by me cottage and pick 'em up?"

"Our men will get them."

"How many men 'ave you got here, Sam? You've got a team lookin' for Rich. There's no tellin' what shape he'll be in. We've got an operative with information you need to 'ave who's waitin' to leave the country—and he might lose both feet. I don't even know how he remains lucid, to be quite honest about it. We've got a third man fightin' for his life in the next room and he's got to get to a doctor soon or he'll be lost for sure."

"What are you suggesting?"

"I'll go after 'em. They're waitin' for me."

"And do what? Have an old-fashioned shoot-out?"

Dylan ran his hand through his hair. "I don't know."

Sam sighed. "Do you have your black bag?"

"Aye."

"Did you go through it completely?"

"Not completely. It was dark when I had it handed to me. I used what I needed out o' it—"

"Did you get Perry's black bag?"

"Aye."

"So you have them both."

"Aye."

"Okay. I'm going to let you handle this—"

"Sam, no!" Vicki's voice was nearly shrill but Dylan motioned for Sam to continue.

"There is an additional pistol in each of those black bags. These have projectile syringes instead of bullets."

"You're tellin' me to shoot 'em with a dart gun?" Dylan raised a brow and his face became ruddier.

"You're a good shot, Dylan. I've reviewed your scores at the firing ranges."

"Aye, but—*a dart gun?*"

Brenda rose from her seat and slipped out the door as Sam answered. "They're tranquilizer pistols. Not darts. Major difference. When they're shot, they'll immediately become incapacitated. They'll know what's going on but they will have no control over their movements."

"And how long will that last?"

"An hour at most for the full effect. Which means we have to get them out of there and restrained quickly. When they become functional again, they have to be out of that village and in jail awaiting trial."

"How many syringes do I have with each pistol?"

Brenda slipped back into the room, carrying both black bags. She handed them silently to Dylan.

"Thank you," he murmured as he rifled through the first one.

"Six. That means with both pistols, you've got twelve attempts for three men. You think you can handle that?"

"Aye—"

"Sam, no," Vicki pleaded. "Dylan, don't do it. Let the other unit get them."

"I can handle it." Dylan turned toward Vicki. "I can handle it, Vicki. I'm not in the mood for suicide."

"Sam—"

"I'll go with him." The voice was husky and strong. All eyes turned toward Father Rowan.

"Father, I appreciate it but I can't—"

"Yes, you can. I'm a decent shot. I've been huntin' since I was a child, as you'll recall. And it'll be more even w' two against three. I know these bad apples and I'd consider it an honor to help put 'em out o' my village."

"Father Rowan," Dylan's voice was softer and he shook his head as he spoke.

"The very least I can do is draw their attention toward me so you can get a good shot. They won't try to kill me. They've done a lot o' bad deeds in their time, but I don't think a one o' 'em would want to kill a man o' God."

Dylan turned back to Sam. "I trust this man w' me life. I've trusted him a'fore w' it. And I'd trust him again."

"If anything goes wrong," Sam warned, his voice firm, "I don't know either one of you. You went there on vacation and you had an old feud with the Hoolihans."

"Understood."

"Having said that," he continued, "I'm watching them now." He turned the monitor so they could view his other screen. It depicted an aerial view of the cottage and the detached garage as well as the surrounding terrain. "One of them—the biggest man—is now in the garage." He pointed to the far end of the cottage. "The second man is at the edge of the house, watching in two directions. The third—" he zoomed in to lowlands on the other side of the drive "—is lying here amongst the weeds or whatever the hell they are, watching and waiting for you to come home. He's in view of the other two so when he gives the signal, they'll all know you're there."

"There are no trees for cover," Dylan said, rubbing his chin.

"That's right. And I'd strongly recommend that you don't go driving up there or walking from the church. They'd have you in plain sight the whole way."

"How were you plannin' on gettin' 'em out once I 'ave 'em subdued?"

"Helicopter. Two are en route to the castle ruins. Once they get to Rich, they'll split up. One goes to the church to pick up Perry and Stephen. The other goes to the cottage to get the Hoolihans. The med unit will take the injured to a military hospital. The other one will take the men to a military prison."

"You can't land at the church," Dylan countered. "It's on a hill where everybody in the village can see what unfolds. It's too risky."

"Then where—?"

"I can help with that," Father Rowan interrupted. "There's a valley about a mile from the church, away from the village."

"But we can't carry—" Dylan began.

"There's a tunnel under the church that leads out to the valley."

"What?"

"It's been there as long as the church 'as. There's been a lot o' turmoil in Ireland over the centuries, you must understand that. And the tunnels from the oldest churches were used to help the unfortunate escape as our lands were pillaged and our people killed or tortured."

"You can spare me the history lesson," Sam said, "but I'll take you up on that valley."

"The villagers may see the aircraft but they won't be able to figure out where it's landed. If we're fast about it and it can lift off fairly directly..."

"They will. It'll be a precision operation."

Dylan groaned. "I'd love to 'ave a mission where somethin' went right for a change."

"But that still doesn't solve the problem of how you'll get to the cottage undetected," Sam said.

A chime sounded and the room became silent. The sound of voices wafted down the hallway. Everyone turned toward Father Rowan.

He glanced at his watch. "The tourist bus."

"The what?" Dylan asked.

"Remember, I told you about the tourists comin' to the village. They look at the sanctuary and they wander around the cemetery for a bit—"

"Ooh," Dylan said, "don't tell me you're allowin' tourists in the cemetery."

"They don't bother a thin'—"

"Don't tell me they're sittin' on *my* bench. Don't tell me that."

"The point is," Father Rowan said calmly, "they're here now."

"Well, tell 'em not today."

"I can't do that."

"Lock the doors."

"I can't do that, either."

"Why? Why can't you do it? It's your church, isn't it?"

"Actually, Mick, it's the people's church. And in all the years I've been here, the sanctuary has ne'er been locked. Not a single day. Not a single hour. And if I ask 'em to leave or I lock 'em out, you know where their next stop is? The village. So they go shoppin' and they go to the cafes and the pubs and they tell all our neighbors that the church isn't open. And then you know what I'll 'ave on me hands? I'll have an entire village drivin' and walkin' to the church like a parade to see what's what. Is that what you want, Mick?"

38

The rain had stopped and the clouds were past the village and moving further eastward. But as Dylan peered toward the heavens, he knew this reprieve wouldn't last. He'd spent a lifetime studying the skies; it was what was done in the rural parts of Ireland, where a man's dinner could depend on the type of weather they had for the day. He remembered well the mornings at the cottage he shared with Alana; stepping onto the stoop with a cup of coffee or hot tea in his hands, warming his insides while he studied the clouds and made his plans for the day.

And today there would be a break in the storms but by nightfall they would be back with a vengeance.

He could see it on the western horizon; the clouds building and roiling. It would take them a few hours to progress across the island but they had another bad night in store.

The tourist bus was stopped a few yards from the stone wall surrounding the cemetery. The crowd had been respectful; about two dozen blue-haired women with balding husbands. They had toured the sanctuary, remarking on the intricate woodwork and original paintings, dropping money into a bowl near the door as they left. They'd wandered through the cemetery, observing the headstones with reverence, occasionally remarking on the markers from the 17th and 18th centuries. They had noted with respect the freshly dug grave of his grandmother, and no one had sat on his bench.

Now they lined up in an orderly fashion as they boarded the bus, which would take them on to the village, where they would have a fine Irish meal and spend their money in the shops. They made slow progress; the youngest might have been in her eighties, he surmised, and it seemed that each required individual assistance.

He looked over his shoulder at Vicki standing in the doorway. Shep sat beside her, watching quietly. Vicki looked pale and fragile. He longed to return to her, to take her into his arms and retreat to a warm room and a warmer bed and sleep the sleep of the just with her beside him. He could sleep away the rest of the day and be awake all night to make sweet love to her.

Instead, he motioned toward the dog. "Make sure Shep stays inside, will you?" he asked. "I don't want 'er followin' us."

Vicki nodded. She seemed reluctant to back away from the door and to close it as long as he remained there. And it was just as well. He didn't want to see her turn her back on him. He didn't want the door between them. And he didn't want to be leaving.

The line continued to grow shorter until Father Rowan and he were watching the last tourist board. He poked his head beyond the stone wall and peered in the direction of the cottage. Father Rowan was right; the angle of the bus prevented anyone at the cottage from seeing the doors to the bus or the people as they boarded it.

He turned once more toward Vicki. He was too far away to say what he wanted to say to her, so he simply motioned toward the dog. The expression on her face said she understood, and she reluctantly called to Shep. Once the dog was inside the church, she closed the door.

He felt alone as he stared at the door, though he was surrounded by people and activity. His priest's collar was too tight and it scratched his skin. But the black cloak was warm against the chill of the air. And it hid the pistols underneath— the tranquilizer as well as his Glock.

"I'm sorry we don't have seats for you," the bus driver said apologetically.

"Oh, not at'al," Father Rowan said. "We appreciate your kindness in providin' a lift to the cottage. Father Maguire can sit up front and I'll have a seat at the back. When you get to the cottage, there's plenty o' room for you to turn around, it bein' a circular drive an' all."

With that, it was done. Father Rowan strolled to the door near the rear of the bus and sat on the steps. Dylan adjusted his cloak and sat on the steps of the door by the driver.

"You sure you're okay there?" the driver asked.

"Aye," Dylan answered. "It's only for a kilometer. We hate to be puttin' you out for such a short distance."

"Oh, these folks will enjoy it. They love looking out the windows."

Dylan chuckled as if he didn't have a care in the world. As if he was a visiting priest and he and the resident priest were simply going back to his rented cottage for a meal. He started to run his hand through his hair but caught himself; the earpiece needed to remain hidden from view.

"Hold on," the driver said as the bus lurched into gear.

He sensed Sam listening through the earpiece and wondered if he could pick up the words of the driver and the roar of the bus' engine. The drive was pitted and old and it felt as if the tires hit every hole and bumped every rock. He held firmly onto the handle at the door, even though the bus was barely moving, and wondered if Sam was watching them on the satellite as they rolled onto the road leading to the cottage.

He couldn't see the cottage on this side of the bus, and neither could Father Rowan. But that was precisely the point.

As they approached the driveway to the cottage, the bus driver remarked, "There's a man lying in the low spot beside the road. Think I should stop?"

"No," Dylan answered. "That would be the village drunk, I'm afraid. Father Rowan will remain on the bus, then, and get off as you come back around. He'll make sure he gets the man home. It happens nearly every night, I'm told."

"Hell of a way to live a life," the driver said.

"Aye, it's a 'ail of a way." He signaled outside the bus and waited for Father Rowan's return signal. He understood.

He felt his heart begin to quicken and his breath grow shallow as the bus wound up the drive toward the garage. When the bus turned further to the right to follow the drive around the garage and back toward the road, he turned to the driver and smiled. "Thank you, my son." With that, the bus slowed for the turn and Dylan hopped off.

He waited as the rest of the bus began to pass him by, nodding to Father Rowan as the priest remained seated.

Then he walked alongside it until they had reached the edge of the garage. When the bus began to turn again, he slipped to the other side and flattened his back against the side of the building.

"The man at the road gave a signal as you passed." Sam's voice was low and even. Dylan knew Father Rowan had heard the same remark; he was now wearing Perry's earpiece.

A few seconds later, Sam continued, "The man at the edge of the house is watching the bus leave. The one in the garage came to the door. Now he's gone back in."

Dylan waited quietly along the back side of the garage. There were no windows here and he couldn't be seen from the house. He knew as the bus made its way back to the road, they would pass by the Hoolihan brother's hiding spot once more. This time, Father Rowan would be seated facing him.

The seconds seemed to pass slowly. Everything hinged on this first contact.

"They found Rich." Sam's voice was deeper. "He's dead."

It was murder then, Dylan thought, that all three of these men would be charged with. Murder of an American tourist and they'd get life for sure. Especially when the authorities found the stash of weapons in their home. They'd be branded domestic terrorists.

The bus reached the road and picked up speed, then slowed again at the spot where the brother lay in wait. Dylan placed his hand against his earpiece, pressing it to his ear even though he knew it wasn't really necessary, in an attempt to hear everything.

The people on the bus were singing a little ditty of a song and if the circumstances hadn't been so dire, he might have smiled at their out of tune melody. Then he heard a popping sound. It was just once and directly following it was the scuffle of feet on the gravel road. He wasn't sure now if he heard what he needed to hear.

A moment later, Father Rowan's voice came through the earpiece. "He's down. It's Ciaran."

Dylan pictured the bus rounding the corner. Ciaran would have laid low beside the road in a deluded attempt to remain hidden from view. But he would have looked. He knew him. He couldn't let the bus go by without taking a good long look at the tourists—tourists he might try to roll later. And as the rear of the vehicle came into his view, he would have been staring straight at Father Rowan's face.

He wondered if he fired the pistol while he was still seated; then scrambled out of the bus and down to the low side of the road where he would pretend to assist a drunk. The syringe was quiet; not quite silent but the popping sound could easily have been mistaken for the bus hitting a rock.

"He's hit in the shoulder," Father Rowan continued. "He moved at first but now he's down completely."

Dylan peered toward the road as the bus picked up speed and continued toward the village, the tourists still singing, their voices carrying now on the wind. There was no sign of Father Rowan. More importantly, there was no sign of Ciaran.

"Stay where you are, Father," Sam said.

"Aye."

"Dylan, the man at the house has gone to the other side. There is still a man in the garage."

He took a deep breath.

"I'd rather you get the man outside first," Sam continued. "But I don't know how you can without the possibility of being seen by the man inside. There are too many windows facing that direction."

"Then I'll be goin' into the garage first."

"When you're at the threshold," Sam said, "you're in a blind spot. I can't see you in the garage obviously so when he's secured…"

"I'll let you know," Dylan finished in a whisper. He moved toward the edge of the garage. The single-wide vehicle door contained a row of windows and he bent down as he moved under them. From where Aidan had been standing just a moment before, he would have been in plain sight. He glanced at the area where Ciaran had been hiding but didn't see him or Father Rowan. He assumed they were lying in the low area on the other side of the road, and he wondered briefly whether Aidan was looking in Ciaran's direction from the other side of the house.

Then all too swiftly, he reached the other corner of the garage.

"All's clear," Sam said.

Dylan rounded the corner. There was one pedestrian door with a grimy window. He moved quickly now, keeping his back against the wall as he drew closer to the door.

"The man at the house is moving back to the side," Sam said.

Dylan reached his hand to the knob.

"He's coming around the corner."

He turned the knob as quietly as possible. It was unlocked.

"You have five seconds, tops."

He transferred the tranquilizer pistol to his right hand and he turned to take the knob with his left.

"One second."

He threw the door open as he stepped into the threshold, his gun ready to fire. The door slammed against the wall as it opened and his eyes tried to adjust quickly to the dark interior. He took a broad step inside as a thunderous roar reached his ears. He saw the lead pipe a moment before it struck him; instinctively he raised his right arm to field it as he tried to jump backward out of its path.

The pipe missed his body but caught his hand, sending the pistol flying through the air. Before he could determine where it had gone, he was slammed on the side of the head with a fist as large as roast mutton. His head reeled with the blow, his ear ringing as the earpiece shattered and flew in all directions. He stumbled, trying to keep his balance, but the onslaught had just begun.

39

Brenda held Perry's wrist in her hand. Frowning, she lowered his hand and reached for his neck. "His pulse is fading," she said. "Sam had better get that helicopter here quick."

Vicki placed another blanket over Stephen and joined her sister. "How did you learn so much about medicine?"

"I know nothing about it," she answered. "I was raised on a farm after Mom and Dad died. They had horses and livestock and I learned to improvise."

"What you did for Perry was more than improvise."

"Don't kid yourself." She leaned back and looked tiredly at Vicki. "How's he doing?"

"He's trying to catch some sleep," Vicki said in a low voice. "He has a strong countenance. He'll make it, I'm sure, but he might lose both feet."

"I figured as much."

Shep wandered down the hall, whining.

"She doesn't like to be cooped up, does she?" Brenda remarked.

"It seems like her pacing is getting worse."

"You think she knows something we don't know?"

Vicki locked eyes with her. "I hope not. I mean…"

"I know what you mean. Why did Dylan say to keep her inside?"

The dog moved back down the hallway, the whine turning to something akin to a controlled, low howl.

"She's freaking me out," Vicki said.

"I've never heard a dog make a sound like that."

The noise grew lower as she moved further from the doorway but a chill had begun to creep up Vicki's spine. She rose slowly and stepped toward the open door as the sound turned to a full howl. She reached the threshold as the dog raced back down the hallway, her teeth bared. As she drew closer to the room where Vicki stood transfixed, she snapped in her direction in a grave warning.

She stepped back into the room as the dog raced past her. Unable to turn away, she poked her head into the hallway just as Shep leapt into the air and crashed through the window at the far end of the hall.

She instinctively cried out and ran into the hallway, dashing to the window to see Shep loping across the meadow between the church and the cottage. She continued to stare even after Brenda joined her; searching the terrain with her eyes, she saw no other movement. She shivered uncontrollably as her sister pulled her back toward the room where the two men lay.

"Dylan can take care of himself," Brenda said gently. "You have to believe that."

Vicki nodded. She glanced at Stephen, who had his eyes closed. In repose, she realized just how sunken his eyes were and how dark the circles underneath. He was much gaunter than his photograph and his clothes hung on him. The blanket hid his blackened feet but the mound was far larger than normal feet should be.

She turned back to Perry. He'd been at the entrance of the dungeons. His jet black hair was thick and a bit unruly, as Dylan's was. And they had mistaken him for the man she loved. Now he was fighting for his life.

And now Dylan was facing those same predators at their cottage.

She whirled around.

"Where are you going?" Brenda asked. Her voice sounded hoarse and urgent in the small room.

"To Dylan. He needs me."

40

The pipe was thrown with such force that once it hit its mark, it sailed out of Eoghan's hands and clattered to the floor with a vicious clang.

Dylan stumbled backward, crashing against open shelves that spewed their contents across the floor. Eoghan Hoolihan had turned into a massive juggernaut as he grabbed a two-by-four and relentlessly pounded him. He smashed against Dylan's upper body and followed immediately with a blow to the upper legs before returning to the torso. The onslaught continued ruthlessly as Dylan tried to buffer the blows with his arms but every strike threatened to knock him off his feet. He staggered backward helplessly and even the stacks of shelves that lined the perimeter could not protect him but became part of the arsenal.

He had been in this situation before, he reminded himself. When he'd first begun boxing, he'd been pummeled around the ring to the crowd's delight. He'd had a particularly bloodthirsty opponent, one he wanted desperately to escape, but the man had kept coming and the crowd's shouts had built to a crescendo. But here, he thought, he had potential weapons.

He grabbed one corner of the shelving and sent it sailing in Eoghan's path but it slowed him only temporarily. He scanned the area closest to him in an attempt to find anything that could reasonably serve as a weapon. Eoghan closed in quickly, backing him around the garage. His eyes were red and bulging and the veins on his neck protruded like ropes. His fists were colossal and they were sprinkled with blood—Dylan's blood, he realized.

The man had one goal: to kill him.

Dylan felt his chest harden and his eyes narrow as he continued in a circular retreat. He kept his eyes locked on Eoghan's but noted in his peripheral vision every object they passed. With the next strike, he dodged and began a counterclockwise movement until he was positioned near farm implements.

The stench of alcohol permeated Eoghan's breath and clothing as he moved toward him. His eyes were glazed now and otherworldly. He began to grin, his uneven teeth snarling as he approached. He was clearly relishing the moment in which he would end Mick Maguire's life.

Dylan seized a pitchfork. He didn't know where the tranquilizer pistol had landed and at this point he sure couldn't look for it. He needed the Glock inside his cloak but he was realizing just how awkward it would be to reach with Eoghan closing in. If it came down to life or death—which it apparently had—he had no choice but to fight to the finish.

Eoghan chuckled. "Ya think a fork is gonna keep you from me?"

"Killin' me won't bring 'er back, Eoghan."

"First, you take me sister. And then you come after me gold."

"I'm not after your gold." They moved in a circumference, Dylan jabbing the pitchfork toward Eoghan as he jumped out of the tines' way. As they neared the doorway, the large man bent to pick up the lead pipe and Dylan rushed him, backing him away from the weapon. But he realized that he couldn't stop the man with a pitchfork unless he was willing to impale him.

His thoughts raced through his head as he contemplated the movements required to get to the pistol without Eoghan getting to him first. He had the pitchfork with both hands and from the squirrely dart in the man's eyes, he knew every second counted. The larger man was waiting for Dylan to make a mistake—waiting for that one wrong move to rush in and finish him off.

He was in a blind spot; a spot where Sam couldn't see him and with the earpiece destroyed, no one could hear him. What he needed was to be out in the open.

He continued the circumference until he reached the pedestrian door. With a grunt and a push of the pitchfork, he simultaneously backed into the open doorway. Once there, he slammed the pitchfork crossways to block the door, holding it in place with his left hand. At best, he had seconds before Eoghan would come right through it like it weighed no more than a toothpick. He awkwardly moved one hand under the cloak to his pistol.

He felt the grip and was about to pull it out when two strong arms came from behind. They grabbed him from underneath both arms and wrenched his hands upward. The pitchfork clattered to the walkway and Eoghan chuckled loudly as he moved into the light of day.

Aidan was as large a man as Dylan; his arms were the muscular limbs of a man accustomed to hard labor and harder drinking. Eoghan was larger than both of them and as he approached, his grin grew wider and more diabolical.

Dylan took a deep breath. As he expelled it, he allowed Aidan's arms to support him as he jumped off the ground and kicked Eoghan square in the chest. The man staggered backward as did Aidan; but the younger brother didn't release his grip on Dylan but only intensified it. As the older brother regained his footing, he came at him like a charging bull. He pulled back a meaty fist, still splattered with Dylan's blood, and with a mighty roar, he moved to slam it into Dylan's exposed chest.

As the fist came at him, he reared up again, his legs reaching underneath Eoghan's extended arm to kick him directly in the chest with the steel-toed boots. Again, the man staggered back, this time with an oath that was picked up by his younger brother.

"Ya gowl, Aidan!" Eoghan boomed. "Hold the man, why don't ya?"

Aidan slammed his knee into Dylan's back, causing him to yelp in pain. Then he wrenched his arms tighter behind him until he thought his shoulder blades would be torn from his body.

"Go for it, Eoghan! Knock the bloody shite out o' the bugger!"

Aidan crammed his knee against Dylan's lower spine again, twisting his back until he was bent backward so far that his kidneys felt bruised and he was completely winded. Eoghan grabbed the pitchfork. Holding it with the tines one above the other, his intent was clear: if Dylan attempted to kick him a third time, the weapon could strike the most sensitive part of his body. But as he approached with his sinister grin and bloodshot eyes, he knew he would be impaled anyway. And Eoghan wouldn't care if the pitchfork went straight through him and tipped his brother; he was that kind of a man.

He had no choice.

To kick again meant to lean back further and he was already bent as severely as he thought possible. But as Eoghan drew closer, he let out an anguished bellow as he forced himself to rear further backward. He kicked the pitchfork out of his hands with his right foot while landing his left heel against Eoghan's chest in the same spot he'd been kicked twice before. There was a resounding crack as the big man boomed in a guttural voice and went down on his knees.

Aidan staggered backward, unwilling to release his grip on Dylan, until they were both pinned against the back of the house. Eoghan was rising, his eyes bloodthirsty, the pain only cementing his resolve. He thundered as he charged him, both hands balled into massive fists.

Dylan rose again but this time, came down hard on Aidan's instep with the full force of his body. Before the man could recover from the sudden strike, Dylan twisted his torso, loosening the grip on his arms and elbowing him in the throat. The hold slackened further and he seized the moment.

He wrestled away from Aidan and Eoghan descended upon him again. Aidan was gathering his strength for another round and as Dylan backed away from them both, he reached for his pistol.

A rush of black and white fur flew through the air, four sets of claws digging into Eoghan Hoolihan's face as Shep brought him down. The battle became one of bared teeth, bloody flesh and an unearthly snarl that grew to the pitch of a tiger.

Dylan grabbed his pistol and turned to Aidan as the other man charged him. He fired as Aidan's arm flew against his, knocking the weapon out of his hand. Dylan rushed the other man with both fists pounding; an uppercut to the chin was followed by a blow to the abdomen and another punch to the head. Back and forth he went, his right fist pounding the man's face while his left one drove at his torso until the man was stumbling back, his head lolling, his feet slipping on the stone walk.

Blood spurted from his face and still Dylan kept coming. Aidan's shirt began to soak with his blood but Dylan wouldn't relent. He pushed the man backward even when his own fists were red with his own blood mixed with Aidan's; he drove him away from the house, away from shelter, away from a crutch he could use to support him. He didn't take his eyes off his, even when the other man's eyeballs began to swell and blood from cuts along his brow ran into his eyes. He didn't stop until the man dropped to his knees.

And then he began kicking his head with the steel toe of his boots, again and again.

Somewhere in the back of his mind, he heard Shep snarling and growling as he ripped Eoghan Hoolihan open. Somewhere he heard Father Rowan's voice calling for reason. Somewhere he heard the uncommon sound of a helicopter's rotor blades approaching the cottage.

It was only when Aidan lay still and crumpled on the ground in a growing pool of blood that Dylan began to slow. When each kick to the head or body brought no more movement and even the man's body ceased to expand with his breathing; only then did he stop.

He turned a furious face toward Father Rowan, who was standing a few feet away, shouting at him, begging him to stop. He held in his hand the other tranquilizer pistol.

Dylan whistled and Shep bounced off Eoghan as if he was a trampoline, landing on the ground a few feet away. Her fur stood on end, causing her to appear twice her size. She was drenched in blood.

With one swift movement, Dylan grabbed the tranquilizer pistol and spun toward Eoghan. The man was coming to his feet, his eyes set on Dylan. Though his face was not much more than bloody pulp and his clothes were in bloodstained tatters, he was not giving up. He was coming after him once again.

As the enormous man charged with a rage that sounded like a lion's roar, Dylan fired. The syringe hit him in the side of the neck, the needle sticking out the side like Frankenstein's monster. And still the man kept coming.

He fired again, hitting him in the chest just above his heart.

His roar grew to a deafening pitch as he ran straight for Dylan.

Dylan stood his ground and prepared to fire again when Eoghan Hoolihan hit the ground with the full force of his body, his fingers landing only inches from Dylan's bloody boot.

41

A boom reverberated through the air like nothing Dylan had ever heard before. He instinctively yelled in Vicki's direction, but his instruction to duck was lost amidst the racket. But as he and Father Rowan went down and he saw the women do the same halfway between the church and the cottage, he saw a plume of smoke billow high into the sky. It was miles away; he surmised it was in the area of the bogs. But the explosion had rocked the earth beneath their feet.

"They're blowing up the dungeons," one of the operatives remarked.

"*They're what?*" Dylan turned to face one of the men who had landed the helicopter on the far side of the cottage. They had cuffed the three Hoolihan brothers and each of them was loaded onto the aircraft. Now as they prepared to lift off, all eyes turned in the direction of the bogs.

"Rich is dead. Sam tell you that?"

"Aye. But—what if there are others kept captive there?"

"He checked with infrared. There's nobody else."

"But he—"

"Instructions were to cave them in. And the ones nearest that these perps used." He nodded in the direction of the Hoolihans.

"All o' 'em?"

"All of them. And you'd better hurry," the man added as he turned to go, "you have very little time to get Stephen and Perry to the other helicopter."

"They're on their way then?"

"They're on their way. Best of luck to you!" With that, he rushed back to the aircraft. The rotor blades had never stopped turning, the engine never ceased; now the man boarded it quickly and as he strapped into the co-pilot's position, it began to hover. They had been on the ground less than five minutes.

Dylan motioned for Father Rowan to follow as he raced toward the church. His chest ached with every breath he took; his legs were filled with a pain that made him wonder how they continued to work at all. And his torso throbbed as if his heart and his lungs were caving in on him.

They met Vicki and Brenda halfway. Somehow he managed to croak, "They're pickin' up Stephen an' Perry in the valley."

Somehow he knew the girls were following but his long legs left them behind. It was Father Rowan who overtook him as they entered the side yard, moving to open the door for him so he barely slowed as he entered the church.

He found Perry still unconscious and barely breathing. Stephen came to a seated position, obviously roused from sleep.

Vicki and Brenda rushed in, pausing at the doorway. It was only then that he saw guns in both their hands. Despite his pain, despite the urgency that faced them now, he smiled. Shep brushed past the girls' legs to stand in front of them.

"Here's what we're gonna do," he said. "Stephen, no disrespect intended but you're nothin' but a bag o' bones. These two girls are gonna help carry you to the helicopter. Put your arm around Brenda's shoulder and the other 'round Vicki's."

He turned to the girls. "You think you can handle that?"

"Of course," they said in unison.

He pulled the blanket off Perry and turned to Father Rowan. "Can you help me get 'im to the blanket?"

Wordlessly, Father Rowan picked up Perry's upper body while Dylan handled his lower body. They laid him onto the blanket and he continued, "We're gonna use this blanket like a stretcher. Can you keep up w' me?"

"Aye."

"Then show us where this tunnel is."

They moved into the cellar wordlessly; the only sounds their own ragged breathing and Stephen's unintended grunts. The naked bulbs shone dimly and Dylan tried not to stumble on the uneven steps as he moved backward along them, one end of the blanket balled into his fists. Father Rowan tried to balance the body as he kept up with Dylan's movements; he had the heavier torso despite Dylan's objections.

Behind them, Vicki and Brenda bolstered Stephen as they moved awkwardly along the steps and into the chill, dark confines.

They moved past the shelves Dylan had seen just hours before; now that seemed like a lifetime ago. They reached the shelves in the far corner and Father Rowan urged Dylan to set Perry down so they could open the door.

Under the priest's instructions, they moved the corner shelving to the side to reveal the stone wall. Dylan turned to him, perplexed, but Father Rowan held up his hand to keep his objections at bay. Then he moved to a large stone near the center and pulled it straight out. More followed, creating an opening about four feet high and perhaps three feet wide.

Shep jumped through and disappeared into the darkness.

Father Rowan reached to the shelving and retrieved two flashlights. He handed one to Brenda and one to Dylan.

Wordlessly, Dylan turned on the light and positioned it between Perry's feet. Then he grabbed the blanket, balling it above his ankles. He nodded to Father Rowan, who had returned to the other end. "Ready?"

"Ready."

Dylan climbed through the entrance and to his relief found the tunnel was nearly seven feet tall. As soon as Father Rowan was through, they began a fast walk that bordered on a jog. Dylan remained beside Perry's feet, allowing the flashlight to illuminate the stone tunnel. It was damp and musty but as they continued, fresh air wafted toward them, circulating with the stale atmosphere.

Behind him, he heard Vicki's and Brenda's footsteps; they were more hurried than the men's and he realized their shorter legs would make them work harder. He glanced back but couldn't see them for Father Rowan's billowing cloak. He realized with a start that he was still wearing the priest's collar and cloak. It was a strange feeling and now he began to feel fatigue set in with a vengeance.

The adrenaline was fading and in its place was the throbbing pain he'd felt as a boxer the morning after. It reminded him of the days when he'd awakened to find his face swollen and blue, his eyes so puffy he couldn't see and his arms so heavy he couldn't lift them. He began to wonder if he could make it to the valley; he felt his feet stumble not once but twice; he felt Father Rowan lurch to catch Perry should he begin to fall.

He had to make it, he told himself. This was his mission. Once the men were aboard that aircraft, he could sink to his knees. He could collapse or he could sleep for the next week. He didn't care about the mess he'd have to clean up at the cottage garage; he didn't care about going through Mam's house before turning it over to the landlord. He only cared about the deepest sleep he could imagine.

He looked for a light to shine into the tunnel like a beacon pulling him closer, but it never did. It was a cloudy day, he remembered; a day in which rains would soon return. He could no longer feel his feet; his legs were numb. He didn't know if he still carried the blanket, balled up in his hands. He could no longer feel his hands at all.

The tunnel made a ninety-degree jog three times, causing him to slow abruptly. At the third turn, the light hit him full force. They emerged from the concealed tunnel entrance to the roar of a helicopter engine and the distinctive rotating of the blades. The air slapped him in the face, the chill awakening him. Three men rushed toward them; two carried a proper stretcher between them while the third carried a medical bag.

They grabbed the blanket from the men with quick precision, placing the blanket and Perry onto the stretcher before retracing their footsteps to the aircraft. The third man nearly lifted Stephen right off his feet as he supported him. The back of the aircraft was open and Dylan came to a stop just beyond it as he watched the activity within. In seconds, they had an IV in Perry's arm and had begun getting his vitals. Stephen was being laid on an adjoining stretcher where an IV waited for him.

One of the men jumped out of the aircraft and closed the clamshell doors. Seeing the four standing just beyond, he sprinted back to them. "We'll take it from here!" he shouted to be heard above the rotor blades.

Shep began barking furiously and ran toward the aircraft.

"Is she one of ours?" the man shouted.

"Yes!" Both Dylan and Vicki replied immediately.

"Get 'er to Sam, will you?" Dylan asked. "He'll know where she's to go."

The man whistled and Shep jumped into the open side door as if she'd been trained to do so. "So you're going to America, girl?" the pilot called as he joined her.

Within seconds, the aircraft began its departure. They watched it hover momentarily and Dylan thought he saw Shep's face grinning at him from the side window.

It was over. He felt a flood of relief coupled with intense exhaustion. He turned to look at Father Rowan, who mirrored his emotions. Brenda's expression was tired but stoic. She was winded and perspiration had popped out across her brow. She wiped it wordlessly. It was okay, he thought; words were not needed.

He turned to Vicki, a tired smile breaking out across his face. But as his eyes fell upon her, the smile turned to a worried frown. She was pale; paler than he'd ever seen her. Her eyes looked like huge amber orbs that grew darker as the whites of her eyes appeared to grow larger. She looked frail and thin, her shoulders shivering in the chill air.

Then before he could open his mouth, her eyes rolled back and she began to fall. He moved toward her as quickly as he could but his legs felt like lead now. As the sound of the helicopter faded into the distance, he scooped her into his arms just as her legs collapsed under her and her head lolled backwards.

42

Vicki awakened to find herself on the couch in Father Rowan's office, a blanket tucked around her and a fire raging in the fireplace. She looked around the room, expecting to see Dylan or Brenda seated at the priest's desk or in one of the chairs neatly arranged in front of it. But she was completely alone.

She rose to her elbows. The last thing she remembered was emerging from the tunnel. A shadowy figure had taken Stephen from them. Her world was filled with blurry images, total exhaustion and a dizzying sensation.

They had carried her back to the church; that much was clear. And as she continued to sit up, she knew it had most likely been Dylan who, after a sleepless night of physical exertion, had carried her in his arms back to safety. The thought of it caused a wave of guilt to sweep over her.

The drapes were pulled apart and now as she sat up completely, she realized the priest's office looked out upon a small courtyard. As her eyes swept across the scene before her, she realized Dylan was seated on a bench beneath a tree, his back to her. In front of him were the priest and Brenda, who was gesturing as she spoke.

She felt her heart sink as she watched her sister. She motioned several times toward the room in which Vicki sat. She splayed her hands and at one point, went down on her knees in front of Dylan, pulling her hands into his. She seemed to be pleading with him, which perplexed Vicki.

Father Rowan appeared to be listening intently but he didn't seem to take part in the conversation. His eyes were focused on Dylan so completely that he appeared as though he wanted to read his mind.

Finally, Dylan pulled his hands away from Brenda and placed both of them on his head, running his hands slowly through his hair. He then placed his face in his hands as he leaned his elbows onto his knees.

Brenda reached for Father Rowan's hand. They stood there for a moment, hand-in-hand, watching Dylan. Then the priest said something to Brenda and they slowly backed away.

Vicki's first instinct was to go to him but there was something deep inside her that cautioned her to leave him alone. She waited for Brenda and Father Rowan to come to her, to tell her what was happening, but if they had returned to the church, they were not near the office. They were leaving them both alone. But why?

As the answer began to dawn on her with a sickening sense of betrayal, Dylan rose. He turned toward the church, wiping his eyes. He looked to the skies for a moment before wiping his eyes again and heading to the door.

She heard his footsteps in the hallway. It was only a couple of minutes before he opened the door to the office and stepped inside. He closed the door behind him, his eyes riveted to Vicki. She remained seated and he pulled up a chair beside the couch and sat down in front of her.

"So," he said, "are ya feelin' better?"

"Yes," she said. Leaning toward him, she made a move to hold his hand but found herself with both her hands placed atop his.

He looked at her for a long moment with red-rimmed eyes. She tried to read the sentiment there but they were a conflict of emotion: sadness, happiness, disappointment, relief.

"It was just such a long night," she said quietly. "I didn't get much sleep and nothing to eat…"

"So," he said again, "when were you plannin' on tellin' me that you're carryin' me child?" Before she could answer, he added, "Or did you think I didn't have the right to know?"

She grasped his hands fully in hers and looked him in the eye. "It wasn't that at all. I tried to tell you—several times—but something always interrupted us."

"How long 'ave you known?"

She swallowed. This wasn't how she'd imagined this conversation unfolding at all. "I found out the morning we left for Ireland."

"And you never told me." His voice was barely over a whisper and his eyes narrowed.

"I wanted to—"

"It was mornin' sickness, wasn't it? Why, all the sudden, you didn't want to eat me cookin'."

"I love your cooking," she said. She moved off the couch and came to her knees in front of him, with his hands still in hers. "Yes. I've been sick in the mornings."

He seemed relieved but also perplexed. "If I had known you were expectin' me child, I'd 'ave never brought you here to Ireland."

"Why?"

He looked at her with increasing puzzlement. "Why?" he repeated. He looked away as if he was trying to form his words. "What if you needed medical attention? We 'ave no doctor in the village. The nearest one is most likely in Dublin. The closest hospital, for sure, is in Dublin."

"I'm okay. I really am. And if I needed a doctor, I'd trust you to get me to one."

Her words seemed to pain him and a lone tear welled up in his eye. "What if the rains hadn't stopped this mornin'?"

"Dylan," she said, her voice firm, "Stop it. You'll never again live through an experience like you had with Alana. Never."

"But—"

"When we get home, we're just a few blocks from the hospital. We could be there in ten minutes if we walked it. One minute if we drove. There are doctors all over Lumberton. Sandy lives right next door."

"I need to get you home as quickly as possible."

"We'll go after we take care of Mam's house. Just as we planned."

"I would ne'er 'ave gone on that mission, you know, last night if I'd 'ave known."

"But—"

"I don't want me child growin' up without a father." The tear spilled onto his cheek and she pressed her face against his. Her arms went around him, one hand running through his hair while the other hugged his neck.

"Please tell me," he said, "you weren't plannin' on doin' anythin' stupid."

"I do a lot of things that are stupid," she said jokingly. But when she looked back in his eyes, his meaning was clear. "No," she said forcefully. "No. I wasn't. I—I just knew—well, the way you felt about children—"

"I'm scared to death o' your pregnancy," he blurted. "I'm terrified, to be quite honest about it. But the child—" As he put his hand on her belly, a soft smile swept over his face. "I don't care if it's a boy or a girl." He looked her in the eye. "I just want to be the best father I could possibly be. I don't want any child o' mine growin' up as I did."

She sat in his lap, cradling his head against her. "Then help me. Help me—learn how to cook. How to take care of an infant. How to—"

"Don't you worry, m'darlin'," he said. "We've got Bennie. She'll do all the cookin'. And when she's got a day off, I'll cook. If you want me to teach you, I will. If you don't, I don't care. And between you, me and Bennie, we'll take good care o' him— or her. Our child shouldn't want for anythin'."

He straightened his back and raised his eyebrows. "Why, I'm a landowner now. You and me, we own a house bigger than anythin' in the village. It's a good place to raise a child. Don't you think?"

"Yes," she said, her own eyes brimming with tears, "it is the perfect place to raise a child."

"And your sister Brenda—"

"What about Brenda?"

"Well, she and I, we've our differences as you well know. But she's always there when she's needed. And I have a feelin' if I happened not to be around but she was there, why, she'd do whatever was needed to help you and our child."

"So you trust her now?"

"I wouldn't get carried away now," he chided. "And you know," he added, "this means Sam is goin' to be a grandfather."

Vicki laughed out loud. "I can't picture that."

"Well, I might end up choppin' his head off if we get home to hundreds o' dead angelfish. But if he lives, I think he might be a decent grandfather."

"You think so?"

"I think so. Aye. I do."

"So we'll have you and me—of course—and Benita. And Brenda. And Sam."

"A whole family." He kissed her lightly and then said, "Darlin', we're both exhausted. Say we get Father Rowan to drive us back to the cottage? I don't want you walkin'."

"Why not? It's only a mile."

He grew serious. "Why, because it's goin' to rain. And you know what they say; if you walk in the rain while you're pregnant, the child will be born with sinus issues."

"What?"

"It's true."

"Where did you hear that?"

"So. We'll get a lift to the cottage. And then, if you don't mind, I want a hot shower—preferably with you—"

"Showers aren't the same as rain?"

"No. They're exempt. And then I want to sleep the rest o' the day and all the night long."

"And food?"

"We've plenty o' food. I'll warm it up whene'er you want it."

She kissed him softly and ran her hand along his five o'clock shadow. Even with red-rimmed eyes, tussled hair and a look of exhaustion, he was so handsome. "Yes," she said. "Let's go home."

43

Dylan sat on the edge of the bed and gazed at the room around him as if seeing it for the first time. The bed seemed so tiny and the mattress so thin and lumpy; and yet he hadn't remembered it that way. The same quilt adorned it that had always been there; it was worn, the material thin in places, the threads yellowed and aged. As he ran his fingers across it, he knew every stitch had been made with love and care. And it would be packed up that way.

The murmur of voices reached him but they sounded distant. Mrs. Rowan was in the kitchen, packing up the food to give to the needy. Brenda was packing the photographs from the living room. And Vicki was in Mam's bedroom going through her jewelry, what little she had, choosing anything that appealed to her.

Absent-mindedly, he patted the pocket of his jeans where the only piece of jewelry he knew he wanted rested. It was Mam's wedding ring. She didn't have a proper engagement ring and the wedding ring probably wasn't worth much, but he knew whose finger he wanted it to adorn. He thought of the ring he'd purchased from Dublin, the one that had been delivered just before they left America. Vicki would have two rings, then, and she could decide how she wanted to wear them.

He hadn't asked her yet. He needed just the right place, the right time. He needed flowers. Music. And candlelight.

He rose and carefully folded the quilt, laying it gently into the box. He went through the drawers of the small dresser and marveled at the clothing Mam had kept. There were his church clothes from his youngest years, so diminutive that he wondered how he could ever have been so young and so tiny. There was his best school clothing, some of it worn in his teens when he was gangly and awkward. He put it all in a separate box, one that would go with the food to the less fortunate.

There was a miner's folding shovel. He smiled. It had been his grandfather's and Mam had allowed him to use it. He suspected she knew all along that he was with the Hoolihan brothers digging for gold supposedly hidden in the bogs. And she knew, and the whole village knew, that they would never find any treasure because there was no treasure there.

Only there was.

And at this moment, it was under tons of peat and debris and God knew what else. Between the cave-in as he escaped and the dynamite used to complete the collapse, it was buried almost beyond discovery. Except he and Stephen knew where it was. And what it was—and how priceless it all must be.

Someday, he thought. Someday he would return; someday soon. And he'd be back in those bogs and digging for gold. But this time, he'll know exactly where to look.

He set the shovel in the donation box and picked up a baseball. He'd been so enamored of American baseball when he was a child. He collected the cards and wondered now what Mam had gone without so he could have the bubblegum and cards every few months. Then one Christmas, she'd given him the baseball. It had been more precious than gold. She didn't have the money for a bat but it hadn't mattered to him. The baseball was enough.

He held it now above the box for the needy but it wouldn't drop from his hand. He held it as if he was weighing it and then gently placed it onto the quilt in the other box. It would go to America then, and perhaps one day he'd have a son who might use it.

A son. The thought was frightening and exhilarating; it filled him with nervous anticipation and thoughtful plans. Or he might, he thought, have a daughter. It didn't matter now and wouldn't ever matter; he would love his child the way he'd always wanted his mother to love him.

Brenda popped her head in the doorway. "It's really quiet here," she said. She waited as if anticipating a response from him. When she got none, she added, "Mind if I turn on the TV?"

"Not at'al," he said. "I think it gets three or four stations. But," he added, "don't let Vicki watch much o' it."

"Why not?"

"Why, if she watches a lot o' the telly while she's pregnant, the child will be born with vision problems."

Brenda looked at him without answering.

"It's true," he said.

"Yeah. Right."

Heavy footsteps started down the hall and Brenda turned. "Well, hello there, Father Rowan," she said, a sly smile crossing her face.

"'alo," he answered. "Is Mick about?"

She stepped away from the doorway. "He's in here." As Father Rowan moved into the room, Brenda said, "I'll be in the living room if you need me."

He cleared his throat as he entered. "How is everythin' goin' w' you, Mick?"

Dylan placed more memorabilia into the box that would go to America. "As well as could be expected, I suppose. It's a sad day, to be sure, clearin' the house o' everythin' that was Mam's. I feel like I've had a cord to this place, you know, even whilst I was in America. And now it's bein' severed."

Father Rowan sat on the bed.

"And how might you be doin'? Are you rested?"

"Just came from the pub."

"Oh?"

"Aye. Thought it might be a good place to find out what's what in the village."

"Might be? It's always been the place for that."

"Aye. And so it has. So. You heard the explosion yesterday?"

Dylan stopped and looked at him. "Aye."

"Turns out, the Hoolihan brothers had a stash o' weapons out in the bogs. It blew up. Probably on account o' gunpowder or explosives they were amassin'."

"But…" Dylan cocked his head and furrowed his brow.

He shrugged. "I'm just tellin' you what the villagers are sayin'."

Dylan continued to go through the clothing in the drawers, placing them into the box for the needy, as the priest's words sank in.

"And it turns out old Aengus went to visit 'is sister in the neighborin' village. And when he returned, his horses had been used. Villagers are sayin' the Hoolihans stole 'em, most likely for cult reasons."

"Cult reasons, 'ey?"

"You never knew about that bunch… Why, I found two horses in the cemetery, wouldn't you know? I phoned Aengus this mornin' and told 'im I woke up and there they were. He came and took 'em home. He thought they'd been ridden hard, from the looks o' thin's. There was blood all o'er one; most likely, we surmised, from a sacrificed lamb."

"A lamb, you say?"

"What else could bleed out like that, and carried across a horse to boot?"

"Did he ask any questions?" Dylan asked.

"None at'al. Didn't look me in the eye and coughed a bit. I believe the man was nervous."

"Did he think—?"

"He was worried o' what I was thinkin', if you want my opinion about it. He goes off to visit his sister and all his horses are used perhaps for a dubious purpose. And there's the priest with an eyebrow raised, wonderin' if he might wish to go to confession."

Dylan chuckled.

"Then there's the matter o' the villagers seein' two helicopters touch down."

Dylan glanced up as he placed more items in the boxes.

"They were American helicopters, o' that the villagers are certain. Rumor has it—on good authority, as you might imagine—that the Hoolihans were plannin' some sort o' domestic terrorism."

"Is that so?"

"Aye. The word is they'd joined a cult, were plannin' to ride Aengus' horses to the government offices and blow 'em up with explosives they'd been storin' in the bogs."

"Anythin' else?"

He shrugged. "Just that they were devil worshippers and had been hypnotized and that's why no one had ever seen 'em in church their whole lives. And then there's the matter o' their plans against the American government."

"And what plans were those?"

"I left a'fore they finished formulatin' 'em but by the morn, they'll have quite a yarn, I'm sure. They'll 'ave 'em linked to every terrorist in the world by the time the week's out." He watched Dylan in silence for a moment before adding, "I suppose you can't inform me o' their real whereabouts, can you?"

"I spoke to me boss this morn. They're in jail—where, I don't know. They'll stand trial for the murder o' an American tourist and attempted murder o' another."

"Attempted murder?" Father Rowan peered at him.

"Aye. It appears the bullet shattered inside o' Perry. It hit a major artery. Had Brenda not stopped the bleedin' when she did..."

"Praise the Lord she was w' you."

Dylan laughed. "That's not a phrase I'd ever 'ave expected to hear."

"You don't care for her, do you?"

"I'm learnin' to."

"But it's Vicki you love."

"I don't know quite what it is about 'er," Dylan said. "Maybe it's 'er gentle ways. But she's got a spine made o' steel, she does, she just hides it well. And she can be so passionate. Or maybe it's the way she cares about children..."

As if on cue, Vicki popped her head into the room. "Father Rowan," she said. "I didn't hear you come in."

"Aye. I was just fillin' Dylan's head w' the rumors from the village."

"Oh?"

"I'll tell you later," Dylan said, "over a romantic dinner. How's that?"

"You have a date."

"Did you find anythin' o' Mam's that you wanted to keep?"

"I want to keep everything," she said. "Everything I touch reminds me of her. I know that I didn't know her long but... I feel connected to her somehow."

"Well, if you go to bed wearin' her jammies, me passion will be Baltic, I can guarantee you that."

Vicki laughed. It always stopped him in his tracks when she laughed; it sounded like bells ringing or angels singing, he couldn't decide which. But it always disarmed him. "I won't be wearing any of her clothes. Unless there's something you want to keep to remind you of her, I'll just be keeping things like her jewelry and a few little knick-knacks. And all the photographs."

"Fine. I'm sure there are ladies in the village who could use her old clothin'. They weren't much but they kept the chill away. Everythin' else will go to the auctioneer."

"Hey, guys," Brenda called from the living room. "You need to get in here."

Dylan opened his mouth to retort something that was probably witty only to himself, but there was something in her tone of voice that stopped him short. Vicki was already out of the room and he and Father Rowan scrambled to follow her.

They found Brenda perched on the arm of the couch watching the old television set.

"What's what?" Dylan asked.

They all gathered around as Brenda gestured toward a late-breaking news story. "A ship was blown up."

"A cruise ship?"

"No. One carrying cargo from China."

"Oh. In China." Relief flooded over him.

She looked at him dubiously. "Not in China. From China. Heading to the United States."

"Well, I'm sure they'll sort it out."

"Well, sort this out: it's the second one in the past hour. Like they're targeting goods heading to the U.S."

"Oh, my God," Vicki breathed.

Dylan spun around to wrap his arm around Vicki. "Have a seat, Darlin'. You shouldn't worry at'al about this. I'm sure everythin' will be fine. And you know what they say."

All eyes turned to him.

"If you worry while you're pregnant, the child will be born with a fretful personality."

They continued to look at him.

"It's true."

His cell phone rang and he reached for it, his brows furrowing. "It's Sam on Skype." He answered the call. "Aye?"

"Dylan, it's Sam."

"Aye, I know it's Sam 'cause I'm lookin' at your face."

"Whatever. Look, we've got a little situation."

"Are you in the fish house?" Dylan asked, peering closely at the screen.

"Yeah. Everything's fine. Look—"

"Is that a cat I see in the fish house?"

Sam frowned. "So what if it is?"

"Cats eat fish."

"Not my cat. My cat does not eat fish."

"What did you feed 'er for breakfast?"

"Tuna, if it's any of your business."

"Tuna is a fish."

"Well, it doesn't look like these fish."

"Does your cat know that?"

"I've got something important to talk to you about—"

"By the way, Sam, we're sendin' you a dog."

"What?"

"Not to worry. We don't want you to keep it. It's my dog. Our dog," Dylan corrected himself, glancing at Vicki. "Just, when it arrives, take 'er to North End Veterinary Clinic, will you?"

"I'm not babysitting a dog and all these fish. I can't do everything around here."

"Just board 'er at the vet's and tell 'em to get 'er all the shots she needs. Oh, and get 'er groomed. I'm sure we won't be here that much longer. And when we get home, I'll take care o' everythin'."

"That's what I called to talk to you about."

"Oh?"

"I need Vicki."

"Well, she's sittin' right here."

"No. I need her here. I've got another mission for her."

"Ooh. I'm not so sure—"

"Can she hear me?"

"Yes, Sam," Vicki broke in. "I can hear you."

"Stephen arrived in the States. I've been with him all day."

"How's he doing?" she asked.

"He's in the hospital; they've got him stabilized. But they haven't decided yet what will happen with his feet. Good job, by the way."

"And Perry?"

"He's in critical condition. Listen, I can't discuss this over the phone, even a secure line. It's too complicated. I need you both back here as soon as you can here."

"If Stephen and Perry are there," Dylan interrupted, "where's me dog?"

"I don't know. I'll find out. Don't worry. We've not lost a dog yet. Men, yes. A dog, no."

"How soon do you need us?" Vicki asked.

"I can arrange a flight out tomorrow."

Vicki and Dylan exchanged a long look. He nodded and she said, "That'll work."

"So," Dylan said, "our job here is done? Completely?"

"That's right."

"But we didn't find Stephen's captors. They're still on the loose, as far as we know."

"That's why I need you back here. That's the mission I need Vicki to work."

"But—" Vicki started.

"I've got information from Stephen. And I need you. Dylan; you're on standby for this one, too."

"Have you heard about the ships?" Brenda interjected.

"We're on it," Sam said simply.

Dylan peered into the screen again. "What is that cat doin' behind you?"

Sam turned around and then did a double-take. He blocked the cat with his body as he said, "Nothing. Anyway, I've got to go. I'll email instructions with your flight plans. See you in about twenty-four hours." With that, he clicked off.

"I knew it was a jacked-up notion for Sam to take care o' the fishies," he said. "Well." He turned toward everyone. Mrs. Rowan had joined them in the doorway, a puzzled expression on her face. "I'll be needin' to get the rest o' the things together to mail to me in America."

"I've got the photographs," Brenda said.

Dylan started down the hall toward his old bedroom. As he entered the room, he spotted Vicki out of the corner of his eye continuing to Mam's room. Father Rowan had hung back and now he heard him speaking to his mother in low tones.

So, he thought. That's that. His eyes took in the boxes that represented his life in Ireland. So that's what it's all boiled down to, he thought. Two boxes. A worn quilt, a baseball and a few things that most likely looked like junk to anyone other than himself.

The curtains were pulled back and he found himself gazing out the window at the meadow for the last time from this vantage point. When he returned to Ireland—and he would have to now, on account of Vicki hadn't gotten the sight-seeing he'd promised her—this home would be rented to someone else. He hoped they would love it as much as Mam had.

He wandered closer to the window. The sky was darkening; there was a storm brewing to the west. It brought back memories of all the times he'd stood in this spot and gauged the day's activities from the looks of the sky. It was always raining in Ireland, he thought.

The mists of Ireland were something alive, something that could soothe a man's soul or destroy it; something that cloaked a man when he wanted to be hidden or obscured that which he needed to see. It could soak into the bones on the coldest of days or sweeten the skin in the warmest of hours.

And no matter where he traveled or what he did, he knew now the land, the culture, its people and its myths would remain a part of him. They were inseparable, he thought. And he wouldn't want it any other way.

A Note from the Author

Like all my books, this one has elements of fact mixed in with fiction.

The amber panels Dylan discovered while escaping from the dungeons were inspired by The Amber Room. Known as "The Eighth Wonder of the World," the amber walls were created in Prussia in the early 1700's and gifted to Tsar Peter the Great of Russia in 1716. Once in Russia, it was expanded until it covered more than 55 square meters and contained more than six tons of amber. The amber panels were backed with gold leaf and contained intricate gold embellishments; it was reportedly worth more than 142 million dollars.

During World War II, the Germans disassembled the room to transport the priceless art to Germany, but it was never seen in public again. To this day, it remains a mystery where such valuable treasure could have been hidden. In 2003, the Amber Room was rebuilt in Russia based on old photographs of the original room, funded in part by a German company.

Dylan also mentioned the tension between England and Ireland during both World Wars. Ireland was still trying to escape from English rule when World War I broke out and there were some who tried to help the Germans in an attempt to prevent England from winning the war. By the time the Second World War erupted, Ireland had been divided into two and the Republic of Ireland had been formed. The rift between the two countries had not yet begun to heal and the Republic was anxious to put distance between themselves and England. Although they declared neutrality, many throughout the Republic of Ireland and Northern Ireland were concerned if England prevailed over Germany, they would renege on their agreement and place the entire island under their rule once more. An underground movement formed to assist the Germans. In Northern Ireland, it went as far as arming the Irish Republican Army with German weapons, but England successfully prevented the Germans from ever conquering Ireland.

The bog wood that Dylan tried to find for making furniture dates back at least 5,000 years, which makes it more ancient than the pyramids in Egypt. In some areas, entire forests have been found buried by the bog mud and peat. There is a lack of oxygen in the peat, which allows the trees underground to remain virtually intact.

To date, more than one thousand preserved bodies and skeletons have been discovered in bogs throughout the United Kingdom. Some of the oldest date to 350 to 400 BC. It's said the mummies of the bogs inspired Bram Stoker, a Dublin author.

Thousands of artifacts have been discovered in the bogs, including tools dating to the Bronze Age, jewelry, ornaments, clothing and weapons. In 1825, two potato farmers discovered gold-covered bronze objects, including hundreds of javelins, axes, pendulous ovoid bronzes, horns of bronze and even cauldrons of bronze. In a separate finding elsewhere in the bogs, twenty-four trumpets and forty-three axes were found among over a hundred items. To date, more than 50 Bronze Age hoards have been discovered. Charcoal found in hearths unearthed from the bogs date back more than 9,000 years.

The technology called Ground Penetrating Radar System is in use today. As Sam described in the book, it is based on sonar technology but is capable of penetrating through buildings and even underground.

The three-dimensional models that are achieved from computer output are also available and used in Intelligence. It utilizes the same technology as many computer games.

When Dylan spoke about his wife's labor, he mentioned a storm in which rains continued for days, eventually causing the flood walls to break. This was an actual storm that occurred in October 2011, in which many areas experienced such severe flooding that some villages were cut off from the rest of the country. Bridges were washed out, gale warnings were issued and gusts of 110km were recorded.

It is also true about the lack of medical care in some rural villages and the waiting list to see a doctor or receive hospital care, though those with private insurance fare better, as do foreign visitors.

The computer procedure Brenda used to unscramble the dungeon and the story she told of law enforcement using the technology to unscramble faces obscured on the Internet is based on real technology in use by federal law enforcement today.

About the Author

p.m.terrell is the pen name for Patricia McClelland Terrell, the award-winning, internationally acclaimed author of more than sixteen books in four genres: contemporary suspense, historical suspense, computer how-to and non-fiction.

Prior to writing full-time, she founded two computer companies in the Washington, DC Metropolitan Area: McClelland Enterprises, Inc. and Continental Software Development Corporation. Among her clients were the Central Intelligence Agency, United States Secret Service, U.S. Information Agency, and Department of Defense. Her specialties were in white collar computer crimes and computer intelligence.

A full-time author since 2002, *Black Swamp Mysteries* is her first series, inspired by the success of *Exit 22*, released in 2008. *Vicki's Key* was a top five finalist in the 2012 International Book Awards and 2012 USA Book Awards nominee. The series will have six main characters whose lives are forever intertwined through events or family ties: Dylan Maguire, Vicki Boyd, Brenda Carnegie, Christopher Sandige, Alec Brodie and Sandy Stuart.

Her historical suspense, *River Passage*, was a 2010 Best Fiction and Drama Winner. It was determined to be so historically accurate that a copy of the book resides at the Nashville Government Metropolitan Archives in Nashville, Tennessee.

She is also the co-founder of The Book 'Em Foundation, an organization committed to raising public awareness of the correlation between high crime rates and high illiteracy rates.

She is the organizer of Book 'Em North Carolina, an annual event held in the real town of Lumberton, North Carolina, to raise funds to increase literacy and reduce crime. For more information on this event and the literacy campaigns funded by it, visit www.bookemnc.org.

She sits on the boards of the Friends of the Robeson County Public Library and the Robeson County Arts Council. She has also served on the boards of Crime Stoppers and Crime Solvers and became the first female president of the Chesterfield County-Colonial Heights Crime Solvers in Virginia.

For more information visit the author's website at www.pmterrell.com, follow her on Twitter at @pmterrell, her blog at www.pmterrell.blogspot.com, and on Facebook under author.p.m.terrell.

Other Books in the
Black Swamp Mysteries Series

Exit 22 (2008)

Christopher Sandige is a political strategist on his way from Washington to Florida when he is involved in an automobile accident at Exit 22 in North Carolina. Stranded for the weekend, he meets a beautiful but mysterious woman and becomes embroiled in a double homicide. He now must decide whether to trust the woman he is falling in love with even as evidence mounts against her and he is swept into a world of shell corporations, bank fraud and the oil industry. Now he is being pursued by a dogged homicide detective and a hired assassin – one who wants to arrest him and the other wants to kill him. And time is running out.

Vicki's Key (2011)

After a botched mission, Vicki Boyd leaves the CIA and moves to a new town to work for an elderly lady. But when she arrives, she finds that Laurel Maguire has suffered a stroke and is confined to her third floor bedroom and her nephew has arrived from Ireland to care for her. Vicki quickly falls in love with the charming Dylan Maguire but all is not what it seems to be in Aunt Laurel's rambling old home. And when the CIA arrive to recruit her for one more mission, she finds her past and her future are about to collide—in murder.

Secrets of a Dangerous Woman (2012)

Dylan Maguire's first assignment with the CIA is to interrogate recently captured Brenda Carnegie. But when she escapes again, it's clear that she had help from within the CIA's own ranks. Now she's in Dylan's custody again and he's learning the secrets she keeps could topple the government unless they can identify the rogue agents—and eliminate them. Joining forces with Vicki Boyd, he discovers Brenda's true identity and he realizes his mission has just become *very* personal.

The Pendulum Files (scheduled for release in 2014)

Shipments of goods bound for America are being destroyed at an alarming rate, plunging the country into a chaos of shortages. As maritime events unfold, one man holds information on the battle for control of the United States Government and its future. Now it's Vicki's and Dylan's jobs to piece together the information Stephen Anders and Dylan risked their lives to protect. And when a hired assassin mysteriously disappears from prison, they find themselves turning from the hunters—to the hunted.